that they were so close was not lost on Brad. He leaned

ov   d her, his tongue pushing her lips apart. "You mean I was
stu   to let you dance with another man?"

                moaned. The roughness of his morning beard against he
he   was doing dangerous things to her hormones. He kissed
he: ing for her answer. "Usually I would only get to dance a
co   s before…."

                ped smothering her neck in kisses and asked, "Before
wh

                he would stop now while she still had enough willpower
to   re you got in a snit."

                his large body on top of hers. He kissed her deeply, his
bo   moving against hers. "Well, I promise from now on, I will
be   partner you're going to have, and I'm not just talking about
da

                lle opened her mouth to tell Brad it was much too early for
th   ds of declarations, but she wasn't given the chance. He took
he   h in a gentle, but powerful kiss that sent her hormones on
hi   . He pulled her closer to him so that now they were body to
bo   tongue mated with hers with a hunger that shocked
M   If she thought his earlier kiss was the bomb, this one was off
th   1.

DO OVER

CELYA BOWERS

Genesis Press, Inc.

Indigo

An imprint of Genesis Press, Inc.
Publishing Company

Genesis Press, Inc.
P.O. Box 101
Columbus, MS 39703

Copyright© 2007 by Celya Bowers

ISBN-13: 978-1-58571-241-0
ISBN-10: 1-58571-241-8
Manufactured in the United States of America

First Edition

Visit us at www.genesis-press.com
or call at 1-888-Indigo-1

DEDICATION

This book is dedicated to my mother,
Celia Mae Bowers Shaw Kenney.

ACKNOWLEDGEMENTS

I dedicate this book to my loving mother, Celia Mae Bowers Shaw Kenney. Even though she's not here with me in the physical, I know she's close to me in spirit.

To my family: Darwyn Tilley, Jeri Murphy, Earl Kenney, Sheila Kenney, Kim Kenney, Shannon Murphy, Yolanda Tilley, Celya Tilley, and Rod Kenney, thank you for all the encouragement.

I would like to thank my readers: Melody Alvarado, Kathryn Strickland, Huini Mwangi, Brandye McCool, Judy Brown, Kenneth Portley, Annette Freeman, and Natasha Swindle.

To my inner circle: Cherry Elder, Erica Black, Eulanda Bailey, Sharon Hickman-Mahones, Lester Brown, De Andra Garrett, Darlene Ramzy, Michella Chappell, Linda Hodges, Roslin Williams, Northa Hollins, and Lisa-Lin Burke, you guys are a blessing to know and thank you for keeping it real for me.

To my good friend, Navy Chief Petty Officer, Lawrence Leonard, thanks for all the jokes and keeping our country safe.

A big welcome to the world and our family to my great niece, Kennedy D. Tilley, I know the future will hold great things for you.

To those of you in Celya's Corner: Sherry Ramsey, Stacey Plummer, Gail Surles, Winston Williams, Veta Holt, Jacoby Stennett, John Brown, Jessica Kenney, Sherry Kenney, Deborah Kenney, Janet Kenney, Elliott Charles, Nely Gonzales, Kyra Zavala, Kimberly Williams, Kerry Elder, Marnese Elder, Lesley Paine, Paula Washington, Mary Thompkins and Mary Bell, thanks for being great supporters!

To the members of Dallas Area Romance Authors (DARA), and North Texas Romance Writers of America (NTRWA), thank you for all the knowledge I have gained on the writing craft.

To the members of the Sizzling Sisterhood Critique Group: Angela Cavener, Diane O'Brien Kelly, and Shaunnette Smith, thanks for your insight and all the great conversations.

To my agent, Cheryl Ferguson.

If I have forgotten anyone, please charge it to my head. It only works on occasion!

CHAPTER 1

London, England

"I don't look him, Brad."

Brad Killarney looked at his wife of five years across their breakfast table in their London flat. This was about as close they could get to intimacy with two small children. Luckily, the kids were still asleep.

Michelle was as beautiful as the day he'd met her six years ago. Her flawless brown skin was the color of honey and smooth as silk, her shoulder length black hair was pulled back in a ponytail. She didn't like anywhere near her forty-five years, which made Brad feel much older than his forty-eight years.

"I don't like him," she said again. "He's around here all the time. I thought the reason he came to London was to oversee your replacement while he got acclimated, not to hang around me and the kids in the park."

He did not want to have the same conversation he'd been having with Michelle every morning for the last two months. "Baby, I've known Frank for almost ten years and he's my boss. He just wants to make sure the transition goes well. I thought you were ready to get back to Arlington, Texas. We've been living in England for almost three years, and all I heard was how much you didn't like it."

Michelle sighed. "No, you heard me say how much I didn't like doing everything on my own. The only time I see you is at breakfast, and that's only because the kids like to sleep late. I thought your schedule would have eased up when your replacement arrived two months ago, but it seems like you work even more now."

He poured a cup of coffee. The rich aroma seemed to calm his nerves. "Look baby, Frank is like my mentor. He recommended me for the job in Arlington. You know what that vice presidency will mean for us. I'll be the first African-American in an executive position at Herrington Global Investments." He ticked off the more solid points on his fingers, hoping Michelle would see the light. "There'll be more money for the kids' college funds and more retirement money for us. Besides, we'll be near your parents and you'll have more free time."

"More free time for what? Do you have any idea what I do each day?"

Brad finished his coffee and rose. This was going to be an all-out fight and he needed to be at work. "Baby, I can't go into that right now. I'm going to be late for the morning meeting, and you know how I hate being late to anything. Why don't you hold that thought and we can do this tonight?"

Michelle folded her arms across her chest, a true sign she was going to be livid. "We can't hold this for tonight, your boss is staying for dinner. Remember? He invited himself for dinner last night."

Brad had forgotten. "Okay. How about after he goes home? We can hash all this out then." He kissed her on the cheek. "Right now, I gotta go. It's raining again. I'll definitely be glad to feel some hot Texas weather and not see rain every day."

"I'll be happy to get away from your boss," Michelle grumbled. "It's just not natural he wants to hang around me and the kids instead of you and the other guys at the office."

He had to soothe his wife's worried tone. "Honey, he just misses his family. You know he just remarried last year. He probably just misses his wife; I would miss you if the role was reversed."

"You might just get your wish."

Or at least that was what he thought Michelle said.

"What?"

Michelle waved him away. "You're going to be late."

Brad decided he didn't have time to dwell on it at the moment, but he'd get to the bottom of his wife's suspicion of the man he most respected.

A few hours later, Michelle heard the doorbell rang. She didn't have to ask who it was; she already knew. Glancing in the hall mirror, she finger combed her hair, then hurried to the door.

Frank Sims stood in her doorway, and he wasn't dressed for a day at the office. His lean, rangy frame was dressed for a day at the park. He smiled at her before she motioned him inside.

"It's Friday, so it must be a day for the park." He sat down on the couch. "Where are the kids?" He winked one of those blue eyes at her. "Did you send them away to have your way with me? I'm going to tell your husband," he teased.

Michelle laughed. "No. They were watching television. They'll be happy to hear that the park is on the agenda today. Make yourself at home, I'll be right back." She started for the hallway.

"No." Frank rose and walked down the hall. "I'll get them."

Michelle watched his retreating back and groaned. Frank was walking wide-legged and hunchbacked and making gorilla noises, heading straight for the children. Michelle heard the happy squeals of laughter. That should have been Brad.

"Uncle Frank!" Peri yelled. "Uncle Frank! Me! It's my turn!"

Before Michelle could go investigate Frank appeared in the hall with Preston riding high on his shoulders and giggling. Peri followed them to the living room. That should have been Brad spending quality time with his children, but it wasn't. It was his boss. And there was the problem.

"Hey, what's this?" Frank wiped the tears from Michelle's face.

"Nothing." She nodded to the children. "It just makes me happy to hear them sound so happy."

Frank rolled his eyes to ceiling. "Sure. We'll talk about it later," he said in a low voice. In a much louder, cheery voice he said, "I think it's time for the park."

Once the children were occupied playing with the other kids from the neighborhood, Frank started the inquisition. "Okay, Michelle, what's going on?"

She opened her mouth to speak, but closed it. What could she say? She didn't like this man hanging around her and the kids every day, yet he knew her better than her husband did in some ways. Brad would tell her she's overreacting, but something about Frank didn't sit right; however, he was her husband's friend and boss, so she had to respect their relationship.

"Michelle," he prodded. "I've known you for five years, you're troubled. I can see it in those beautiful brown eyes. Brad loves you, you know."

"I'm sure he thinks he does."

Frank shook his head. "He does. I know he's working a lot lately, getting ready for the transition, but when's the last time you talked to him? I mean really talked."

When would there ever be time? Michelle shifted on the bench seat and faced Frank. His pale face featured looked more drawn than usual. He always looked like he was one meal from starvation, but today he looked even worse. Michelle rooted through her bag for some food. She handed him a granola bar.

He refused it. "When, Michelle?"

"I can't remember," she lied and unwrapped the treat. She took a bite, honestly trying to remember when she and Brad did anything just for the sake of doing nothing.

"Before Preston was born," he guessed. "You know my first marriage failed because I shut down. I quit talking to her and that's when our trouble started."

"I just want Brad to realize he's missing his kids growing up. You know we married late. We were both over forty when we met. He's missing all the important things in life for the sake of his job."

"I understand. Have you had this conversation with your husband?"

"No, and I don't intend to. His job is very important to him."

"Well, his family should come before any job. But I know what he's going through," Frank said in Brad's defense. "He's worried about college funds, retirements, and probably every other thing in this world. You have to tell him what you're feeling, Michelle, or it's going to bottle up into something neither of you want."

"I think it already has."

Brad didn't like the atmosphere in his own house. He'd come home early, hoping to smooth some of the troubled water with Michelle, but all hopes were dashed when he noticed his boss was sitting on the couch playing with his children.

"Daddy!" Peri called as she slid out of Frank's lap and ran to him.

"Hey baby." Brad picked up his four-year-old daughter and hugged her thin frame. She smelled like freshly baked chocolate chip cookies. "You smell good."

"Uncle Frank made us cookies while Mummy slept. She didn't feel good."

"Where's Mummy?"

Peri pointed a finger to the kitchen. "Fixing chicken."

Brad smiled. Some things never changed. Friday was chicken night. He let Peri down when he saw Preston, his two-year-old son, toodling toward him.

"Da-da." He stretched out his chubby arms for Brad to pick him up.

Brad scooped his son up and gave him a fierce bear hug. "Hey, man. You haven't been giving Uncle Frank fits today?"

Preston chuckled and grabbed his father by his ears and pulled. "Oh, man. We're going to have to cut those fingernails soon." Preston had a fierce grip and sometimes didn't know the power of his own torture.

Frank rose and walked toward him. "Yeah, I was telling Michelle that earlier. Little bugger got me by the hair when we were leaving the park," Frank said in a light tone.

"Uh, yeah." Brad adjusted Preston in his arms and strode into the kitchen. As he entered the small room, Michelle was putting a casserole into the oven.

"Frank, I appreciate your help earlier. You don't know what having a real adult conversation meant to me."

"No," Brad drawled, "why don't you tell me?"

Startled, Michelle slammed the small oven door closed and spun around. "What are you doing home so early? I didn't expect you until…"

"Until you and Frank have another conversation? Just how adult was this conversation?"

Michelle regained her composure quickly. "Brad, don't start. He's your friend and boss. You wanted me to be nice to him. I'm being nice."

He opened his mouth to tell her his thoughts on being nice when Peri tugged at his pants leg. "Daddy, are you fighting with Mummy?"

"No, baby. We're just talking."

Michelle nodded in agreement. "Yes, Peri, adults just have louder voices than children. Why don't you take your daddy in the living room and show him what you and Preston made at the art gallery this afternoon?"

"Okay, Mummy."

"This isn't over, Michelle," he whispered as Peri grabbed his large hand.

"Oh, you can bet the house on that one."

Brad allowed his tiny daughter to lead him out of the kitchen and upstairs to her room. Maybe the move back to Texas would help this bump in their marriage. Brad knew Michelle was the woman for him, and he would do anything to make sure she realized that.

Two months later
American Airlines flight from London to Dallas, Texas

Brad stared at Michelle, not believing for one moment she'd just shattered his world. They were sitting side by side in first class on the transatlantic flight for home, or what he thought would have been home. "What did you say?"

Michelle sat the in-flight magazine on the tray table and faced him, speaking just above a whisper. "I said when we land, my parents will take me and the kids to their house. I think we need some time apart."

"This is because I didn't have your back about Frank, isn't it?"

"If it hadn't been Frank, it would have been someone else."

Brad involuntarily smashed the can he held in his hand. "What are you saying?"

"Brad, you treat me like I'm a comfortable pair of shoes in the back of the closet. You just know I'll be there, and that's partly my fault. I let you treat me that way. But when Frank was with us, he played with the kids, and he talked to me like I was a regular woman. All I ever wanted was a little recognition from you."

"You're my wife."

"Yes, and I love you, but I can't live like this anymore. I can't live another day craving something you're not willing to give me."

Brad tried his best not to let the tears fall, but this was his family Michelle was talking about splitting up. "What about the kids?"

"I would never keep you from seeing your kids, you know that. Whenever you want to see them, you can."

"Michelle, you know I can't live without you."

She wiped tears away as well. "I know you think you can't."

DO OVER

Two months later
Arlington, Texas

Brad Killarney stood at the window in his corner office of Herrington Global Investments in downtown Arlington, Texas. How did his life get so out of control? Here he was, six months past his forty-eighth birthday and preparing to embark on one of life's most painful processes. He was going to have to find a divorce lawyer.

"Hey, man. How's it hanging?" Alex Cole walked into the large corner office. He sat in the chair, not giving Brad a chance to answer. "Have you come up with that master plan to win Michelle back yet?"

Brad shook his head. "Oh man. I royally screwed up."

"You're not going to tell me that you actually planned on going through with that divorce mess? Now what are you going to do?"

Brad stared at his friend. "I don't know. She hadn't spoken to me since we returned. Any messages about the kids have been relayed through her mother, Emily the Horrible. Surely she'll listen to reason. After all, it was a mistake."

"I'm sure she'll take you back," Alex said.

"I'm not," Brad countered.

Alex crossed the room and stood next to Brad. I think you should talk to Michelle first and go from there. You're going to have to do some major crawling, so you might as well get ready." He whispered, "Diamonds never hurt, either."

"Michelle Shaw-Killarney," her mother's soft voice broke in to Michelle's thoughts, "you're going to have to get over this thing. So your marriage has ended. That's no reason for you to spend two months moping around the house. You act like the world has ended." Her mother poured a cup of tea and placed it before her.

Michelle inspected her mother's flawless brown skin as she placed a platter of lemon scones and tea sandwiches on the table. Even at the age of sixty-five, Emily Shaw was a knockout. Diahann Carroll would be jealous. "I know, Mom. The kids adapted to the change quicker than I did. I know Brad has moved on." After two months she still missed the aroma of his aftershave or the sight of his dreamy hazel eyes staring back at her in the morning.

Emily watched her daughter. "I know it's hard, but life must go on. You have two small children to look after."

Michelle wiped her eyes. "Yes, it was my choice to separate from Brad."

Emily doctored her tea, something she didn't start drinking until she visited Brad and Michelle in England when Preston was born. Now it was high tea in Arlington, Texas, every afternoon. "This isn't about Brad. This is about you. If you don't mind me saying so, I think you and Brad were having trouble way before you realized he was neglecting you."

Michelle glanced at her mother. "You were an ocean away. How could you tell?"

Emily took a long sip of tea, watching her daughter over the rim of her prized Royal Doulton cup, before she finally commented. "A mother knows."

Michelle played with her cup of tea. Everything in front of her reminded her of England and how happy she was then. "I feel lost," she admitted.

"Well, this is the time to find yourself. You're forty-five and it's time for you to find out what makes you happy. You've spent the last five years being Mrs. Brad Killarney, wife of an executive and mother to your children. It's time for you to find Michelle. Your car is paid for, so you don't have to worry about looking for work just yet. You can stay here as long as you like. I say this with a mother's love."

Michelle instantly braced herself for her mother's brand of tough love. "What is it, Mom?"

"You've put on a little weight. I bought you a membership to the gym. Do you think that soon-to-be-ex-husband of yours is moping around his apartment? He's probably got a new woman already."

She knew she had put on weight. Most of her jeans were snug and bordered on uncomfortable. "Okay, you win. I was thinking of starting my business again. I've only been out of the real estate business for five years, it shouldn't take to long to rebuild."

Emily shook her head. "I think you should take an art class. You always loved it. You used to paint. Why don't you try that?"

"I'll need an income," Michelle countered. "I didn't want to take any of Brad's money, but he insisted on paying child support."

"That's why I wanted to talk to you," her mother said in a quiet voice.

Michelle didn't like that. Her mother only used that voice when she wanted to tell Michelle something bad. "Don't tell me the money I told Jeremy to invest for me while I was in the UK went belly up?"

"On the contrary. It did quite well. Plus, your father and I have been talking."

She was using that voice again, Michelle thought. "What is it, Mom?"

"Well, we want to travel, since he retired last year. We didn't want to sell the house, and this way we won't have to. It'll be like you're house sitting. We'll put some of our furniture in storage and you can use some of your furniture. So it will at least feel like your home. We'll stay in one of the smaller bedrooms when we're here."

"Mom, I can't." Although her childhood home was more than large by today's standards, with six bedrooms, three bathrooms, and a three-car garage, she couldn't think of putting her parents out of their own home. Her father and grandfather built the two-story house over a half a century ago.

"Well, we're leaving on a cruise next Monday, so you don't have any other options."

Now that sounded like her mother. "I guess I don't." Michelle sighed. "How long will you be gone?"

"Two weeks. It's a seniors' cruise. You know, one of those over-sixty things."

Michelle had noticed her mother packing some luggage the last few weeks, but just thought she was packing away clothes to make room for Michelle and the kids. As the idea began to appeal to her, she decided her mother was right. She could do something she liked with her time.

"Okay." Michelle took a sip of tea and smiled. "I think I'll start my new life by going to the gym today."

CHAPTER 2

Brad left work early, hoping to talk to Michelle without the kids present. Surely they were in daycare, he reasoned as he drove to the large house. But he was sadly mistaken. After he rang the doorbell of her childhood home, he heard the squeals of his children running to the door.

"Daddy!" He heard his four-year-old daughter yell when she peeked through the side curtain. He laughed at her accent. The British inflection mixed with Texas drawl was an interesting sound. But he loved hearing it.

The front door opened and he prepared himself for the sight of his wife. She was always careful to be upstairs or somewhere else when he picked up or dropped off the kids. He wondered how much Michelle had changed in two months.

But he wouldn't find out today. Instead of his wife's face, he saw his mother-in-law. "Hello, Emily." He coughed and shuffled his feet. "Is Michelle home?" How could this little woman frighten him with just a facial expression?

Emily stood at the door, waving him inside. "No. She's out. Is this your day for the kids? I thought you picked them up on Fridays."

He smiled. "No, I didn't come for the kids. I came to talk to my wife."

Emily shooed the kids to another part of the house before speaking. "I think you mean ex-wife, don't you?"

He knew it would be an uphill battle, he just didn't think he'd have to start with her mother. "Okay, Emily. I get it. You're pissed at me." He sat down on the couch, noticing the suitcases on the dining room table. "Who's taking a trip?"

"I believe that's none of your concern," she said shortly. "Why don't you spend some time with your children while you wait for Michelle?" Emily walked to the hallway and called the kids before he could answer.

Soon his reasons for living were standing before him. Peri seemed like she had grown since last week. Preston jumped in his lap with a thud.

"It's not your day, Daddy." Peri sat beside him. "Mummy said your day was two more times away," she said, still using the British version of *mommy*.

She was so smart, just like her mother. "I know, baby. I came to talk to Mommy. Where is she?"

Peri shrugged her small shoulders.

Brick wall. He would just have to wait until Michelle came home; hopefully his mother-in-law wouldn't throw him out of the house before she did.

Emily walked into the living room, her jaw firmly set for battle. "So, Bradley, how have you been?"

He figured she was only being hospitable because the kids were in the room. "I've been doing horrible. I miss my wife and kids."

"Well, isn't that special," Emily said in a dry tone. "Is that why you haven't spoken to her since your return from England?"

He glanced at his daughter. She looked back at him with those big, innocent brown eyes. He had made so many mistakes in the last year. He had to start somewhere. "I'm not doing this here," he told Emily defiantly.

"Well, you'll have to do it somewhere. And you didn't think of that before, did you?"

He was about to open his mouth and break the rule that he and Michelle had about not fighting in front of the children, but he heard the back door open and close.

"Mummy!" Peri exclaimed, heading for the rear of the house, followed by Preston.

Emily stared at her opponent. "Well, looks like you're about to get your chance to talk with Michelle."

Brad didn't answer her. He knew Emily would light into him if he did. He braced himself for the image of his wife. Would she throw him out on sight? Or would she let him pour out his feelings, then throw him out?

Michelle walked into the living room and stopped cold. Dressed in workout clothes of shorts, T-shirt, and tennis shoes; she looked gorgeous. When did she start working out? He imagined he was the last person she wanted to see. Her next words cemented that fact.

"What are you doing here?" She had Preston in her arms and Peri was holding her hand. "You're supposed to call when you want to see the kids," she said in an accusatory tone. "No drop in visits, you promised."

He tried to keep his temper under control. "Look, Michelle, I came here to talk to you. I've already been through the Spanish Inquisition." He nodded to Emily. "I just want to talk. And I'm not leaving until I do."

She nodded and put Preston on the floor. "Peri, take your brother into the den and watch TV."

Soon the kids were gone and Emily left as well, muttering something about watching *Divorce Court* on TV.

Michelle and Brad sat on the couch. Opposite ends, of course.

"Okay, Brad. What do you want? I have to get dinner ready for the kids, then give them a bath."

"I wanted to tell you that I'm sorry and I still love you."

She laughed, but it held no humor. "Well, should I just count my lucky stars now or in divorce court?"

"Funny. Real Funny." Brad took a deep breath. "Look, I wanted to talk to you about our marriage."

"What do you want to talk about? I haven't gotten around to finding a lawyer yet. Dad is checking around for me."

"No," he shouted. "I don't want a divorce."

Michelle shook her head. "Well, I certainly don't plan on being separated for years on end." She tried to settle her breathing, so he wouldn't know how much those words turned her inside out. He scooted closer to her, the familiar scent of his cologne filling her senses.

"I came to say I was wrong and beg your forgiveness."

Michelle stared at him. Now she was mad. "I'm tired of you pretending I don't matter. Just like now, you think you come over here say you're sorry and I'll be willing to take you back. It's not going to work."

"Shell, come on. Try to see it from my side."

"What side would that be?"

"Michelle, I was completely wrong."

"Wow. There's a revelation. A man was wrong. Should I call CNN or CNBC?"

"Michelle, I'm here right now. Saying that I'm sorry. What more do you want?"

What did she want? "I want you to suffer like I have suffered every night for the last two months."

"How do you know I haven't? How do you know I don't suffer every night when I crawl into my bed and you're not there? I miss seeing your bubble bath in the bathroom. I miss seeing your perfume on the dresser, your nail polish on the vanity. Most of all I miss seeing you waiting for me in our bed."

Michelle was tongue-tied. In their five-year marriage, Brad never expressed raw emotion. That kind of passion never made it to their bedroom. Not even during their brief courtship, nothing came close to what he was saying right now.

She spoke in a whisper. "No, Brad. We must continue with the proceedings. If we stop now, this could happen again. We don't have the one thing that a strong marriage needs. This has to be a partnership. My life is just as important as yours."

"Shell, I love you. I never stopped loving you and I will love you always. I love you more than anything besides our kids."

"Enough to take me for granted."

"Shell. Please. God. Listen. I just made a mistake. Can't you see that?"

"How did you arrive at this conclusion? I know you didn't wake up this morning and decide you were going to treat me the way I deserve to be treated." She wondered at the sudden change of heart.

He wiped his eyes, took a deep breath and spoke in a whisper. "I decided that I wanted my family back, and nothing or no one would prevent me from getting what I want."

"So what do you want?"

"I want us to give it another try."

Michelle shook her head. "I can't put the children or myself in that predicament again."

"Shell, let's just start with dinner. Just you and me. We need to discuss the kids anyway."

"What about them? They're fine."

He stared at her with those dangerous eyes. "What about their daycare? What about when you start to work?"

She leaned back in a relaxed position on the sofa. Finally she felt a moment of triumph. "I'm not going back to work. At least not yet, so the kids are fine."

"Where are you going to live?"

"Here. Mom and Dad are going on a cruise. I have everything under control. Just keep your end of the bargain."

He nodded, digesting the information. The wheels were in motion in his brain. She felt it as he shifted his position in the sofa and faced her. "You never gave me an answer about dinner. Can we have dinner tomorrow night?"

She hesitated, but knew it was useless against him. They would have to have this talk at some point in time. "Okay, Brad. I'll meet you for dinner tomorrow night. Where?"

"I'll pick you up. I want to show you my apartment." He smiled at her.

"I think you're supposing a lot." *That's good, Michelle, maintain a cool front. Don't give him any hope.* "We're having dinner to discuss the care of our children, that's all."

His lips formed a thin line. "Right now, I don't suppose anything," he admitted. That sure, cocky tone was gone, replaced by a voice full of doubt. "I'll pick you up at eight." He rose, walked to the hall and called the kids.

After he kissed them goodnight, he left.

The minute Emily heard the door close and Brad drive away, she walked into the living room. Michelle knew the evening would only get worse.

"Your father is taking the kids to McDonald's for dinner so we can talk."

Michelle nodded. "I know you want to know what Brad and I talked about."

She shook her head. "I heard what you talked about. I'm very proud you held your ground. Men are so wishy-washy anyway. Are you sure about being alone with him? Remember, you didn't date long. You were helpless against his charms then, not that I can blame you. He's all man with that smooth chocolate skin, those hazel eyes, and that body."

"Mom, I sure hope you're going to make a point with this conversation."

"What I am saying, dear, is we both know you'll take him back. Just make sure you make him crawl, and that this is what you truly want."

"What if I don't know what I want?"

Her smile told her the answer. "You know what you want. The same as every woman in the world. You want a man to love you as much as you love him."

Brad entered his apartment, smiling. Okay, so the thing with Michelle hadn't gone as planned, but it hadn't been a disaster. He had made some headway.

He tossed his keys onto the marble countertop in the doll-sized kitchen and checked his phone messages, the first of which was from his sister, Melody. She called every day since his return to Arlington, to see if he and Michelle had reconciled. She would be happy with today's progress.

He decided to give her the good news right away. "Hey, Mel."

"Bradley. Do I have a sister-in-law again?" Her voice was both teasing and serious.

"You've always had a sister-in-law," he reminded her. "Actually, I saw her a little while ago, and we're going to dinner tomorrow night."

"That's great, Brad," Mel said. "I knew you guys would work this out."

"Well, don't get too excited yet. It's just dinner."

"If you hadn't been so stupid in the first place, you wouldn't have to be dealing with all this now. May I suggest diamonds?"

He felt his temper rising. "Why doesn't anyone take my side? I'm just as much a victim in all this, too. She could have just told me I was taking her for granted instead of letting this fester into a separation. And why is everyone telling me to buy diamonds?"

"Because you're an idiot," she joked. "But you have seen the error of your ways. You know nothing says 'I'm sorry' like a diamond ring and matching earrings. Goodnight." She hung up before he could respond.

Brad got a bottle of beer from the refrigerator and went to his desk to tackle the large pile of mail he had been neglecting.

He had expected Michelle to continue using the credit cards, but the monthly statements showed no activity by her. What was she using for money? True, she was living with her parents, but she still needed cash for incidentals. The statements for their joint checking and saving accounts revealed she had not used any of those funds, either.

Why did it bother him so? Most men would have been happy. But he wasn't most men. He believed in taking responsibility, and she wasn't letting him take his.

He sifted going through the remaining bills, paying the ones due online, he went to his bedroom.

A lot was riding on tomorrow night. It would have to be extra special. Who was he fooling? He needed a damn miracle. What he really needed was a do-over.

The next morning, Brad went to work determined to plan the best evening Michelle had ever experienced. He went straight to his friend's office.

"Hey, Alex."

Alex smiled at Brad, curious. "Man, you're seriously beaming. I take it you talked to Michelle. She took you back, right?"

"Apparently, you must know a different Michelle," Brad replied. "No, she didn't take me back, but she did agree to have dinner with me tonight."

Alex frowned. "Who's keeping the kids if you guys are pretending to date?"

"You know she's living with her parents. Her mom will probably keep them. Man, that woman gave me the blues yesterday."

"What did you expect? She's going to welcome you with open arms? It's a wonder she didn't shoot you."

"I know. I need something that's going to knock Shell's socks off."

Alex rubbed his clean-shaven chin. "Well, sit down. Let me pull up my notes." His fingers began flying over his keyboard. "Let's see, what is our objective?"

"For my wife to take me back."

"Well, Brad, since the separation is your fault, you can't be subtle. What's her favorite food?"

"No brainer. Italian."

Alex nodded. "Okay, find the most romantic Italian restaurant in Arlington. Is she meeting you?"

He was proud of that part of his plan. "No, I'm picking her up. I wanted her to see my apartment. I figured if I could get her there, I could talk to her."

"And try to take her to bed?" Alex shook his head. "Bad plan."

"What's wrong with it?"

"It says I know I was wrong, but I really miss the sex. Now if you took her to your place and didn't make any passes at her, you'll impress her." Alex snapped his fingers. "I have the perfect plan."

"What? I hesitate to guess."

"Call one of those people who will prepare the meal and leave. Go pick Michelle up, and when you return the apartment will have the aroma of her favorite food. Excellent."

Brad mulled the plan over in his head. It sounded good. Alex wasn't the office Romeo for nothing. "But there's no way I can find one of those people today."

"I just happen to know one."

"You would." Brad extended his hand. "Give me the card. I'll call before my meeting."

Holding back a retort, Alex grinned and handed him the card. Brad wanted to check Michelle's financial status, but he would have to be crafty. Since he was an investment banker, the company didn't allow running credit analyses. Only the brokers had such access. And Alex. "Hey, I need a favor."

"Yes."

"I'm trying to find out what Michelle is using for money. She hasn't touched any of ours since we returned."

Alex shook his head. "You know, you might be a whiz at investments and corporate tax shelters, but when it comes to women—namely your wife—you're dense."

Brad took offense at his friend's blunt assessment of him. "What the hell do you mean?"

"You treated your wife as if she didn't exist. She tells you she didn't like Frank hanging around so much, but she knows you guys are friends from way back, so she keeps her opinions to herself. You don't spend any time with her or the kids."

"So?"

"This is about pride," Alex continued his lesson in romance. "You pretended your family meant nothing to you, now she's showing you how little you mean to them. She's not going to use one penny of that money. If she did, that would be something that you'd be holding over her head. Think about it. When you guys met, she did have her own business, remember?"

Brad nodded. That seemed a lifetime ago. "Yeah, she had a real estate business. I still don't see where this is going."

"Patience. You will." Alex stood and began walking around the room. "When you guys married after only six months of dating, she sold her business—at your insistence, I might add. What kind of return was that?"

Brad shrugged, remembering. He was so happy that after only a few months of marriage, Michelle had become pregnant with their first child, he hadn't asked for specifics about the sale. Michelle agreed, wanting to concentrate on being a stay-at-home mom. "I don't remember."

"Guess."

"I don't know." Brad feigned innocence. "I was just happy we were starting a family; I didn't care if it was two dollars."

"Word in the financial community was she cleared six figures. She was the realtor most of the professional athletes in the Dallas/Fort Worth area used. There were bidding wars for her client list when she put her business on the market. She probably put that money into some kind of fund, because she didn't need it, and I'm sure you were too proud to use it for anything. Not that you needed to. It's probably a nice nest egg by now, if she did invest it. She could probably live off the interest alone."

"I really hadn't thought about that." Brad's heart sank as he remembered Michelle's brother, Jeremy, was also an investment banker.

Alex continued. "So, no, I will not run a credit analysis on your wife. It will only lead to more problems for you later."

Brad smiled. Good old Alex. Always the voice of reason. "Thanks, man."

Brad opened his office door and tensed. Frank was sitting behind his desk. "What can I do for you, Frank?"

He smiled at Brad. "Just wanted to say how good it is to have you back in the States. I hope everything is working out for you."

"Everything is just fine," Brad said. "I'm settling into the position. I'm looking forward to our first executive meeting next week."

"I understand you're going through a divorce. I thought being back in the States would help you guys. You know sometimes living in a foreign land can wreck havoc on a marriage."

"We're just separated," Brad said. "I know it'll work out in time."

Hours later, Brad rang the doorbell at Michelle's house. He smiled when he heard the kids running to the door, but his smile vanished when he heard his mother-in-law's voice. He straightened his tie as the door swung open.

"Well, Brad, on time as usual," Emily said, motioning him inside. "Please visit with your children. I'll tell Michelle you're here." Emily walked away before he could answer.

He and his children went into the living room. Brad sat on the couch with his son on his lap.

"Daddy, where are you taking Mummy?" Peri asked.

"It's a surprise."

"You mean it's a secret?"

"Yes. Have you been a good little girl for grandma and grandpa?"

"Yes, I have. PaPa says we're a joy. He took us out for lunch today."

Where was your mother? But he couldn't ask his four-year-old daughter that, could he? "Where was your mom?"

Peri shrugged. "It's a secret," she giggled as she left the room with her brother in tow.

"What secret is she talking about?" Michelle asked, walking into the living room looking like a vision in a figure-hugging pink linen dress. The v-neck sleeveless dress fell just above her knees, showing off her smooth legs.

He smiled. She was beautiful. The pink high-heeled strappy sandals called attention to her shapely calves and pedicured feet. He'd forgotten how sexy she looked when she set her mind to it.

Her usually shoulder-length dark hair was now streaked with blonde highlights. She'd always worn her hair straight with the minimum fuss, but now she had a head full of loose curls. And she wore gold hoop earrings. That's new, he thought. She'd always worn small, delicate earrings that were usually obscured by her hair. The earrings and the new hairdo made her look ten years younger. Or was it the dress? "You always did look nice in pink."

"Thank you," she said, clearly flustered by the compliment. "I'll just say goodnight to the kids and I'll be right back."

"Aren't they my kids, too?" Brad countered, not knowing why. "May I say goodnight, or is it not allowed?" He chastised himself for getting defensive.

She shot him a look of pure disdain. "Yes, you may say goodnight. I would never use the kids against you." She called them into the room and gave them a hug.

Brad watched the interaction. Something didn't seem right. The children acted as if they were used to their mother going out at night. He didn't like that. Or the fact that Peri asked for a doggie bag. After he hugged and kissed his children, the kids went upstairs.

Michelle got her purse. "Ready?"

She motioned for him to walk to the front door. "Bye, Mom. Be back soon." She opened the front door and waited for him to exit.

But Brad wasn't going out like that. "I got it." He waved her through the door and followed. As soon as the front door was closed, he heard the deadbolt lock click.

"Man, Emily doesn't waste any time locking that door, huh?" He laughed.

"I guess not."

He led her to the Range Rover, being careful not to touch her. He opened the door for her and waited for her to slide into her seat before closing it.

Patience, Brad, he reminded himself as he got into the truck. The familiar scent of her perfume had already filled in the air. God, she smelled good.

"We have a little time to spare before dinner. I thought I could show you the apartment," he lied.

"This isn't a trick, is it?" Michelle asked, looking out of the window.

"Why would this be a trick? Shell, come on. Yeah, I know I screwed up. I'm trying to right the situation."

"I don't think you can."

"Will you at least let me try? All I'm asking is that you give me a do-over."

CHAPTER 3

Early separation décor, Michelle thought when she saw Brad's apartment. None of the pieces really went together. The brown leather couch was fighting the plaid love seat for attention.

"Well, I see you still have your flair for decorating." She plopped down on the loveseat. "What did you do? Raid your sister's house?"

He smiled as he started toward the kitchen. "Did she call and tell you? Would you like something to drink?"

Perhaps a glass of wine would help her to relax. "White zin will be fine."

"Of course." He soon returned with a tray, holding a wine glass, a chilled bottled of wine, and a bottle of beer.

"I see we both still drink the same thing."

"Shell, it's been two months since we separated. Not two years."

"True," she said, sipping the wine. "What smells so good? It smells like fettuccine. I thought we were eating out?"

He sat next to her. "Yes, we were. But I didn't want to have a discussion this important in a crowded restaurant."

"Yeah. Here, in the privacy of your apartment, there are no witnesses."

He opened his bottle of beer with a sharp twist of his strong hand. He took several swigs before venturing an answer. "Shell, I didn't invite you to dinner to have a war. I just want to talk. Nothing else."

"So you cooked?"

"No. I hired a personal chef. She was pretty good."

She didn't like his faintly self-satisfied smile. "Was she pretty?" She immediately chastised herself for asking. It advertised she still cared and would be easy pickings. She couldn't have that. "Did you explain the reason for the dinner? You're afraid I'm going to take all your precious money in the divorce."

He set the beer bottle down with a little too much force. "Goddamn it, Shell. I told you. I don't want a damn divorce. What do I need to do? Hire a skywriter? A translator? What?"

The unbridled emotion he unleashed startled Michelle. Was he sorry? Really sorry? Was he kiss-your-feet sorry or I-haven't-had-sex-in-a-while sorry? How would she find out?

"I don't know what you need to do, Brad." She took a long sip of wine, hoping to calm her nerves.

He turned and faced her. "When did you start feeling neglected?"

"When you started spending so much time at work. After Preston was born, you were barely home."

He nodded. "I know. I was just trying to give you all the things that you wanted."

"What I wanted was a husband. What I got was a workaholic who forgot he had a family."

"I didn't forget. I was supposed to be providing for my family." He picked up his beer bottle and chugged the rest of the contents. Slamming the bottle on the table, he stood, looking down at her. "Why don't we pick this up later? The food is getting cold. Let's eat," he said, pointing to the dining room.She followed, trying to hide her confusion. She sat down at the table while he went to the kitchen.

He returned with the first course and they ate in silence. Michelle was in deep conflict. Her heart was fighting her brain and was in the lead. She coughed and shifted in her chair.

"Don't think that I'm taking you back," she announced. "I realized we could at least talk about what happened between us. You can see the kids as much as you want. No one would ever prevent that. All I ask is that you not take them around your girlfriends."

Brad was a smart man. He knew when not to push. This was one of those times. "I understand. I can ask the same of you."

"Yes," she agreed, eating the last of her salad.

Michelle didn't know how they made it through the rest of the meal without hurling more insults at each other. But with miracles being what they were, she didn't question it.

They sat on the couch sipping wine and listening to classical jazz on the stereo. Brad maintained his distance and never tried to rush her.

"How do you like being back in Texas?" It was the best she could do in the small talk area.

"Shell, we know each other. You don't have to ask idle questions."

"I really want to know. Remember when your transfer to London came through? You fought tooth and nail not to go. You complained the first six months after we got there."

He smiled, thinking back to those days. "Yeah, then I started to enjoy it. Pretty soon I was going to the pub with the blokes for beer," he said, using the British slang for *men*. "God, I miss that life, now."

Michelle missed England, too. Preston was born there. They lived across from the park, and Brad started playing rugby. He felt younger than he had in years. She remembered bundling up the children and tramping over to the park to watch him get covered from head to toe in mud and grass. He always complained about the pain the next day, but he refused to give it up.

"When did we stop communicating, Brad?"

He knew exactly when—right after he got the promotion. "Let's try to figure out how we can fix it instead of when it happened. I'm ready to do whatever it takes to make you understand how sorry I am and how committed I am to this marriage."

"Would you quit your job?"

"Yes."

She didn't believe that. "You would quit your job at Herrington Global just like that? You've had that job over twenty years. You're a vice president of investments, for goodness sake!"

He fixed his hazel eyes on her. "I would quit my job and look for a new one, if that's what it took for us to be a family again."

Maybe he was serious. Maybe this was a trick? She was too confused to consider any other options. "I'll think about it."

He smiled. "Thank you."

It was contagious. She found herself smiling back. "What are you thanking me for? I haven't given you an answer about reconciling."

"You said you would think about it." He put his wine glass down. "I had better take you home before you realize what you've done."

Michelle nodded. "Yes, you had better."

Michelle woke late the next morning. Usually her internal clock woke her just after sunrise, but today that internal alarm wasn't working.

She put on her robe and went into Peri's room. Empty. Preston's room was the same. Her mother had taken to fixing the kids breakfast on some mornings, claiming she was giving Michelle a break. And that was exactly where she found her little darlings.

Preston was in his high chair munching on a large pancake, eating it like a tortilla. He smiled as he noticed his mother. "Mama," he said around another bite of pancake.

"Hi, baby." She kissed his forehead. "You'd better slow down, Preston. You're going to turn into a pancake." She tweaked his chubby cheek with her thumb and forefinger.

He laughed but continued eating.

"Hi, Mummy," Peri said between bites of pancakes. Her pancakes were topped with whipped cream, nuts, and sliced bananas. "Grandma fixed us pancakes."

"Yes, they look delicious." She kissed Peri on her forehead before walking to the cabinet and getting a plate. She handed her plate to her mother. "What happened to 'I can't fix those kinds of things anymore'?"

Her mother put three large pancakes and two slices of bacon on her plate. "I don't know. I just felt like cooking this morning, instead of the usual oatmeal or cold cereal. I didn't want them bothering you, since you got in so late last night. I take it all went well."

"It went okay." She walked to the table and sat by Peri. She dug into the heavenly pancakes. Unlike her daughter, Michelle's pancakes were topped with butter and maple syrup and looked like a breakfast food instead of dessert. "These are good, Mom."

Emily joined them at the table. "I've asked Jeremy to help you with the kids while we're away. You know, just in case." She winked at Michelle.

"Just in case what?"

"Don't make me say it in front of your kids."

"Mom, I'm not taking him back." She knew that was a lie. She knew she would take him back when she saw him two nights ago.

"Hey, I'm not the one you have to convince. He's picking up the kids tonight?"

"Yes, he is. Since you and Dad are leaving Monday, I'm going to ask him to bring them back early."

"So you're going to face him this time, and not leave a note of instructions for me to relay?"

"Actually, I was kind of hoping that you would ask him. I have an aerobics class I just can't miss."

"Now, Michelle, I bought the membership for you. I go to that gym, so I know the schedule. No ma'am, it's time for you and Brad to stop dancing around each other and talk."

"We talked last night."

"I know that. But this hiding from him when he shows up has got to stop. Face your demon, which in this case is Brad. You don't want him having the upper hand, do you?"

"No. I know I have to face him, and I might as well start with tonight."

"Mummy, Daddy is here!" Peri announced, running to the door a few hours later.

Michelle laughed at her daughter. "Honey, calm down. You'll tire your daddy out before he even gets inside the door." She wiped her hands on her jeans and opened the door. Why was she nervous?

"Hey." He looked tired and frazzled.

"Hi." Michelle waved him inside. "Bad day?"

"Horrible. Don't want to talk about it." He headed straight for the couch and sort of dropped down.

"I wasn't asking," she snapped. "I'm sorry, Brad. That was uncalled for. You do look like somebody opened a can of whup-ass on you." She sat down beside him on the couch.

Peri joined them on the couch. "Honey, why don't you go watch TV with your brother while I talk to daddy? I'll call you when he's ready."

"Okay."

"Is there any chance of me getting something to drink?"

"Not while you're chauffeuring our children around. You can have a soda, coffee, or tea." Michelle waited for his choice.

"How about a glass of juice?"

"Okay, be right back."

When she returned his eyes were closed. He almost looked like an innocent little boy, and she felt a centimeter of ice melting around her heart. She sat next to him and placed the glass on the table. He opened his eyes.

"If you don't feel like taking the kids this weekend, that's fine. I was going to ask you to bring them back early Sunday, anyway."

He sat up and faced her. "Why?"

"Mom and Dad are leaving for a cruise on Monday and I wanted us to spend Sunday night together." *Like a family*, she said to herself.

He grunted. "Sure, Shell. I'll bring them back around noon. That way you can have family time with your parents and our kids."

"I knew you would take it the wrong way. It's just that they'll be gone for over two weeks. Since we've been back they've been with the kids every day."

He stood and started to pacing the room. "I take it you haven't given any thought to last night."

She didn't want to admit last night was all she thought about, but she couldn't form the words. "I was kind of busy with Mom today."

He didn't want to push the issue. The old Brad would have pushed her for some kind of answer by now. "I'm not trying to rush you." He called the kids. "My mom wants you to call her."

"Did you explain about us being separated?"

"No, Melody ratted me out. So Mom is really pissed with me."

The kids ran into the room, and Michelle went to get their miniature bags. She bent down and hugged them fiercely. "Be good for daddy." She rose and faced Brad, smiling. "You make sure you don't let them pig out on chocolate again." She took another tentative step towards him. "If you want to talk later, I'll be willing to listen."

A flicker of hope lit up his eyes. "Well, I just might take you up on that. You might see that I'm serious."

He was so close she could feel his breath warming her skin. It felt marvelous. She waited for him to take the initiative and kiss her.

He didn't. He picked up the bags and led the kids out the door.

"Bye, Mummy." Peri's voice was the only one she heard before the door closed.

But Michelle didn't let that last scene rattle her. She changed into workout clothes and left for the gym.

When she first saw Bodyworks Gym, she couldn't believe her mature mother was a member. Bodyworks lived up to its name. Buff bodies populated the gym in muscle-hugging outfits.

Michelle always enjoyed the view. It made up for that sometimes painful time she spent on the Stairmaster and treadmill, as it did tonight. As sweat poured down her face, almost obscuring the view, one of the buff bodies smiled at her.

"Michelle Shaw, is that you?" a woman's voice asked.

Michelle turned to see whose voice it was. "Oh my God!" It was her old school friend, Pamela Ryan. She jumped off the Stairmaster and ran over to her friend. "Pam, I haven't seen you in years!"

"I know. I got transferred to Tokyo about ten years ago," she said.

"Wow. Tokyo. I couldn't imagine living there."

Pam stood directly in front of her. Pam was almost six feet tall and towered over Michelle's five-eight frame. "It did take some getting used to, but once I did, I loved it. Momma told me you were living in England."

"Yes, but I just came back about two months ago. I miss it. So are you married?"

"Just divorced. My job was sending me back to the States, and he didn't want to leave Japan."

"Oh?"

"Well, his family was there and you know those Japanese are all about family and tradition. I worked hard for that promotion. We have three kids—six, four, and two."

"I'm separated," Michelle confessed. "We're trying to work it out. We have two kids, four and two. He has them tonight."

Pam smiled. "We should work out together. What's your schedule like?"

Michelle was embarrassed to admit she was lost. "Well, I'm not working right now. I'm living with my parents."

"When I first got back, I took a little time off to get my bearings. So I guess your time is pretty flexible, huh?"

"Yeah."

Pam pulled out a business card from the pockets on her shorts. "Here's my card. I know what you're thinking. Yes, I'm anal enough to carry business cards around on the exercise floor."

"You're just focused," Michelle reassured her friend. But she did think it was very strange. How could Pam choose her career over her marriage?

CHAPTER 4

Michelle had just stepped out of the shower when she heard the phone ring. She wrapped the towel around her body and picked up the nearest phone. "Hello."

"Hey, I didn't catch you in the middle of someone, did I?" Brad laughed, knowing that wasn't possible.

"No." She should have lied. "What's wrong? How are the kids?"

He chuckled. "Will you just relax? They're asleep. You said if I wanted to talk, you'd listen."

"Yes, I did." So he decided to take her up on her offer? She sat on the bed and tightened the towel around her. She unwrapped her hair and let it fall freely to her shoulders.

"Am I keeping you from something?"

"Dressing. I just got out of the shower," Michelle said.

"I could always come and help you."

"Brad," she groaned, praying he hadn't heard the hope in her voice.

"I know. That was way over the line. I'm sorry."

"That's okay. What did you want to talk about?"

"My day."

"Okay, Brad, how was your day?"

Taking a deep breath and began. "I had an argument with Frank today, which got me in hot water with the new regional director."

"What happened?"

"Well, Frank asked me if I had the specs for the upcoming executive meeting yet. You know as vice president I have access to all the financial reports, and I have to approve them before they go out to the shareholders. Well, Frank told me to give him my access codes, so he could make sure they were right. That's a direct breach of ethics, and I would be fired for doing that."

"What did you do? And do you still work there? Now we're both unemployed," she gasped.

"Classic Shell. How bad is it? You're such a pessimist," he teased, ignoring the seriousness of the issue. "I still have a job, but the director told me that although I was right to stand my ground, Frank is still my immediate supervisor and I should always take what he says as a directive. I told him to stuff it, and I wasn't giving anyone my access codes."

Michelle knew Brad was a stickler for office policy and took his duties as vice president seriously. "Is this normal? It would seem that Frank should have access."

"Herrington has this check and balance thing going on. No one person has access to everything. I may have access to that part of the report, but I don't have access to the actual investment companies. So if something goes missing, the blame will be easy to place. Like if the funding disappeared, they'd look in my direction. If the mutual bonds disappeared, they'd look at Frank."

She understood. Being of the business world before she married Brad, she knew all too well about how easily a scandal could start. "So what happens now?"

"I have to attend a workshop about teamwork next week. After that I was fit to be tied for the rest of the day."

Michelle released the breath she hadn't realized she had been holding. "Man, when you want to talk, you really want to talk."

"Yeah. Really sorry for putting all that on you. I guess I just wanted to vent. It felt good to talk about it."

Michelle didn't answer. She could feel his charm already flowing over the phone line and heading straight for forbidden territory.

"Shell?"

"I'm sorry," she said, snapping back to the conversation. "It was nice talking to you."

He laughed. "So what were you doing that necessitates a shower?"

Was he just being nosy or what? "Why?"

"I don't know," Brad whispered.

"Well, if you must know," Michelle teased, "I was at the gym."

"You're not going to Bodyworks, are you?"

"Yes. It's great." She laughed, as he groaned.

"Yeah, I've heard what a meat market it is. I've heard that guys walk around with almost no clothes on," Brad said, almost sounding jealous.

She decided a little baiting was in order. "Well, yeah, that part is true. I've never seen so many firm young bodies prancing around. It's the best gift my mom ever gave me."

His silence stretched until it began to get on her nerves. "Brad?"

"Yeah, I'm here."

"What?"

"I just don't think you should be working out there alone. Maybe I should join you?"

She realized he was jealous, "No, I like it. I'm finding my independence."

"I know, and I don't like it. Goodnight."

Michelle went to her art class Monday evening, prepared to change her life. This is just the start, she told herself. Earlier that day, she had waved good-bye to her parents, and her recently divorced brother moved in to help her with the kids, or so he claimed. Michelle knew he needed to be around family while he was trying to mend his broken heart.

As she opened her sketchpad, she wondered if Peri and Preston had driven poor childless Jeremy crazy yet.

"Is this seat taken?" A masculine voice interrupted her thoughts.

She knew that voice. She had only heard it every day for last five years. "What are you doing here? You hate anything remotely pertaining to art," Michelle said in disbelief.

Brad slid into the seat beside her, smiling. "Your mom told me about this class last week. She thought it might be good for me. She actually enrolled me in the class and told me I had better attend if I knew what was good for me."

"That woman." Michelle laughed. Her mother had gotten her pretty good over the years, but this time she had outdone herself.

"I'm glad I took her advice. Who's watching the kids?"

"Jeremy."

Laughing, Brad opened his sketchpad. "Jerry hasn't had a whole lot of experience with small children, has he?"

"Since we've been back, he's been spending a lot of time with them." Michelle looked around the room. "I can't believe Mom did this to me."

Brad leaned closer to her and whispered, "You said you wanted me to show you how serious I was about getting back together. I'm here with you taking this class. Doesn't that mean something?" He caressed her hand. "Hey, where are your wedding rings?"

He was quite serious, but she felt like playing with his head. She shrugged. "I'm sure they're in one of my jewelry boxes at home," she said casually.

"I still wear mine." He held up his left hand; the gold band shone brightly against his brown skin.

"Good for you," Michelle said sarcastically. "My husband finally remembered he was married."

"Please," he begged, "let's not start that again."

"You're late." Jeremy had just come down the stairs as Michelle came in. "I thought that class was over at nine."

Michelle set her canvas bookbag by the stairs. "I was tricked by your mother. Brad was there."

Jeremy laughed. "So that's why she wanted his phone number. That sounds like Mom. Don't be mad, Shell."

"I was at first, but after we finished trading insults, I remembered how much we actually have in common."

"Sounds like somebody is getting the reconciliation bug."

"Not hardly." She started up the stairs. "Did the kids give you any trouble?"

"No. They tried to pull a fast one, telling me that you hadn't fed them. But I knew better. I told them we could eat salad for dinner."

Michelle laughed. "Oh, my poor babies."

"Those little munchkins have met their match. Now they're asleep," he laughed. "So, since it's almost midnight, where have you been?"

She stopped walking and turned to face her brother. "I think I'm the older one here. I don't think I have to explain myself to you."

"No, you don't, but I'm asking you as a friend."

That got her. Jeremy, her thirty-nine-year-old divorced brother, was her friend as well as an irritating relative. "Well, friend, after the class was over, Brad asked me to have coffee with him."

"It takes three hours to have coffee?"

"You know, you sounded just like Mom when you said that. We talked about our former lives."

"And?"

"I don't want to go back to that life. This time it's going to be all about Michelle." She continued up the stairs. "Goodnight."

The next day while looking over some investment reports, Brad found that Frank failed to do his job, leaving Brad to clean up his mess.

He took the reports and headed down the hall to Frank's office. The door was open, Frank fiddled with his prized possession—a Monet reproduction on the wall. Brad cleared his throat, startling Frank, who recovered quickly and waved Brad inside the spacious office. Brad sat down and placed the flawed report on Frank's desk.

Frank had the nerve to look angry. "What's this?"

"This is the quarterly report, and it's missing about two million dollars," Brad said, enjoying the surprise on his boss's face.

"I thought you were going to look for it. That is part of your job as vice president."

"But your job as president is to avoid this kind of error in the first place. We could always discuss this with the regional director or the CFO to see what could be done."

"Are you suggesting I did it deliberately?"

"Even you wouldn't be stupid enough to sabotage a report of this importance. This isn't just about you and me. This involves the entire company. If something like this was leaked to the press, we could all be on CNN or *Money Matters*—or in jail."

Frank took a cursory look at the report. "Let's meet tomorrow night and go over this. I have a meeting tonight."

Brad instantly thought of Michelle. He couldn't miss class. "I can't tomorrow, I have a meeting."

"Can you reschedule?"

"No, I can't." Brad stood firm. That class was the gateway to his future. No one was going to prevent him from going. "We can work on this tomorrow during the day. I'll clear one of the conference rooms, unless you've got something else going on?"

Frank thought better of forcing the issue and caved. "Okay. Tomorrow afternoon."

Walking back to his office, Brad ran into Alex—literally.

"Hey!" they both exclaimed.

Alex saw the report in Brad's hands and worriedly asked, "You didn't go see Frank alone, did you?"

"Yes, I did. Don't worry. No bloodshed." Brad motioned to Alex to follow him to his office.

"What is it?" Alex asked, noting Brad's hush-hush manner.

Brad leaned forward in his chair and spoke in a low voice. "I think something big is going on and somehow Frank is involved. In going over the report, I've discovered there's some money missing. It could be nothing, but I've got a bad feeling it is something, and I'm not signing off on this until I can figure it out."

"Did you ask Frank about it? You know, maybe he just transposed some numbers or something."

"On three different accounts? We're going over it tomorrow afternoon." He grinned, suddenly remembering the surprise on Michelle's face when he sat by her in art class.

"I take it art class went well."

"Yeah, after the usual insults. We went for coffee afterwards and we talked for hours. You know, like two adults. We talked about us, not about work or the kids, just us. God, I miss talking to her. We hadn't talked like that in a long time. I want that part of our life back."

"All in good time, my friend. Let's go over those numbers and see what's going on."

Wednesday afternoon, Brad phoned Michelle, but Jeremy said she was at the gym. Frank walked into his office just as he hung up.

Frank flopped into the nearest chair. "Are you ready to go over the report?"

Brad nodded and retrieved the file. "Yes, I have reserved the conference room upstairs. Let's go."

"How are the proceedings coming along?" Frank asked as they entered the elevator.

"What proceedings?" Brad asked, pushed the up elevator button.

"Divorce. Like I told Michelle when I was visiting you guys, communication is the secret to a good marriage. I treated her like a possession, not an asset." Frank smiled as he entered the glass elevator. "I failed my first wife and she'll never forgive me for what I did to her."

"Wow, that's too bad. How long have you been divorced?" Brad asked, pushing the button for the floor above.

"I guess about five years. Seems longer. I was just going through the motions until I met Claire a few years ago. This last year has been the happiest of my life. Claire is my best friend. We talk constantly."

Brad noticed the wistfulness in Frank's voice. "Sounds like she's made you happy."

"Happy doesn't begin to describe what I'm feeling. Sometimes I still can't believe she picked me to marry. She could have had any man in Texas, but she chose me."

Brad could agree with the sentiment; he felt exactly the same way about Michelle. He just had to make her realize they were meant to be together. "Let's just get this over with, shall we?"

CHAPTER 5

After his nerve-wracking meeting with Frank, Brad was sure an entire bottle of aspirin would not have helped his headache.

In addition to the two million dollars missing in securities, there was another million missing in mutual funds. Brad would have to put in some overtime to track the missing funds.

He checked the time. If he didn't leave now, he wouldn't have time to shower and change before art class. He threw the report into his briefcase and headed of the door.

Talking as he walked, he gave last minute instructions to his secretary. "Mary, I'm leaving for the day. If anyone needs me, call my cell."

"Yes, Mr. Killarney."

He barely made it to class on time. He spotted Michelle sitting alone. He slipped into the chair beside her. "Hey."

She smiled at him. "Damn. I owe Jeremy twenty bucks."

He thought she didn't believe in him, but she *really* didn't believe in him. Somehow that took the wind out of his sail. "You thought I wouldn't show up? I'm hurt." He was smiling until he noticed what she wore. "Did you just come from the gym or something?" he asked, eyeing her nylon shorts and T-shirt. The reserved Michelle he knew wouldn't have dared show that much leg in public.

"Actually, I planned to hit the treadmill after class."

He didn't like that idea. "Will the gym still be open? You know, most gyms close at nine or so." He knew that was not the case.

"Of course it will still be open. It's open twenty-four hours a day, seven days a week."

"I think I should go with you."

She shook her head. "No, Brad. I'm sure you have other plans. You don't have to go. I'm not your responsibility anymore."

The answer to that declaration would have only started a fight in the middle of art class. "I know you're not technically my responsibility, but you're still my wife and the mother of my children. So I will go with you."

"Dressed like that?" She pointed at his polo shirt, slacks, and casual shoes.

She had him, and he knew it. "Well, I would have to change first."

After class, Michelle followed Brad to his apartment. He changed and convinced her to let him drive her to the gym. Part one of his plan was working out great. Even Alex would have given him high marks for this part.

"You have a membership?" Michelle asked as they produced IDs for the receptionist.

"Yeah, I'm a new member, too." He neglected to mention that Emily had also informed him about the gym and suggested he join.

"You don't need to work out," Michelle said, walking to the treadmill area. "I mean, I didn't think you had time to work out, what with your promotion and all."

"Nice backtracking, Shell. Thanks." He hopped on the treadmill next to hers. "Hey, want to race? I jog on this sometimes," he lied. He had been to the gym only one other time—when he signed up for his membership.

"No. I just started working out. I'm not that advanced. I can barely walk on this, let alone run."

Brad couldn't believe they were bantering instead of trading barbs. He decided it was time to up the ante. "You know, if you want to work out late, I could come with you.

"That's okay. I already have a workout partner."

Brad's heart lurched. That's why she was pushing so hard for the divorce. "Of course you do. I was just offering."

Michelle knew she should correct the impression she left with him, but the woman in her was enjoying his crestfallen reaction.

"How long?" he asked, jabbing the buttons impatiently.

"Forty minutes." She set the controls and began her stride.

She was in her comfort zone, blood pumping and heart racing. She had almost put Brad out of her mind, except for the noise he was making.

He punched the controls again and began running on the treadmill. He was actually jogging. She initially thought he was kidding. She watched as sweat poured down his face, drenching his T-shirt. She barely noticed when her time was up.

Brad watched her intently as he dried his face. "Thanks, Shell. I was feeling stressed, but that helped me a lot."

"What do you have to feel stressed about?" She dried her face. "I don't shower here. Do you?"

"Same ol' Shell. Afraid of all those germs in the public shower?"

Michelle laughed. "Yes, I'm still the antibacterial specialist. I just can't bring myself to shower here."

"Me neither. Being married to you for five years, I guess the germ thing rubbed off on me. I even have the handwash stuff in my briefcase," he said, enjoying the smile tugging at her lips.

She playfully slapped his sweaty arm. "Let's go." She pulled him out of the gym.

A familiar feeling came over Michelle during the drive to Brad's apartment. Hunger. In her rush to get to class, she had not eaten. Her stomach rumbled a reminder.

"Wow. Somebody sounds hungry," Brad teased.

"Yeah. I forgot to eat today."

"I could whip us up something."

I just bet, she thought. "I don't know, Brad."

"Oh, come on. I'm not asking for sex. I've been really good. It will be just a little snack, not an orgy." He winked at her.

Michelle knew better, but she let Brad fix her something to eat. They sat in his small kitchen and ate turkey sandwiches.

"Well, Brad, I'm surprised. I didn't think you knew what healthy food was. I was envisioning greasy hamburgers, with a mountain of cheese."

"People change, even if just a little," he said between bites.

There was something about the way he was looking at her across the table. *No, Michelle, it's only because you've been with him all evening.* "That's true. I think I've changed. I don't think I'm the same woman you left two months ago."

"Yeah. I'm finding that out."

The next morning, Michelle woke to the sounds of her two-year-old singing his favorite song of the month—the 'I Love You' song from Barney.

"Good morning, honey." She sat up and hugged her son. "I bet you're hungry."

He nodded. "Unca Jemee had to go to the office. Can we have cakes for breakfast?"

Michelle nodded. "Just let me get dressed. I bet Peri is watching cartoons?"

He said, "Dunno," and wiggled down off the bed. He opened her bedroom door and went down the hall, yelling for his sister.

After breakfast, Michelle took the kids to the park for a little playtime. She also wanted to work on her assignment for art class. It was early summer, so the weather wasn't too hot. North Texas was known for scorching hot summer days that regularly passed the hundred-degree mark. But this promised to be a good day.

She kept an eye on the kids as they played on the jungle gym. As always, she also kept an eye out for strangers. She spotted a face, but it wasn't that of a stranger. She only wished it was.

Frank Sims sat on a wooden bench near the playground, a briefcase resting next to him. He had chosen a spot where he could conduct the last part of his business discreetly.

At the most, he had another week before his "mistake" would be found out. Brad would be sure to tell the chief financial officer about the missing money, and the board of directors would launch a full-scale investigation. He would be exposed. Frank just needed a way to keep Brad quiet.

He'd recommended Brad for the job because he seemed the most likely candidate. Frank thought he could use his friendship with Brad to his advantage. He had forgotten what a stickler Brad was for the rules. Brad believed in doing things right, and if that meant he had one less friend in the world then so be it. Frank needed access to the financial prospectus on the company so he could fudge the numbers, but Brad wouldn't hear of it.

His contact was dressed in business attire, looking like a million bucks. Frank knew that because that was what was in the briefcase. He neared Frank and took a seat on the bench next to him. "This is your idea of discreet?" the man asked, gesturing at the kids playing.

"Yes," he answered, placing a hand on the briefcase to make sure it hadn't somehow mysteriously vanished.

"There are children and their nosy stay-at-home moms all over the place," the gentleman pointed out.

"Let's just finish this transaction. This is the last one. No exceptions." Frank stared into cold blue eyes, determined to make his point stick. He wasn't going to jail for stealing money he didn't get to enjoy. If he was going down he was taking this man with him.

"Oh no, Frank. This is not the last installment of your payment. No, I expect payment to go on as usual. It's not over until I say it's over."

"My new vice president is a hands-on kind of guy. He refused to give me access to the report. I can't fix the numbers if I can't get to the report."

"Get rid of him."

"I can't get rid of him. It would raise too many questions. He's the fourth vice president in the last year. If there's one more accident people will get suspicious." Frank thought for a moment. "I could set him up."

"You get rid of him, or he'll get rid of you. I've worked too long and too hard to have you screw this up now. Payment next month as usual." He picked up the briefcase and left.

Frank swore under his breath as the man disappeared into the distance. "I'll find a way to keep Brad quiet and a way to keep that monkey off my back, too," he promised himself.

He looked around the park and saw the answer to half his problem.

Seeing Michelle with the children brought back the memory of his wife earlier that morning when she informed him she was pregnant. He'd been given a second chance. He had to fix all the wrongs he'd committed in the name of teamwork and move forward.

The first thing he had to do was fix Brad and Michelle. It was his fault for hanging around them so much, but that was the only way for the plan to work. He had to meet in the park, and Michelle was the perfect cover. He escorted them to the park, met his contact and no one was the wiser.

"Hello, Michelle." He sat next to her on the park bench. "I see you're adjusting well to the single life."

She scooted away from him. "What are you doing here? Aren't you supposed to be at work or something?"

He scooted closer to her. "Yes, I was just taking a little break and I saw you. I love coming to this park," he said. "It's miles from work and I can just sit there and reflect on things. How are you and Brad?"

"We're fine."

"Michelle," he said as he picked up her hand and caressed it. "We both know that isn't true. Just remember if you want to talk, I'm ready to listen."

"Thank you, Frank."

He wondered if she noticed the man he was with. Could she put two and two together and come up with three million dollars? He was just about to ask her when he noticed the shocked expression on Michelle's face. But she wasn't looking into his eyes, she was looking past him and above his head.

"Why is it every time I turn my back for one minute, you're either holding my wife or trying to get her to leave me?" Brad asked.

Frank thought of the question and knew Brad could and would beat him to a bloody pulp. He outweighed Frank by at least fifty pounds, and Frank guessed most of that was muscle. Brad, dressed in a blue suit and an angry scowl, grabbed Frank by the arm.

"You don't think I know what you're up to, but I do." Brad wrestled Frank to the ground, pounding him with his fists.

"Brad!" Michelle screamed. "Brad, stop!"

Brad was enjoying his moment of triumph. He had Frank right where he wanted him. He pounded Frank's face until Michelle's frightened voice penetrated his rage. What was he doing? His kids were watching their father beat another man senseless. Suddenly, he stopped.

Brad walked to Michelle as she sat on the park bench, using her body to shield her children from the violent scene. She jumped when Brad touched her.

"Are you okay? Did he hurt you?"

Michelle turned accusing eyes on him, breaking his heart. "Frank was just offering his ear for conversation. He wasn't trying to make a play for me. He knew we were separated and offered help. Why couldn't you have reacted this way a few months ago? Like when I first told you I didn't like him hanging around because I didn't trust him. But you kept insisting he was harmless. Now he's going to file charges against you for assault."

Brad knew otherwise. Frank wouldn't dare, especially with the information he had on him now. Frank got up, dusted himself off, and left the park. "I'll be okay. I'll help you get the kids to the car." He picked up his son and hugged him. Nothing in the world could compare to the feeling of holding his child.

"Would you care to tell me what that was about?"

"I'll tell you later. I want to make sure you're okay."

She buckled the kids into their car seats. Her hands shook as she tried to buckle her own seatbelt.

"Move over. I'll drive." Brad started to get into the car.

"No, I'll be fine. We'll be fine. I just need to get my bearings." She took a deep breath. "See. I'm okay."

He didn't want her to leave in her shaky state, but he knew she would never let him drive her home. "I'll follow you."

"Whatever you feel is best." She closed her car door and started the engine.

She pulled off, and he headed for his truck. He called his secretary and told her he would be out for the rest of the day. He drove to Michelle's, knowing that he would have a lot of explaining to do.

By the time he arrived at her house, the kids were out of the car and in the house. He rang the doorbell and waited for Michelle to open the door. "You didn't have to follow us."

"I know I didn't. But I wanted to." She was getting ready to feed the kids. They were already seated at the dining-room table. "What's for lunch?"

She read his mind. "Just soup and sandwiches. You wouldn't want any, would you?"

He took off his jacket and threw it onto the couch. "I would love some soup." He walked ahead of her to the table and sat by Peri.

"Daddy's eating with us! Are we fixed?"

Brad and Michelle exchanged surprised looks. "What do you mean, honey?" he asked, looking into his daughter's hopeful face.

"Are we a family again?"

CHAPTER 6

After Brad left, Michelle stretched out on the couch, finally able to relax. Lunch had been difficult enough with his intense staring at her; with Peri's innocent but probing questions, it had become unbearable.

She had been so busy trying to make sure the children were shielded from external forces that she had forgotten about the internal ones. Every Friday, Brad picked the kids up and brought them back on Sunday. They *were* a broken home.

They could thank Frank for that. *No, be honest, girl, your marriage was going by way of the wastebasket before Frank Sims showed his ugly face. He just helped to speed up the inevitable.* Had she and Brad really grown that far apart in such a short time? Were they just taking the easy way out by separating and, ultimately, divorcing?

"Mummy, Daddy's at the door," Peri said, tugging on her mother's hand.

"What's he doing back here?" Michelle wondered aloud. She walked to the front door and got her answer.

Looking very relaxed, Brad had changed from a suit into jeans, a polo shirt, and tennis shoes.

"What are you doing back here?" she asked, letting him inside. As he walked past her, she caught a whiff of his cologne.

He joined his daughter on the couch, smiling up at Michelle. "I thought we could talk while the kids are napping."

Michelle had to do something or that sexy grin of Brad's was going to make her do something silly. "How do you know they haven't had their nap already?"

"In less than an hour? Come on, Shell, even I am not buying that one." He pulled his yawning daughter onto his lap. "I think it's naptime for somebody," he said, trying not to laugh at Michelle's not-so-subtle attempt to avoid being alone with him.

Michelle reached for Peri. "You're not sleepy. Are you? How about some chocolate?"

Peri's eyes lit up, but the day's events had worn her four-year-old body out. Yawning again, she hugged Brad's neck and closed her eyes. Preston was Michelle's last hope, but he, too, had grown awfully quiet in the last few minutes. Michelle turned around to see her son asleep on the floor.

Brad tried to stifle his laughter. "Why don't we put the kids to bed? I'll be a gentleman. I promise." He gathered Peri up and started for the stairs.

What choice did she have? "All right." She picked up Preston, and they headed upstairs. "Peri's room is to your left," she whispered over her shoulder.

They met up in the hall after she had put Preston down. "I wouldn't have expected them to have their own room," he said quietly.

"Mom insisted. She said it wouldn't do to have them start getting in the habit of sleeping with me."

Downstairs, they sat on the couch, she at one end and he at the other. Michelle watched him watching her. "They'll be asleep for awhile. So what was that in the park?"

Brad took a deep breath. "Pretty much a continuation of what I told you last week. Frank is supposed to compile the numbers on a mutual fund report, and I have to check it. But when I did I found there was a discrepancy in the numbers. Frank and I met yesterday for a little while to figure out where he made the mistake, but all he talked about was his wife."

Michelle didn't see the problem. "So he loves his wife. I don't really see the problem."

"I know I screwed up, Shell. You don't have to remind me at every turn, do you?"

"Sorry, Brad, but you make it sound like there's something wrong with Frank being in love with his wife."

"That's not the problem. Actaully, she just found out she's pregnant. And that's all he talked about. How he was going to be a better father this time around."

"So maybe he just transposed some numbers or something," Michelle said. "It's possible. He's human, not a computer."

"That's what I thought, too. I mean, I've known Frank a long time and he's always been dedicated to his job, but lately he seems distracted. So today when I heard him tell his secretary he had a doctor's appointment, I decided to follow him."

"Stalking is a crime, Brad. Even if it is your boss."

"Be serious. Frank Sims has never been sick a day in his life. He's thin as a rail and he's always exercising."

"Maybe he has cancer," Michelle suggested.

"That's really not the point here, Michelle. The point is that I knew he was lying and followed him to the park. He was talking with some guy, I couldn't tell who it was."

"I didn't see him until he was walking toward me."

He moved closer to her. "I know that, Michelle. I saw him talking to you and I snapped. With all the strange things that had been happening at work, I just snapped. I didn't want him touching you." His voice was a low, sexy timbre, and throbbed with sexual tension. "I know you didn't do anything to warrant his attentions, and I am not accusing you. I am telling you what I did today and why I was knocking the holy crap out of Frank," Brad explained caressing the inside of her hand with his thumb.

"Sorry." It felt too good to be this close to him. She wiggled her sweaty fingers free. "Continue."

"I don't know if I can. A lot of it is bad vibes. I can't go to the board with bad vibes. I don't have anything concrete until I can go over that report with a fine-toothed comb. I've known Frank a long time, and this just doesn't make any kind of sense."

"Does he know that you know?"

Brad shrugged. "I don't think so."

Michelle shuddered at the things Brad hadn't said. "You should tell somebody."

"Who, Shell? Most of the company knows that Frank and I have known each other for years. It was partly his recommendation that got me this job. I've got to have concrete evidence."

"I think three million dollars is pretty concrete," Michelle said. Of all the days for her to take the kids to the park, it would have to be that park in particular where Frank Sims would met his partner in crime. "Okay, how much trouble are you in? Are we in danger?"

He hesitated. "Danger might be a strong word. I would definitely be careful. Since we're taking the art class together, I can just pick you up."

"No. I'm not going to let him dictate my life. He's not going to make me a hermit."

"I didn't say you had to be a hermit. Just humor me."

"You're just using this to get back together," Michelle said accusingly.

He grabbed her hand and massaged it. "I know this about you. I can't use anything to get you to take me back."

"Really? I thought you just assumed I'd take you back."

"I know it's all up to you. I can say I'm sorry only so many times without sounding insincere. I just have to show you how I feel." He leaned over and kissed her gently on the lips.

Her brain told her she should stop this madness. But her lips were ruling her body at the moment. His lips teased hers apart and his tongue devoured her.

Michelle arms crept up to circle his neck and drew him closer. She couldn't stop if she wanted to, and she didn't want to. He whispered against her smooth skin, nuzzling his face against hers, "I've missed you."

"Brad, please stop," she whimpered.

He chuckled. "You'd sound more convincing if your hand wasn't under my shirt, and caressing my stomach. You're giving me such a hard-on." He pulled her onto his lap.

She let herself go, she knew that. She was lost with a few kisses and the feel of an enormous erection. How to reel herself back in? She was drowning and was going down for the third and final time. Brad's hands slipped further under her shirt. His fingers moved in a circular motion on her stomach, creating delicious shivers of excitement. She wanted to so badly. But she couldn't.

"Brad, the children," she moaned, finally regaining some composure.

"Are asleep," he finished for her. "Please," he whispered against her ear. "I need you, Michelle."

It was the events of the day that had them both out of control, she thought. She couldn't let the insanity of the day continue. Someone had to call a halt to this madness.

She slid off his lap and sat beside him. "Brad, I can't."

"I'm not going to push you. You think that's all I want from you, don't you? I do want you, Michelle, and not just for sex. I want you because I love you and we were meant to be together."

"I just don't want us rushing into something that we'll regret."

He picked up her hand and kissed it. "I'd never regret anything that we do together." He stared into space, collecting his thoughts. "Now what?"

"I do want you, Brad. I just don't want the past to happen again. I'd been so unhappy the last year. I kept hoping things would get better, but they didn't."

"All you had to do was talk to me," he said.

"I know. That's easier said than done."

He turned and faced her. "Okay, since we're both here and the kids are asleep, let's hash this out. I want to start that clean slate now."

Just like Brad, she thought. No muss, no fuss, just the facts. "Okay, Brad. I'll start," Michelle said.

He reached for her hand. "Shoot."

CHAPTER 7

Michelle woke up to strange noises beside her on the couch. It didn't sound like Preston. It sounded more like Brad snoring in her ear. They were lying spoon fashion on their sides after their heart-to-heart talk that afternoon.

They must have fallen asleep somewhere in their list of demands. Michelle decided that they had both voiced their concerns about the marriage and, to her surprise, they were almost the same.

Except for her staying home with the children. Michelle was ready to reclaim her life in the workplace, which Brad was totally against. Brad was traditional all the way. They came up with a compromise of Michelle working part-time until the kids were in school.

Michelle wanted Brad to work less and spend more time with the children, and that was where the talks broke down.

"Why don't we table this until later?" Brad suggested as they lay snuggled on the couch.

She yawned and agreed, closing her eyes.

Now, however, Michelle was ready to resume the discussion. She nudged Brad awake. "We have something to talk about."

Brad stretched and nodded. "Yes, I can only imagine the issue. You want me to give up my job."

"You offered to the other night. What was that? Just idle promises?"

He sat up and reached for his shoes. "No, it wasn't idle talk. I meant that. I want to be all that I can for you and the kids, but I have to work."

"We don't need the money," Michelle said.

"What about what I need? You said you're ready to reclaim your life, but you're asking me to be idle and I can't do that."

"What about the kids? I don't want Preston wondering why his father never had time for him. He's only two, and these are his formative years. I want him to know you."

"He knows I'm his father."

He was missing the point, as usual. "Brad, any man can be a father, it takes a real man to be a dad. I'm asking you to be a dad and put your son above your job."

He stood and looked down at her. "How dare you accuse me of neglecting my son. I know I screwed up in London by working too much, and I'm paying for my sins every day that we're not together, but I'm trying. One day you'll see I'm really trying to change." He stalked out of the house.

Later that night, Michelle read the kids a bedtime story and put them to bed. Then she allowed herself to wonder where Brad was. He hadn't called. Not that she expected him to, but an apology would have been nice. She went downstairs to talk to her brother. He was a man, after all, and maybe he could give her insight on her husband's behavior.

"Any word from Brad?" Jeremy asked, looking up from his laptop computer, smiling. He pushed back from the desk and stretched his six-foot frame.

"He hasn't called. Not that I expect him to," Michelle lied.

"Liar."

"Yes, I guess so," Michelle admitted. "Anyway, he was just being a man."

"I take offense at that statement. I would never neglect my family for the sake of my career. You just let those bad feelings build up until they exploded."

"I know that now. I also know I've changed during our short separation. I want some of my old life back."

"And Brad sees this as bad?"

"I want to have a life outside of my children and husband. Is that so bad?"

"I don't think so. Look, Brad is almost fifty. He's just got a tradi-tional view of marital roles. He'll come around. You'll see."

"How can you be so sure?"

"Because even though he was an idiot and made all the wrong choices, he's busting his chops to show you he can change. I suggest you do the same, big sister." He stood up. "We'd better go to bed. They had a lot of candy and junk today. Tomorrow won't be fun."

Michelle yawned. "I'm really tired."

She was awakened by the doorbell. Who could it be? It was seven in the morning. Putting on her robe as she rushed downstairs, Michelle was ready to read Brad the riot act for coming over so early to apolo-gize.

She opened the front door, simultaneously asking, "What is it?"

Two men dressed in department store suits stared at her with a questioning look on their faces. "Michelle Killarney?" They held up their badges for identification. Arlington Police Department.

A feeling of dread came over her instantly. Oh, no. Her parents. Something happened on the cruise ship. She leaned against the door. "Is this about my parents?"

"Ma'am?"

"My parents are on a cruise. Did something happen to them?"

"No, this isn't about your parents."

"Then what is this about?" She remembered she hadn't change the license plate on her Lincoln Navigator since returning to the States. "If it's about the plates on my car, well, we've been back from the United Kingdom just a few months...."

One of the police officer held his hand up to stop her babbling. "Ma'am, do you know a Bradley Huntington Killarney?"

Oh, this was so not good. "He's my husband. I mean we're sepa-rated. What's this about?"

"We're trying to contact him, that's all. Do you know Frank Sims?"

"He's my husband's boss. Has something happened?"

The officers looked at each other before the more talkative one replied, "What would make you ask that, ma'am?"

"Uh, I don't know." *Bad move, Michelle. Real bad. Now they think you have something to hide.*

"We have witnesses who placed you in the park yesterday talking with him. Your husband attacked Mr. Sims. Now Mr. Sims has a nine-inch blade sticking in his chest."

"Oh, no!" Michelle slapped her hand over her mouth to stifle a scream. Brad was awfully mad yesterday. But he wouldn't take a life. Brad was going to investigate, not kill, Frank.

Keeping his expression blank, the officer, "Can you tell me where you were about ten last night?"

"Why would I need an alibi for last night?" Michelle asked, not believing the officer's line of questioning.

"Because you and your husband were the last people in contact with the deceased, and you both have a clear motive and ample opportunity. So where were you last night between the hours of ten and midnight?"

She didn't like his attitude. "Well, between nine and eleven, I was talking to my brother in the den here." She pointed to the open door down the hall. "From eleven to twelve I was taking a bath."

"You take an hour for a bath?"

Jeremy joined them at the front door. "You don't know my sister and her bath ritual. Please, come in, gentlemen." He directed the officers to the living room.

In her shocked state she had forgotten to invite them inside. She also realized she was in her robe. "Do I have your permission to get dressed?"

The officers nodded. "Yes, ma'am, you can get dressed. Just don't get any ideas about taking a trip out the bathroom window."

"From the second floor?" Michelle asked as she headed upstairs. She checked on the kids, hoping the doorbell hadn't woken them. Thank goodness for small favors; they were still sound asleep. Yesterday must have tired them out, too. Hopefully, the police would leave soon.

She dressed in jeans and a T-shirt and went back downstairs to face the two officers.

"Well, was my alibi solid enough or do I need to elaborate on my bath time?"

"Near as we can figure, Mr. Sims died around ten-thirty. You were here with your brother. But we do need to speak with your husband. When was the last time you saw him?"

"Yesterday about three."

"What kind of mood was he in? Was he angry? Was he violent?"

"He was angry, but it was because we had a fight, not anything to do with Frank."

"What did you fight about?"

"I don't think it has anything to do with this," Michelle said, her hands on her hips.

"Mrs. Killarney, we have a man with a knife in his chest. I think any information you can give us will help. You could be charged with obstructing justice by withholding information."

"The fight was about our marriage," she said.

"I understand Mr. Sims was the cause of the separation," the officer stated.

Oh, boy, that was a loaded statement. "Yes and no."

"Ma'am?"

"Our marriage was already troubled before Frank Sims became Brad's boss. We were living in England, and Frank came over to check out operations. He ended up spending most of his time with me and the kids, instead of at the office with my husband. Finally, I had had enough of babysitting the boss."

"Did you separate in England?"

"No, we didn't separate then. We separated when we came back to the States, which was about two months ago."

"I see. Were you and your husband trying to reconcile?" The officers were taking turns asking questions.

She shrugged. "I guess," she allowed. "We were trying to iron out some of our problems yesterday."

Jeremy laughed, attracting the attention of the officers and Michelle. "Sorry."

"I take it you have spoken to your husband on more than one occasion," the officer said.

"Yes."

"Did he mention anything about Frank, or about the financial report?"

"Vaguely."

Both officers glared at her, letting her know that they knew she wasn't telling the entire truth. But they were going to let her be for now. "Thank you for your time. If you happen to hear from your husband, please let us know." One handed her a business card. "You can reach me day or night."

She stood also. "Is he being formally charged?"

"We need to question him. That's all, ma'am. The quicker we can eliminate him from our list of suspects, the better for him."

"So, he *is* a suspect." She opened the door for the officers. "Brad might be a lot of things, but he's not a killer."

"His boss, who was instrumental in ruining your marriage, is dead. He was seen beating the same man in the park, and three million dollars in investments is missing," the officer said, holding up three fingers. "That's why he needs to come forward. Good day, ma'am."

Michelle closed the door and leaned against it for support. Oh, my gosh. This was serious. Frank was dead and Brad was a suspect.

She pushed herself away from the door and walked heavily back to the living room. Her brother was just finishing a call. "Do you think he's guilty?" Jeremy asked.

She shook her head. "No, of course not. He was mad yesterday, but he wasn't that mad. I don't think he could get that mad."

"I just tried his house, but there's no answer."

CHAPTER 8

Michelle, confused and worried, plopped onto the couch and tried to process the news she'd just received. Would Brad kill Frank? Was he capable of murder? Not her Brad. Not the idiot that accused her of cheating on him.

She heard the kids coming down the stairs. She forced a smile on her face and walked to meet them. "Good morning. How about McDonald's for breakfast?"

"Yeah!"

"Okay." She raised her hands up in surrender. Please quiet down, she prayed silently. It was too early in the morning. "I'll be up to help you get dressed in just a few minutes." She smiled as they ran off in the direction of the stairs.

She saw the quizzical look on her brother's face. "I know. I'm letting them eat fast food for breakfast. I think the occasion calls for it. Why don't you come with us?"

Jeremy declined, saying, "Why don't I go by Brad's apartment and see what's up?"

"Don't you think the cops are casing his place?"

"Maybe. But this doesn't sound like Brad, or at least the Brad I know." Picking up his keys, he headed for the door. "I'll call if I find out anything."

Why didn't she believe in Brad as vehemently as Jeremy did? Shaking her head, she went upstairs to help Preston get dressed. Peri could usually pick out her own clothes and dress herself. After both children were dressed, they headed for McDonald's.

At McDonald's, Peri and Preston gobbled down their food and then headed for the play area. As she sat drinking her coffee, her cell-phone rang.

"Hey, Jerry. Did you find him? I just thought he might be at work or with a client or something." She knew that was unlikely. Brad hadn't dealt with clients in ten years.

Jeremy's voice alarmed her. "No, he wasn't here. Something doesn't feel right about this. His bed doesn't look slept in."

"How did you get into his place?"

"He gave me a key when he first moved in. Anyway, his place is neat as a pin and his car's not here, either. Maybe you should call his office."

"Okay. Will do." Brad's secretary picked up on first ring and, upon hearing Michelle's voice, pretended the call was from a client.

"I'm sorry, sir. Mr. Killarney is out of the office today." Then she hung up abruptly.

"Sir?" That could only mean that the police were there, Michelle reasoned. But where was Brad? If he wasn't where he should be, where could he be?

She took a sip of her coffee, which by now was cold. How long had she been sitting there like a zombie? She took her tray to the disposal bin and went to get her kids. "Come on, guys."

She strapped the kids into their car seats and headed for home. "The hospital," she murmured, "I should check there."

"What, Mummy?" Peri asked.

"Nothing, baby." She turned the car around. Arlington, a mid-sized city, had three major hospitals in the area.

She phoned her brother. "Hey, did you check any of the hospitals?"

"No, I wasn't thinking in those terms."

"I'll begin checking hospitals. I'm sure it's a wild-goose chase, but I've got to try."

"Which one are you going to first? I'll come get the munchkins."

"You don't have to," Michelle said. She had momentarily forgotten about the two children. "I know you still have clients to see."

Jeremy laughed. "Yeah, and you're looking for your missing husband. I'll meet you at Kennedy Memorial Hospital in twenty minutes."

She drove into the hospital parking lot and waited for Jeremy. "Uncle Jeremy is coming to get you guys," she said, spotting his black BMW turning into the space next to hers.

She hopped out of the Navigator and quickly unbuckled the kids. Her brother also had the spare car seats in his car. With the kids safely buckled in, Jeremy drove off.

Michelle walked into the waiting room and went directly to the information desk. "May I help you?" a pleasant young woman asked.

"I was wondering if you could tell me if you have had any admissions since yesterday afternoon. He would be an African-American, about six-two, athletic build, hazel eyes, age 48." A beautiful physical specimen, Michelle almost added.

The young woman's eyes lit up at the description. "You know, last night a fortyish black man staggered in here covered in blood. He had hazel eyes. As a matter of fact, your description comes pretty close to this patient's."

Michelle steadied herself, hoping against hope. "Is there any way I can see him? He could be my husband. He's missing." She left out such tiny details as the murder of his boss and the missing money.

"Let me make a call." The woman picked up the phone and began making inquiries. Turning to Michelle, she said, "Someone will come down and get you."

Michelle nodded, bracing herself for the possibility that it might not be Brad. It was a double-edged sword. On one hand, she wanted it to be Brad, so the mystery would be solved. But on the other hand, she hoped it wasn't Brad in the hospital and covered in blood.

"Someone will be here shortly."

Michelle stepped aside, as there were other people in line. She called her brother with the news while she waited. As she ended the call, she saw a man in a white lab coat approaching.

"Ma'am, I'm here to escort you to the intensive care unit." His sympathetic eyes told her this was very, very bad.

He led her into the elevator and pushed the button for the fifth floor. Michelle whispered a prayer as the elevator began moving. *Please don't be Brad. Please don't be Brad. Please don't be Brad.*

The orderly took her to the ICU, informing the duty nurse that she was here to see John Doe.

"John Doe? No, I'm looking for my husband."

"That's the name we use when they come in with no identification," the orderly explained.

"Oh, dear," Michelle gasped. Where was his identification? So many things didn't make sense. The attendant pulled back the curtain, and there he was: it was definitely Brad lying in bed, unconscious. His head was bandaged. His lips were swollen. It looked like someone had beaten him senseless. A doctor was leaning over him.

"Ma'am, can we talk outside?" he asked.

"Yes."

Michelle followed him into the hall. "What happened to Brad?"

The doctor was as clueless as she was. "I don't know. According to our admitting records, he showed up here last night covered in blood. He's got some cracked ribs and a concussion. Someone worked him over pretty good. He hasn't been conscious, so we haven't been able to talk to him."

"What time was he admitted?"

The doctor looked at Brad's chart. "About ten."

Michelle took a deep breath, relieved. At least he hadn't killed Frank.

Who killed Frank Sims?

Michelle certainly wanted to know, as did the police, his company, and probably his relatives. But for now, here she was sitting in the ICU by Brad's bed. She should call her family. Using the cell phone was out, as a large sign in the hall read: Please do not use cellphones on this floor.

Michelle found a pay phone just outside the ICU waiting room and called Brad's globetrotting sister, Melody, or Mel, as she was known. Michelle was surprised that she was actually in town.

"What do you mean he's in the hospital?" Melody demanded.

Michelle summed up the events of last twenty-four hours for her sister-in-law, ending with Brad storming out of the house yesterday afternoon.

"So have you guys reconciled?"

"No, Mel. We both had had a bad day. I guess you could call the fight a stress reliever. Then this happened. We were just ironing out some of our problems."

"I'll be over straightaway."

Michelle returned to Brad's room and found him exactly as she had left him. He lay there, unaware of all the trouble waiting for him. He hadn't moved one inch in the time she was gone. She looked at the scanner recording his brain activity and at the respirator helping him breathe. He barely looked like himself.

She gingerly lifted his limp hand. *Please wake up,* she pleaded. *We need to find out what happened to you. And most of all, we need to know what happened to Frank.*

Michelle felt someone touching her hand. She must have dozed off, she thought. Her eyes popped open. "Brad?"

He was watching her. "What? Who?"

"Shh, don't try to talk. You've been through an ordeal." She rang for the nurse.

The nurse burst into the room, pulling back the curtain. "Well, I'll just be darned. John Doe is awake."

"His name is Bradley Killarney." Michelle wanted to set the record straight. "He's my husband."

"I am well aware of that," the nurse smiled, taking Brad's vital signs. "Mr. Killarney, my name is Nurse Brown," she said loudly. "I'll be taking care of you."

Why is she yelling? Michelle wondered. "Is something wrong?"

Ignoring her, the nurse continued talking to Brad in that loud, annoying voice. "Mr. Killarney, do you know where you are?"

Brad shook his head very slowly.

Okay, that's normal. Nothing to worry about, Michelle told herself. Then she heard him whisper something to the nurse.

"Who is Mr. Killarney?" He barely choked out the words before an alarm in the room went off.

A response team rushed in, pushing Michelle aside. She was asked politely but firmly to wait outside. Figuring there was no use protesting, she went to the waiting room.

She was soon joined there by Brad's sister, Melody. Looking like an ad in a fashion magazine in her Anne Klein suit, Mel hugged Michelle warmly. She was forty-nine and had never been married, choosing a career over marriage and children. She was one of the strongest women Michelle knew.

"I'm so glad you're here, Mel. Some kind of alarm went off, and they kicked me out." Michelle started crying. "I don't know what happened."

"I know. Let's just hope for the best. I know Brad is getting the best of care." Mouthing 'I'm sorry' to Michelle, Mel answered her ringing cellphone.

"Mel Killarney. No, I don't think you should sell. You should let it ride another week. Have I ever lost your money? Good. I'll be in touch." She summed up her caller's angst in a few choice words. "Men, they're always nervous when a CEO is caught with his pants down."

Mel was an investment banker, as were Brad and her brother, Jeremy. How did she end up amid these financial geniuses? She started laughing.

"What was that?"

"You'll think it's silly. I was just thinking that you, Brad and Jeremy are investment bankers."

Mel easy laugh filled the empty waiting room. "Yes, dear, that is silly."

"Mrs. Killarney?" Brad's doctor stood in the doorway.

"Yes," she answered, reaching for Mel's hand for support. "This is my sister-in-law, Melody Killarney."

He nodded a greeting. "Please, sit down." He sat down across from the women and addressed Michelle. "There's been a development in your husband's condition."

Expecting really bad news, Michelle tightened her grip on Mel's hand. "What's wrong with him?"

"He has retrograde amnesia. I believe it is due to the trauma he received yesterday. As soon as some of the swelling in his brain goes down, I'm confident that his memory will return. The question is to what degree."

"You're telling us that even when his brain returns to normal, he still might not remember his family or what happened yesterday?" Mel asked in her banker voice.

The doctor looked from one woman to the other. "Yes, that's what I'm saying. The stress of not knowing you, Mrs. Killarney, and finding you in his room holding his hand, frightened him and caused his heartbeat to accelerate."

"Just spit it out!" Was that Michelle's usually patient voice screaming at the doctor?

"He's slipped back into a coma."

Wanting to be with Brad, she headed for his bedside. The nurses were apparently getting him ready for something. "What are you doing?"

"We're moving him to a room. Looks like he might be with us a while before he's able to go home. He'll be in room 443." They shooed Michelle out again.

She returned to the waiting room Mel was talking on her cellphone, but ended the call when she saw Michelle. The ultimate multitasker, she began speaking as if Michelle had been there all along.

"Michelle, I know it looks pretty dim right now, but I know my brother. He's too stubborn to let this get him down. After you left, that cute doctor said that the swelling might be gone in a few days. I know he's listed as John Doe, but I'm sure the cops would like to know you've located your husband."

Michelle shook her head. "I forgot. They're going to arrest me yet!" She dug in her purse and found the small business card they had given her. She called and asked for the detective on the case. "This is Michelle Killarney. I found my husband. He's at Kennedy Memorial Hospital. Yes, I will be here."

Mel looked at her with those hazel eyes. "I take it they want to question both of you. I don't understand the whole thing about Frank."

"I'm just glad that Brad was in the emergency room here at the time Frank was being stabbed."

"Do you think my brother killed that idiot?"

"No, Mel. The police hinted that he was a suspect because of the fact Brad got into a fight with him in the park the day of his murder, and then there's the missing three million dollars."

"Talk about movie of the week."

Later in the evening, Michelle went home to face her children. It was almost dinner time so guilt, rather than nutritional value, decided the menu for dinner: hot dogs and French fries.

"Mummy, where's Daddy going to live?" Peri asked, happily munching on a French fry.

"Why?"

"Well, Uncle Jeremy said Daddy hurt his head. Someone will have to take care of Daddy."

"Aunt Melody will take care of Daddy."

"But she's always gone. That's why we don't have cousins," Peri reminded her mother.

Michelle almost choked on her hot dog stuck in her throat. "Well, maybe Granny and Papa will come take care of him."

"But why can't he come live with us?" Peri asked in a child's reasonable voice. She had finished her hot dog and fries and was drinking her glass of milk.

Why couldn't he recover there? Because that's an invitation to disaster, she wanted to say aloud, and there was the matter of his missing car and wallet. If he couldn't remember anything, how could he protect himself from his still-at-large assailant?

"Mummy?"

She looked at her daughter. Peri's little face was demanding a response. "Well, honey, we have to wait for Daddy to wake up from his nap." Peri looked skeptical, indicating to her mother that she didn't believe the part about the nap. "Why don't you and Preston go watch TV?" Michelle took Preston out of his high chair and set him on the floor. That put a temporary end to Peri's questions, giving a bit of a reprieve and a chance to think uninterrupted.

First, she needed to talk to Mel about Brad. Maybe she wanted to take care of her brother herself. Or even his parents might want to come and take care of him. That would leave Michelle free of any responsibility.

She mulled several scenarios, but in her heart she knew as well as she knew her name that Brad would be recovering at her house.

CHAPTER 9

After her brother promised to see to the children, Michelle left for the hospital. But first she took a detour by the police department.

"I would like to speak to someone about a missing vehicle."

The desk officer looked up from his hot dog and coffee. "Your vehicle was stolen?"

"Well, not exactly. My husband was attacked yesterday, and his vehicle is missing. I was wondering if it had been reported as found."

The officer turned to his computer and started asking the usual questions. "What kind of car?"

"Range Rover."

The officer was shaking his head even as he entered the data. "I'll be surprised if that turns up. It's probably already chopped up and sold for parts," he said. "Did he have an alarm system on it?"

"Yes. The truck was only about two years old. We got it in England. It still has UK license plates on it. Maybe that would make it stand out."

"If the plates haven't been switched already, which in all likelihood they have. What side was the steering wheel on? If it's on the right, that would definitely make it stand out."

The officer had taken the wind out of her sail. The Range Rover was probably just a hunk of metal by now. "No. It's on the left. He special-ordered it when we were in England," she added for no particular reason.

"Well, let's see what we can find out." He continued punching keys, but his expression told Michelle his search wasn't finding anything. "I'm sorry, ma'am. I don't have any Range Rovers listed as found."

"Well, it was just a shot. Is it possible to contact me if it's found? It's really important to me."

He smiled a yes. "The database is updated after midnight. I'll leave a note for someone to call you if it shows up."

She knew the likelihood of an overburdened police officer calling her was practically nil. Still, she could hope. "You can call me at this number." She scribbled her home and cell numbers on it. She thanked the officer and left.

Michelle was yet reliving the day's events when she returned to Brad's room. His sister was at his bedside. "Hey, has he woken up or anything?"

Wiping her eyes, Mel said, "No, not a peep. But the doctors did say the swelling had gone down a little."

"Are Mom and Dad coming?" she asked of Brad's parents.

"Yes, but they can't get here for at least two weeks. They're in Hong Kong on one of those tours."

That sounded odd, even for her traveling in-laws. "Why is it going to take so long?"

"You know that mess they had over there a few months back with that international spy? Well, if they were to leave suddenly for the States, apparently it would raise a red flag and the Chinese government might brand my sixty-nine-year-old parents as spies. So I thought it best they continue the tour. I'll keep them posted."

Michelle vaguely recalled a sensational story about the Chinese government charging a young couple as spies because they wanted to leave the country suddenly. "Yes, I guess it's for the best."

"I'm sure it is," Mel said firmly. "I can't believe that he hasn't woken up. Wonder where his car is?"

"I went by the police station to see if it had been reported abandoned. No luck."

Mel flashed that annoying smile. The one that told her she was about to ask her a monumental favor, and it probably concerned Brad. "I'm glad you're here, Michelle, even if you and Brad aren't officially back together. But I'm sure it's just a matter of time."

"Why on earth would you think that? Just because of yesterday? We only talked about the changes we both wanted, and nothing is settled yet."

"Oh, please," Mel said, knowing full well Michelle was not being honest with her. "We both know you hold onto the key to that particular vault with a vengeance. Maybe that's what you're telling yourself, but I know the truth. Besides, you're here now."

Michelle, at that moment in time, hated her sister-in-law, mainly because she knew Mel was right, damn it. But damn if she would admit it.

"Mel, just because we had one good afternoon, that doesn't make up for the months of fighting and neglect."

Of course, Mel ignored her sister-in-law's denial of the obvious. "I know you and Brad were having some bad times before Frank came onto the scene. But I do know that Brad loves you and he wants to be back with you."

"If you just wanted me to let him stay at the house while he's recuperating," she smiled, "all you had to do was ask."

"Thank goodness, I didn't know what to do. Mom and Dad can't get here, and I'm due to leave for England for a business trip. I wouldn't ask you this, but I've been working on this merger for a year. I have to be there for the closing of the deal. I don't want to have to put my little brother in a rehab center."

"I don't know about him staying with me." Michelle was backtracking fast. "I don't think I'm qualified to care for him. Can't you hire a nurse or something?"

"He needs to be around the kids. Maybe that will speed up his recovery. His memory may return tomorrow, or next week, or next month. There's no guarantee. I think if he's around the kids and you, it will help him heal faster."

"So you want me to babysit him? What about his rehabilitation?" Michelle didn't really want Brad in the house. She knew it would only lead to trouble, but she didn't want to let her sister-in-law down. So she was grasping at any reasonable way out.

But Mel was way ahead of her. "I'm going to hire a therapist to come to the house and work with him. Look, Michelle, you would really be helping me out. You know this is a busy time of the year for me. I've got some really big deals going on right now. If he's with you, I know he's being looked after and that would be one less thing I have to worry about."

Michelle knew how busy Mel's life was. She had one of the most successful investment firms in the state and was constantly out of town. There was no way she could afford to take time off to be with Brad. Michelle felt herself weakening. "I have to discuss this with Jeremy first."

"He already agreed," Mel said, smiling triumphantly.

"You got me," Michelle conceded, just as her cellphone rang. "Hello."

"Mrs. Killarney? This is Sergeant Jones. You talked to me earlier about a missing Range Rover."

"Yes. Did you find it?" Michelle asked, trying to stay calm.

"Yes, ma'am. A security guard at Herrington Global reported it. He said it had been there since last night."

"Oh dear." Frank was killed in his office at Herrington. "Could I come look at it?"

The officer hesitated. "Usually, we're not supposed to. But if you hurry, I can let you look at it before it's inventoried. You won't be able to take anything with you because it's evidence."

"Thank you. I'm on my way," she said, already heading for the door. "That was the police," she told Mel. "They found Brad's truck. I'll come back tomorrow as soon as I get the kids settled."

"Okay," Mel said. "I'll see you tomorrow."

Michelle entered the police station and headed straight for the desk. "I appreciate this, officer."

He came from behind the desk and looked around the busy reception area. "This way, please." They headed down a narrow hall. He whispered, "This is against departmental regulations, but you seemed very concerned."

The officer placed his hand on Michelle's back when they came to a secured area. Was this young man trying to hit on her? Or was he just guiding her? She had made it very plain that it was her husband's truck she was reported missing. "Was his wallet in the vehicle?"

"I don't know."

It occurred to her that this officer was sidestepping a lot of regulations just for her. Or was he? "Why are you helping me?"

"You don't remember me, do you?"

Michelle took a closer look at him as he unlocked the door to the properties room. He motioned for her to walk ahead of him. And there it was. Brad's "other woman." A black Range Rover, as clean as it would be on any given day. He would never let it get dirty. He loved that car.

"You don't remember selling me a house about six years ago?" the officer asked. "I had just gotten married, and it was our first home. You usually handled the sell of more expensive homes, but because I was a friend of Jeremy's, you helped us. When you came in last night, I wasn't sure if it was you or not, and you seemed distressed enough without me playing old home week."

It all came rushing back to her. "Dryson Jones. Now I remember. How is your wife?"

Dryson smiled. "I'm afraid the house was more solid than the marriage. I've been divorced about three years. The last time I talked to Jeremy, you were living in England."

"We came back about two months ago. I'm sorry to hear about your marriage." Michelle reached for the door handle, but Dryson stopped her.

"Here." He handed her a pair of latex gloves. "Wear these, so you won't mess up the prints that are already there."

"Of course," she said, pulling the gloves on and opening the door. The scent of Cool Water, Brad's favorite cologne, filled the car's interior, causing her to smile.

"What are you looking for?" Dryson asked, slapping on a pair of gloves. "Maybe I could help you find it."

"That's just it. I don't really know what I'm looking for. All I know is that he stumbled into the hospital yesterday, beaten and covered in blood, and his boss was killed yesterday. I guess I'm hoping for a clue or something. Or even his wallet."

"I see." Dryson opened the hatch door in the back and began searching. "Holler if you find something."

"Okay," Michelle answered, opening the glove compartment, which contained the expected—insurance papers, the truck's registration and manual, passport, notes for a meeting. And a piece of wadded-up paper. She smoothed it out and found her mother's seldom-used cellphone number on it. "That woman has a lot to answer for."

"What?" Dryson called from the rear of the truck.

"Nothing. Just cursing my mother."

"Oh, is that all?" he laughed.

Michelle moved her search to the console. It contained a personal digital assistant, cellphone, and several music CDs. She checked the last calls. One was from Jeremy, the traitor. Another call was from an unfamiliar number. Using her cellphone, she dialed it. The answering machine clicked on after four rings. "You have reached Frank Sims, president of investments. Please leave a message."

Startled, she quickly snapped her phone shut. Frank had called Brad at seven. He was killed three hours later in his office. Had Frank attacked Brad, and then was killed himself?

Michelle shook her head, somewhat overwhelmed by all the possibilities.

"Hey, I think I found his wallet."

Michelle slid out of the front seat and hurried to the back of the truck. Dryson held up Brad's small Gucci wallet. She had purchased it in Paris for his birthday. "That's it."

"How did he get separated from his wallet?" He flipped through it. "It wasn't a robbery. His credit cards, cash, and ID are still in here." He counted the money in the wallet. "Was your husband in the habit of carrying around five hundred dollars in cash?"

If she explained why she thought Brad had that much cash, she would have to explain everything. Dryson deserved the truth, considering all the regulations he had broken for her. "Well, actually, we're separated. Have been for the last two months."

"What happened?"

Michelle's laugh held no humor. "I guess we had been having problems ever since our son, Preston, was born. Brad started working all the time. He never had time to take a trip or anything. Then his boss came to England to check out operations. But instead of him spending time at the London office, he was spending it with me and the kids."

Dryson asked. "Didn't you tell your husband?"

"Yes. I told him that I felt uneasy with Frank around so much, but Brad just blew me off. He and Frank have been friends for years. Finally, I had had enough and told him I wanted to separate. Since we've been back, he usually takes the kids on the weekend, and that's probably why he had so much cash in his wallet."

Dryson shook his head. "What's he doing? Trying to buy your kids off? I have a son, and I don't spend that kind of money on him."

"I know. I think he's overcompensating for the separation. He's been begging for a reconciliation."

"Do you want him back?"

"I've bent your ear enough with my problems." Michelle wanted to drop the subject and get back to searching the truck, but Dryson wanted to talk.

"It's okay, Michelle. Believe it or not, my situation isn't that far removed from yours. My marriage was over after Taylor, my son, was born. It was over before that, but she had gotten pregnant and I tried to do the right thing. We should have divorced after the first year. By the time we did divorce, we hated each other."

"How did it affect you?"

"I was an undercover narcotics officer, but my ex started trying all kinds of things to get me back. I had been working on this bust for about eight months. She blew my cover by showing up at the stakeout. I was shot."

"Oh, my."

"Yeah. It took about six months for me to heal. Since my cover had been blown, I got transferred to robbery division. She was all but stalking me. Funny isn't it? I'm a cop, and she was stalking me. That's how I ended up on the desk. She can't come inside the station."

"What did you do?"

"I first filed an order of restriction prohibiting her from coming within one mile of me or my house, unless I initiate the contact. I sat her down and explained that I didn't want her, because I couldn't trust her and she had endangered my life. I could never forgive her for that."

Michelle was thankful that at least Brad wasn't like Dryson's ex. "Did she ever get the hint?"

"Yes, thank goodness. She finally moved on and has since remarried. They live here in Arlington, so I can see my son often. The guy's real nice."

"I'm glad it worked out for you." She hoped she and Brad could eventually resolve their problems, too.

He watched her, smiling. "I know that look. You're taking him back."

"How do you know that?"

"You're in a police substation, late at night, going through his truck looking for clues."

Reality knocked. "You got me."

He patted her shoulder. "Don't feel bad, Michelle. It happens to the best of us. Hey, we'd better get back to searching."

Michelle nodded, grateful for the diversion. "Thank you for sharing your story. It helps to know I'm not alone." She walked back to the front seat. She wanted to go through Brad's PDA. Knowing how anal he was about details, she knew he would have put the meeting with Frank on his calendar.

She was right. There it was: Frank at seven. He had only scheduled thirty minutes for the meeting. He even had an entry to visit her at eight. But he didn't keep that one.

"That's probably all we're going to find." She peeled the gloves off. "I do appreciate this, Dryson."

He met her at the front of the truck. "Yeah, I don't think there are many clues. This stuff will be tagged later. I'm sure the police will want to talk to you again." He escorted her back to the front lobby.

"I intend to cooperate fully. I just want to know what happened to him yesterday." She left the station and headed home.

CHAPTER 10

The next morning, Michelle walked into Brad's hospital room and got quite a surprise. He was sitting up in bed. The smile she had fallen in love with greeted her as she sat down next to Mel.

"Well, I guess he's doing all right. He looks good. When did this happen?"

Mel didn't answer her, but Brad did. "You know, I can hear."

"Oh, my gosh. I'm sorry, Brad. I didn't realize. Just yesterday, you were unconscious."

He gave her a dazed look that said he wasn't all the way back.

"Brad, do you know who I am?"

He searched her face for a clue. "No, I don't remember you."

"How do you feel?" Michelle asked, not knowing what else to say.

Brad touched his forehead. "Why is this here?" he asked, pointing to the bandage covering most of his head. "My head feels as if someone hit me with a sledgehammer. I keep hearing bells ringing."

Michelle touched his leg. "I'm sure that will clear up soon. What's the last thing you remember doing?"

He stared at her for a moment, then, as if a cloud had cleared, he smiled. "I know who you are now."

He would remember them having a fight. "Who am I?"

"I went to see you about a house."

Michelle suddenly went cold. "You have a good memory. Do you remember anything else?" Why was he remembering things from six years ago?

He scrunched up his face, thinking. "Yeah. I took you out for dinner, then breakfast." He smiled again. "I feel we have some kind of connection."

She looked at Mel. Brad's high-powered, high-maintenance sister had tears streaking her normally flawless makeup. "What is it, Mel?"

"Let's talk in the hall. Honey, we'll be right back," she told her brother.

Brad nodded.

Once in the hall, Michelle faced her sister-in-law. "Okay, Mel, what's going on? Why does he remember things that happened six years ago and not yesterday, or his name?"

"The doctor came by this morning. He was impressed that Brad was sitting up and talking, considering his condition yesterday. He says the amnesia Brad has is common. He remembers certain things. He remembered when I moved to Texas at his insistence. He can remember dating you, but not marrying you or having the kids. He probably won't remember the details of the attack."

"Isn't that like selective amnesia?"

"In a way. But he's not remembering anything current. He doesn't remember living in England. He doesn't remember our parents, or the fact that they're free spirits. The doctor said that Brad's memory would return in stages. If his memory keeps improving, that means there's no brain damage."

"Brain damage? Where did that come from?"

"One of the blows he received almost cracked his skull. That's why he was bleeding so. But try not to call him by his name. It seems to make him go all loopy."

Michelle didn't like the look in Mel's eyes. Something she hadn't said or done. "What else?"

"Well, they want to dismiss him tomorrow. There's really nothing else they can do. It's a waiting game."

"Tomorrow is Sunday. I won't have a sitter for the kids. Jeremy will be gone all day, to some kind of frat thing he's had planned for months."

"I'll bring him to your house," Mel said. "Thanks a lot for this. I'll do anything you need doing. I'll hire a therapist to help with his recovery."

Michelle had a lot to do. "I'll get the spare room ready and break the news to the kids."

Sunday afternoon, Michelle tidied the spare room, making sure everything was in order for Brad's arrival. She then joined her children on the couch downstairs.

Now for the hard part, she told herself. Preston crawled onto her lap and hugged her. "Okay, guys, we need to talk before Daddy gets here."

Peri turned away from her cartoons and face her mother. "What, Mummy?"

"Well, Daddy isn't completely well. He still has a headache, and he doesn't remember certain things. We're going to play a game. Instead of you calling him Daddy, call him Honey."

Peri was confused. "Why can't we call him Daddy? He can't remember us? He doesn't love us anymore?" Tears flowed down her face. "Why doesn't he love us?"

Michelle hugged her daughter. "No, baby. He still loves you, I mean, us. He had an accident and hurt his head. Sometimes when you hurt your head, you forget things for a while. We want him to get well, right?"

Peri nodded, and stopped sniffling.

"So we'll call him honey. Okay?"

"Okay."

"If he acts like he doesn't know you, don't worry, it will come back to him," Michelle reassured her daughter.

"Is this like Felicity's granddad? He pretended Felicity's dad was in the army with him and they were at war. He called him a Yank."

Michelle looked baffled. Then she remembered. Felicity was one of Peri's London friends. And her grandfather had Alzheimer's. "Sort of," she said.

In the two months they had been back, this was the first time she had heard Peri mention anything of her friends in England. "Don't you miss your friends in England?"

"Yes, but Daddy, I mean, Honey showed me how to e-mail and talk to Felicity when I go to his house. But how will I talk to her now?"

"Once we get Honey settled, I'll get Aunt Mel to sit with you and I'll try to get the information off his computer." She smiled at Peri's happy face. "Wait. Why don't we call her before he gets here?"

They went into the den, where Michelle looked through a box she hadn't unpacked yet and found her London address book. She leafed through the book and located Felicity's number. She dialed the number and, when the connection went through, she handed the phone to Peri. It was good to hear her daughter's excited squeal. A bright spot in a gloomy day. "Peri, don't forget to get her e-mail address."

"Okay, Mummy."

Brad stood to one side as his sister rang the doorbell. The two-story house looked familiar, but it gave him a cold feeling. This was definitely not his house. At least he didn't think it was.

He needed to sit down; his head had begun to hurt. Hopefully, someone will open the door soon.

"Who lives here? Why can't I go home?" he asked, hearing the doorknob turn.

Mel looked at him. "How do you know this isn't your home?"

He shrugged. "I just know." The door opened slowly, and the woman who had visited him at the hospital greeted them. Two small children stood on either side of her. Great. All he wanted to do was lie down, and she had two small, probably troublesome children with her.

"Hi, Mel." She greeted his sister but not him.

"Hi, Aunt Mel," the kids said in unison.

Both women were watching him closely. "Honey, why don't you go inside and take a seat," his sister suggested.

He did as he was told. The house seemed oddly familiar. Something about this house, he thought. The children joined him on the couch, while the women stood at the door talking in low tones.

"Honey, how do you feel?" the little girl asked after having stared at him for longer than he could take.

"My head hurts."

"Why don't you go to your room and lie down."

"I don't live here, do I?"

"No," the little girl said. "But Mummy said that you were going to stay with us until you got well."

He was relieved when she and the boy went to find their mother. Brad closed his eyes, hoping the pain would soon pass. Hopefully, his sister would be ready to leave soon.

The women came into the living room. His sister sat next to him.

"Honey, you're going to stay with Michelle and her children until you get better."

He looked at Michelle standing before him. She was pretty, but she was still a stranger. He leaned closer to his sister. "I can't stay here. That's not proper. We're not married."

Michelle also sat down. "Do you remember? We dated a long time ago."

He nodded.

"We're like old friends," she smiled.

"But what about your children? What will their father say?"

Michelle and Mel looked at each other, smiling. Michelle finally said, "He's out of the country right now. He won't mind."

Brad decided his sister really wanted him to stay, and she hadn't led him wrong yet. "All right, I'll stay."

The women sighed with relief. Michelle rose. "I'll show you to your room." She called the kids as she neared the stairs. "Come on, guys, we're going to show Honey his room."

Three hours later, Michelle sat on the couch, sipping a glass of wine. Having Brad in the house was a little more difficult than she had expected. He looked so helpless and lost when his sister kissed him good-bye.

"What was I thinking?" she asked the TV remote.

At least now the kids and Brad were asleep, giving her some much-needed private time. She went to the floor-to-ceiling bookcase to find something to read. Apparently, since retiring, her mother had taken to reading amateur-detective stories. Michelle laughed, trying to imagine her mother as a mature detective trying to solve a whodunit. She selected the book by mystery maven Agatha Christie from the shelf.

She then made a pot of tea and settled down for what she hoped would be a good read. Initially, she wasn't sure the plot would interest her, but she found herself comparing the murder in the book with Frank's demise. She fell asleep with those thoughts.

Michelle felt someone tapping her on the shoulder. Michelle opened her eyes. Brad stood before her, smiling. "What's wrong?" She straightened up and patted the space beside her.

Sitting, he said, "I was bored just lying in bed. Your kids are still asleep."

It hurt he didn't know his own kids, but Michelle tried not to focus on that. "Would you like something to read to fill the time?"

He shook his head. "No, I would actually like to talk. Maybe it would help me to remember." He leaned back on the sofa. "I feel we have some kind of connection."

"You shouldn't try to force your memories. The doctor said they would come back in time. Forcing it will only make your headaches worse." She checked her watch; it was six. "It's time for your medication. Dinner won't be for another hour. We usually have dinner at seven." She knew that the medication would make him sleep.

He rubbed his forehead, trying to ease the pain. "I don't know which pain hurts more—the pain in my head or the pain in my stomach."

"You have several cracked ribs. It'll probably hurt for a few weeks." She stood up, taking his hand. "Come on."

He snatched his hand away. "You think I'm stupid, don't you? That I can't remember how to get back to my own room."

She didn't want to upset him, which might cause a relapse. "No, I don't think you're stupid. You're one of the smartest men I know. Honey, I just want you to know that we all know this is difficult for you and no one is trying to rush you," she walked toward the stairs.

He reluctantly followed her. "I guess I'm a little edgy. I can feel that I'm usually doing something else, but I can't remember for the hell of me what it would be."

You usually had the kids, she thought. From what Peri has told her they would have dinner at McDonald's or some other kid restaurant. "It'll come back." She started up the stairs.

She walked past her room, but he stopped. "Why do I feel like I've been in this house before?" He smiled. "I have a good feeling."

You should, she thought. She didn't want to bring up the day they actually talked about reconciling, fearing it might trigger something he wasn't ready to remember. She continued walking until she got to his room.

By the time he entered, she had his medication on the bedside table with a glass of water. She realized as she watched him take the medicine that in their five-year marriage, he had never been sick. Had never needed her for anything other than tending to his children and being an ornament on his arm at social affairs.

She closed his door as he got settled in bed. Although the circumstances weren't ideal, it felt good to actually be needed by the man she loved.

CHAPTER 11

Michelle was in the kitchen, preparing dinner, when her brother arrived home. "Hey, how was frat day?"

Jeremy smiled. "Tiring. Taking those munchkins out for lunch and male bonding is getting to me." Jeremy's fraternity took a group of fatherless boys to lunch and games every couple of months.

She took the chicken out of the oven. "I think it's great what you guys do. Those boys might not have any other male influence in their lives."

"I know. Brad had said he was going to start doing it, too, since he was a member, once you guys got your stuff together."

"Who knows when that will be?"

"Yeah. Especially now. How's he doing?"

"Okay, I guess. In some ways he's typical Brad, in other ways, he seems different. I like this Brad."

"Yeah, I think this is what you guys need. The food smells great. How long before dinner?"

"Thirty minutes. Hey, are you still going to watch the kids and him while I go to class and to the gym?"

"Sure."

The first part of the week dragged by. Michelle was going nuts sitting at home all day, especially since she had to watch her every word around Brad for fear of accidentally unlocking a painful memory. She was grateful that Jeremy was babysitting so she could attend art class.

She kissed the kids good-bye and started to leave when Brad stopped her. "Are you coming back?" he asked, standing between her and the door.

"Yes, but I'll be gone a few hours. Jeremy will be here with you and the kids."

He nodded, leaned down and kissed her softly on her lips.

"Honey, what are you doing?"

"I don't know. It seemed like the right thing to do," he said, smiling devilishly. He moved out of her way. "I'll see you later."

Michelle eased out the door. Amnesia or not, he still had it. He was a great kisser.

Michelle came home to a quiet house, entering through the back door. Her brother was at the kitchen table. "How did everything go?"

A sly smile tugged at Jeremy's lips. "I think Brad is doing pretty well. We watched a baseball game together. At first, he didn't remember a lot of the rules, but after a while he could remember his favorite team." He was clearly in a teasing mood, grinning at her as she made herself a sandwich. "You know, you could have told me that you told him that your husband was out of the country."

"Oh, no," Michelle said, frowning. "He didn't want to stay. He said that it wasn't right for him to stay here. So I had to tell him a little untruth."

"A little warning would have been nice. Is there anything else I need to know?"

She joined him at the table. "No, I think that's it. I do appreciate you keeping up the fib. Why was he asking about my husband?"

"He told me he kissed you, and he knew he shouldn't have. So now you've got to tell him that you and your 'husband' are separated. See what happens when you lie?" He burst out laughing.

"So now on top of him not remembering, he's feeling guilty about kissing his own wife," Michelle sighed. "Great. Just great."

By the grace of God and Jeremy's help, Michelle made it through the week. Brad was improving, remembering bits and pieces of their short courtship. He still didn't remember that they had married or that they had kids.

Today, without any prompting, he had gone upstairs after breakfast to take his morning medication. His stomach had been giving him trouble. She knew he would sleep for a few hours, allowing plenty of time for her to take the kids to the park. Jeremy was working on something at home and had agreed to keep an eye on Brad while she was out.

At the park, she took out her sketchpad, intending to work on her assignment for the next week's class. Instead, she made a list of the clues to Brad's beating and Frank's murder. There weren't many. She dialed Brad's office on her cellphone.

"Mary, hi, this is Michelle. I know the police had Brad's and Frank's offices sealed off. Have they finished searching yet?"

"It's nice to know Brad is staying with you while he recovers. There are some evil people in this world. Who could have done that to him?"

Michelle liked Mary. She had been Brad's secretary before they had relocated to England and, by a stroke of good luck, he was able to rehire her when he returned to the Arlington office. "Yes, Mary. Have they finished?"

"Oh, yes, but Alex has locked both their offices until the auditors have finished as well."

"Thank you, Mary." She then rang Alex. After updating him on Brad's progress, she told him what she needed.

"Now, Shell, you might find more than you're bargaining for," Alex warned her.

"I know about the missing money." Same ol' Alex, always looking out for Brad, she thought.

"Oh?"

"Brad told me about it when he got into it with Frank the first time. It doesn't look good for him right now. I just want to know where he was those missing hours. I won't disturb anything."

"Michelle, only because I love you. Why don't you meet me up here about nine?"

"Okay."

Precisely at nine, Michelle parked the Navigator in front of Herrington Global. The security guard waved as she walked past him to the bank of elevators. The building seemed eerily quiet.

The elevator opened on the sixth floor. Dressed in jeans and a T-shirt, Alex was waiting for her.

"Hi, Alex. Thanks for doing this." She kissed him on the cheek. "I'm sure Brad will appreciate this once he comes back to himself."

"I take it no one knows you're here." He looked at her outfit. "Were you on the way to the gym or something? Brad mentioned you had joined the gym."

She ran a hand over her smoothed-back hair, which was pulled into a ponytail. "I had to tell Jeremy that I was going for an intense workout. I couldn't tell him what I was really up to. Jeremy would have told me not to come or worse he would have insisted coming with me."

Alex led the way down the hall to Brad's office. "We don't have much time. The auditors will be here first thing in the morning. I know you haven't been in Brad's office since you guys returned from England." He paused, smiling. "Just for the record, I told Brad he was neglecting you."

"I figured the personal chef was your idea. Brad's too rigid to think of something that romantic."

Alex laughed as he unlocked Brad's office. "Yeah, I guess you know me too well. You think you guys will get back together?" He stood back and let her walk in first.

"I don't know, Alex. It might be a while before he's back to normal. He doesn't even remember the kids or marrying me."

"I know Brad. He might be separated from you, but he still wears his wedding ring. He didn't buy any new furniture when he got the apartment. It was mostly hand-me-downs from his sister and me. I could tell he didn't plan on staying there long. He didn't sign a lease. He's paying month to month."

Alex walked directly to Brad's desk. He picked up the photo on his desk. "Look, he has your picture on his desk."

She had already noticed the photo from their honeymoon in Greece. "You could have just put it there."

"True, but you know that's not my style. I'm not into props." He pulled out the top drawer. "What exactly are we looking for?"

Michelle, her brow knitted, said, "I have no earthly idea. I was just hoping maybe there was something he found out about the missing money and that's why he was attacked. I guess I'm looking for anything related to that report."

He nodded and began rummaging through the drawer. "Notes for art class, plans for the kids, four tickets to the circus, and four tickets to the baseball game. I see a Disney World Cruise brochure. Hmmm. This doesn't sound like a man in search of a divorce."

"Maybe a new girlfriend?" She knew that wasn't so.

"Shell, you must be kidding. Almost since you guys separated, he's been trying to figure out how to get you back. You know you guys are meant for each other. How many people meet as you did and then marry?"

She thought about that often. It had been a dream day. Brad had walked into her real-estate office looking for a house. He had just been transferred to Dallas from Boston. After showing him houses all day, he asked her out for dinner later that night and had charmed her right into his bed. Six months later, they were married. "I know what we had was special. But I feel like I lost me when we got married. I want to find myself before we get back together."

"What do you want?"

"I want my life back. I want to be needed. I don't just want to be his wife and mother to his children. I want to be my own person. I was my own person before and had my own business."

Alex smiled. "I told Brad that whole my-wife-is-not-going-to-work thing wasn't going to wash with you."

Michelle scanned the bookcase, searching for some clues. "Hey, look, maybe this is something." She pulled a piece of ledger paper from between two hardback books. "I see Frank's name is all over this." She handed the paper to Alex. "It's dated from last year."

Alex sat in Brad's chair and turned on his computer. "Man, I hope Frank hadn't been taking money from that far back." He downloaded the last report. "Man, I could sure use Brad's brain right now."

Michelle stood behind him. "What is it?"

"This report wasn't finished. It's still in Brad's codes, which he devised so no one could use the information before he could verify it. But I can't decipher it, and the only other person who would have known what was originally on the ledger sheet is on a slab in the morgue."

"It's been a week. Why hasn't he been buried?"

"Because his body was being autopsied. When the coroner released the body no one claimed it."

"What about his wife?"

"Apparently, Frank was hiding some facts about himself from her. She refused to claim it."

"Doesn't he have some adult kids from his first marriage?"

"He does. Apparently, when he and his first wife divorced, it was because of infidelity on his part. He hadn't spoken to his kids in about five years."

"Oh my." Michelle sat down. She actually felt sorry for the dead man. Fifty years old, and no one would claim his body.

Alex was reading her mind. "I know it seems awful, and there's a lot of questions that we need answers to. Things just aren't making sense right now."

"What kind of questions?"

Alex shook his head. "Crazy questions that don't make sense. Like Frank's house. It was a rental. Claire has to move out the end of the month."

"Why? I'm sure he has that mortgage insurance that would pay the house off when he died."

"Nope." Alex looked up from the computer. "Hey, I thought we were trying to find something to clear your husband, not gossip about the biggest moron on earth."

"That's right. Get busy." She looked through Brad's file cabinet, hoping to find anything with the slightest resemblance to a clue.

An hour later, Alex finally gave up. "Let's check out Frank's office."

She followed him across the hall. As he pushed the door open, a gust of cold air hit them. "This even feels spooky," Michelle said, shivering.

Alex went directly to Frank's cluttered desk and pulled out the top drawer. "Man, this guy was a slob. Look. There's ketchup packets, mustard packets, opened salt and pepper packets. I bet the cleaning crew is just going to love it when they have to clean all this up."

Michelle walked to the desk. Frank was a slob. "Can you get into his computer?"

Alex stretched his arms and wiggled his fingers. "I just might, Mrs. Killarney." His fingers began dancing over the keyboard. "His password was too easy. Sex. Amatuer."

Michelle lightly punched Alex on the arm. "You already knew it."

"No, I just remembered him typing in a three-letter password. It wasn't his initials, and I knew it wouldn't be his kids, so I just figured it was what he always talking about."

"Very good, brainiac. Now, is there any info on there I can use to clear Brad?"

"Well, on the day he was killed, his schedule shows Brad at seven. Then OP at eight. But he was killed at ten." Alex looked at her. "You think OP, whoever it is, killed Frank?"

Michelle shrugged, not knowing what to think. "Probably. But did Brad make the meeting with Frank? His car was found here, so at least he showed up for the meeting."

"But who would attack Brad? I mean, he's a big guy. Whoever did it had to overpower him."

"I know. Also, considering the extent of his injuries, there had to be more than one person. He had cracked ribs and several head blows to the head. The doctor said he had been hit with a blunt object. I can't figure out how he got from here to the hospital that is ten miles across town."

"It would be nice if we could ask him some of this."

"Yes, it would help a great deal. But I can't risk him having a relapse, either. Why don't you come to the house this weekend? Maybe it will jog his memory."

"Are you sure?" He continued searching Frank's database.

"Yes, we could bring up some of the things we found tonight." She looked at her watch. "I had better get going. Brad won't go to sleep unless I'm in the house."

"I can't believe he doesn't remember you."

"He remembers when we dated."

Alex turned to the messy desk and grinned knowingly at her. "I think you like him staying there, being dependent on you."

"I like being needed," she conceded, "but wish it wasn't like this."

CHAPTER 12

Upstairs was unusually quiet when Michelle woke the next morning. It was eight and the kids weren't in her room asking for food. Jeremy probably fixed breakfast for them, she thought. She turned over for some well-deserved quiet time and closed her eyes.

Then she remembered Jeremy had a client meeting in Dallas that morning. He was probably already gone. She jumped out of bed, threw on her robe, and flew downstairs, imagining all kinds of disasters. As she neared the kitchen door, she heard the kids' voices. She also heard Brad's baritone.

Peri greeted her as she entered. "Mummy, Honey is fixing us pancakes."

Michelle was too shocked to answer. Brad stood at the stove flipping pancakes like a seasoned cook. He was dressed in jeans and a T-shirt that showed off his strong, muscular back. Darn it. Her eyes finally met his.

"What's wrong? Is this okay?" He looked at her with those expressive eyes.

"Yes, it's fine. You should have wakened me. You don't have to cook."

"Peri said I wasn't supposed to go into your room when you're sleeping," he said, watching his daughter.

A smile hovered on Michelle's lips. He was so adorable in this unspoiled phase, reminding her of the warm innocence of a puppy. Only he was over six feet tall. "It's okay. You may knock on my door. I don't mind. Would you like me to finish this? I'm sure you would like to sit down."

"No," Brad said, "it feels good to do something." He smiled at her and continued his pancakes.

Michelle joined the children at the table. They were still in their pajamas. Just like their mother.

Brad soon placed a platter of pancakes on the table, along with bacon and eggs. "Thanks, um, Honey." She had almost called him Brad. Brad, who hadn't made breakfast in over three years and had always said pancakes took too much time. Brad, who never had time for his children or his wife because there was always a meeting he absolutely had to attend.

"These are delicious," Michelle said. "Where did you learn to cook?" Michelle prodded gently, hoping the question wouldn't trigger an anxiety attack.

He slathered butter on his pancakes as he pondered her question. "I don't know. This morning when Peri said she was hungry, I felt compelled to make her something special," he said, obviously pleased that he had made her happy.

"They're her favorite," Michelle said cautiously. "You're a pretty good guesser. What kid doesn't like pancakes?"

Brad didn't answer and a faraway look came into his eyes. He was remembering something. She could feel it. "Honey, what is it?"

"Probably nothing. I see a woman standing in a kitchen making breakfast. It's a small kitchen and it looks funny."

"Funny how?"

"It doesn't look like this. Not spacious, but not exactly cramped. I see a washing machine in the kitchen. It has a foreign feel to it."

England. He remembered England. Michelle had to fight to maintain control so as to not scare him by crying out joyfully. His memory was coming back. In dribbles, but it was coming back.

"Mummy, we're done," Peri said, interrupting her mother's joyful moment. "Can we go to the park today?"

"Maybe later. Honey might want to do something different. Why don't you and your brother go watch TV."

"Okay."

Michelle took a deep breath and faced Brad. He had had a break-through and didn't realize it. She watched him breathe slowly. "Are you okay? How are those ribs feeling?"

He rubbed his stomach. "A little tender, but I can manage."

Now that sounded like the Brad she knew. Too stubborn for his own good.

Michelle and Brad sat on the park bench, watching the children play. She wanted to ask Brad about his memories of England, but knew she had to tread lightly.

It was the usual Texas summer weather—hot. They wouldn't be at the park long. It was barely ten in the morning and it was already over eighty degrees. Brad, now wearing shorts, looked around the park curiously.

Michelle felt him tense up. "Do you remember this park?"

"No, but it feels like I've been here before. Have I been here with you and the kids before?"

"No," she lied. The last time they had been there, he had gotten into that fight with Frank.

Brad seemed confused and unsure. "It feels like I've been here," he said, turning to her. "Where is your husband?"

His question didn't shock Michelle. But she was surprised he had taken so long to ask it. "I told you. He is in Europe. Actually, we're divorced."

Brad was seemingly trying to decide if she was telling the truth. A funny look crossed his face. He had remembered something else. But she didn't get to probe because the kids ran up to them.

"Mummy, can Daddy push me on the swings? I want to go high. Like when Uncle Jeremy does it."

"No, baby—" Michelle stopped speaking. Peri called Brad Daddy. She hoped he hadn't heard her, but it was already too late.

Tears tumbled down his face. "I'm your daddy. I can't be. I don't have any children. I don't remember children." He stood suddenly and began pacing nervously. "I'm not married. I'd remember children. I'd remember having children." He sat back down on the bench and held his head between his legs.

He was having a panic attack. Michelle picked up Peri and placed her in her lap. "Are you okay?" Michelle wiped her daughter's eyes, but Peri's eyes were fixed on Brad.

"I'm sorry, Mummy," Peri whispered. Then she rested her small head on her mother's chest.

"Don't worry, baby. He'll be fine. Don't worry," she reassured her daughter, rocking her back and forth.

Peri slowly reached out to her father and gently touched his back, rubbing it as Michelle had just done.

"I'm sorry, Daddy," Peri said in a small voice.

Preston, forcing his way into the situation, stood in front of Brad and demanded to be picked up. Brad took quick little breaths and then straightened up, and cradling his son in his arms. He kissed Preston on his forehead, then looked at Peri. "I know." He leaned over and kissed Peri on her forehead. "Thank you."

Peri looked at her father. "What did I do?"

"You called me Daddy."

Michelle was having trouble holding back her own tears. A simple slip of the tongue that could have sent Brad into a tailspin had instead opened another door. She swiped at a defiant tear as it crept down her face.

"I'm your husband."

It wasn't a question. He was making a statement, assessing the information. "Yes," Michelle said. "Do you remember me?"

"No, but I wish I did," he said, taking Michelle's hand and caressing it softly. "I honestly wished I did."

Michelle nodded. She had hoped to question him about the codes she had found in Brad's office. She decided not to press her luck.

"Where did we go on our honeymoon?" he asked, looking straight ahead. "I remember white sand, dark men, and skinny-dipping." He grinned. "And being tired."

Michelle remembered being happy. "We went to Greece. The Aegean Islands. It was very romantic."

"Are we divorced? I know I don't live with you normally, or we would be sharing a bed."

"We are separated."

"Why?"

That was a dicey question. "It's complicated. I really don't want to discuss it in front of the kids."

"Sorry. I wasn't thinking. I guess I was looking for memory triggers." He rubbed his thumb across the back of her hand in a slow, sensual motion.

"It's okay. You can't force your memory back. It will come back, not all at once, but it will come back in time. When—how did you know, or feel, we were married?"

"The night I kissed you. It felt right." Brad shifted Preston in his lap and moved closer to Michelle and spoke in a whisper, "Whatever I did to make you unhappy, I'm sorry."

"I think it was both of us. But we'll deal with that later. Do you remember Frank Sims?"

He shook his head. "Who is he?" He let go of Michelle's hand and rubbed his temples.

"Nobody special," she lied. "I'll bet your head is giving you fits."

"Yes, with all the discoveries I've had today, I do have a slight throbbing, but I wouldn't change it for the world. I have a family."

Michelle couldn't shake the feeling they were closer to the truth than they realized. "Why don't we go home? You can take something for your headache and I can read to the kids at home as well as I can here."

Brad nodded. "Sounds like a definite plan." Brad stood with Preston in his arms. "What do you say, big guy? Ready to go home?" He hugged and kissed on his cheek.

Preston, not used to so much attention from his father, threw his arms around Brad and kissed his father. "Go! Daddy!"

Once they were all in the car and buckled up, Brad asked an unexpected question. "When do you think I'll be able to drive?"

"What makes you think you can?"

"I remember a car," he said. "It was like this one, but different."

Of course he remembered the Range Rover. It was his pride and joy. "Do you remember the last time you were in it?" She asked, starting the car.

"That's kind of fuzzy. I can see it. It's black." He closed his eyes, trying to force more. "That's it."

Michelle reached over and patted his leg. "That's okay." Her hand wanted to linger, but she quickly dismissed the notion and withdrew her hand. But he took it back and caressed and kissed it before letting it go. That one gesture drove her to distraction.

"Mommy, you passed it," Peri complained.

"What?" Michelle couldn't figure out what was going on until it was too late. She had just driven past the house. "Oh, I'm sorry, baby." She quickly turned the car around and headed back.

An hour later, Michelle was able to breathe easy again. Everyone was napping, including Brad. The phone rang just as she had settled on the living room sofa with a romance novel. It was Brad's sister, Melody.

"How's he doing?"

"Pretty good. We had a little setback today. He had forgotten to take his medication this morning, but he's resting now." Michelle didn't want her sister-in-law to worry.

"Has any of his memory returned?"

"Bits and pieces." Michelle put the paperback aside, knowing it would be a long conversation. "Peri accidentally called him Daddy. He freaked out a little bit. He remembered our honeymoon, but little else."

Mel's quiet sniffles slowly became louder, full-out blubbering. Michelle didn't offer any comforting words; there were none.

Mel gradually quieted down. "Sorry, didn't mean to get all weepy on you. But his condition was the reason I called. I've hired a therapist to help with his recovery."

"I don't think he really needs a therapist. His memory will return on its own."

"Yes, but the doctor thinks the therapist might be able to stimulate his memory."

"Is there something else wrong that you're not telling me?"

Mel took a deep breath. "I'm just doing what I think is best for Bradley."

You know what's "best" from Lord knows where, Michelle thought. "I know you're concerned about his health. When are you coming home?"

"Well, I'm in Scotland now. Tomorrow I'm flying back to London to complete the details of the merger. I should be back the latter part of next week."

Michelle felt a wave of relief. Mel had been working on the details of the Hartsberry merger for the last six months. Hopefully, she would be home long enough to help care for Brad. "That's great. I know Brad will be happy to be around someone he actually remembers."

"There's just one little snag."

Michelle knew Melody well enough to know there was never just one little snag. There was probably one big rip in the universe. "What?"

"I'll be home for only a few days."

Michelle had hoped that Brad would be out of the house before she found herself succumbing to his innocent charms. Now she felt trapped.

"Look, Michelle," Mel continued, "when I asked you if he could stay with you, I expected it to be for only a short while, but looks like it's going to be longer than I thought."

"It's okay. The kids are adapting well to him being in the house. He does want to drive. What did the doctor say about that?"

"I don't want him driving yet," Mel said. "Not until his memory has completely returned. Any word on who beat him up?"

"No, nothing," Michelle replied. "I wanted to ask him about it, but he got a headache. Maybe the therapist can ask him."

"You can discuss that when he gets there. I think Brad would feel more at ease with a man than with a woman, don't you?"

"Definitely."

"Well, I've got to rush, so I'll talk to you later. Kiss Brad for me."

Michelle pushed the end button on the phone, and returned to her book. "Like heck I will," Michelle muttered.

CHAPTER 13

Monday morning, Michelle made breakfast for everyone while the kids were watching cartoons. Jeremy walked into the kitchen dressed in a suit and took a seat at the table.

Michelle poured two small glasses of milk and called the kids for breakfast. She laughed as she heard them running to the kitchen. "What will it take for them not to run through the house?"

Jeremy laughed. "A miracle, for one. They're kids. That's what they're supposed to do. Speaking of kids, where's Brad?"

Michelle made a face at her brother. "He's not a kid," she reminded her annoying brother.

"Yeah, like you don't get off on having him all dependent on you."

"I don't. I want his memory to return. Mel even hired a therapist to help him."

Jeremy held his hands up in mock surrender. "Hey, I'm not the one who's married to him and trying to pretend that you want a divorce. Look at you. You're dressed in tight jeans and a very revealing shirt, when usually you would still be in your robe and your hair would be standing all over your head. Today, not a strand is out of place."

She didn't have a response. "Why do I bother trying to discuss anything with you?"

"Because you know I'm right."

"Yes, and right now I hate you."

Having gotten the best of Michelle, Jeremy stopped his teasing and turned to his niece and nephew. "Hey munchkins. Where's Honey?"

Peri looked at the adults. "I don't know. I didn't hear him in the bathroom."

Brad usually took his shower in the morning, and the kids could hear him in the bathroom. Michelle remembered that she, too, hadn't heard the shower that morning. She placed platters of scrambled eggs, bacon, and toast on the table and hurried upstairs to check on Brad.

Michelle listened at Brad's door for a sound. Nothing. Her hand was raised to knock on the door when she finally heard a noise. Actually, it was the more likely a yell.

"Brad!" Michelle, called, knocking on the door loudly. No answer. "Brad!" she called again.

Still no answer. She turned the doorknob and opened the door. She expected to see Brad standing, but he was still in bed and appeared to be sound asleep.

A nightmare.

Maybe it was something from the night this hell began, she speculated. She walked closer to the bed and gently shook him awake.

Brad opened his eyes, screamed and pulled her down on the bed beside him.

This wasn't passion. He was trying to choke her, apparently, thinking she was attacking him.

"Brad, stop." She was gasping for air. "Brad, please." She tried to wiggle out of his iron grip.

"If I let you go, you're going to hit me," he said hoarsely. His eyes were glassy and unfocused. He didn't recognize her.

"Brad, it's m-e-e, Michelle," she sputtered. "Michelle. Your wife." She said, wiggling again. Finally, his grip loosened.

"I'm sorry," he said, sitting up. "I didn't realize it was you."

Michelle couldn't speak; it was all she could do to just to breathe. Still gasping for air, she sat up. "I heard you scream. Were you having a nightmare?"

Rubbing his face, he said, "It didn't feel like a nightmare. It felt real. Like it was happening right now."

"What was it? Maybe it was a key to your past." Michelle started to get off the bed, but he put a hand out to stop her.

"Please."

"All right." No other words were necessary. He was asking her to stay. Michelle knew what temptation it was being with Brad in such in an intimate setting, but he needed her in a different way.

He inhaled deeply and then exhaled. "I was in my truck and I was dialing a number, but I was interrupted. It must have been someone I knew, because I opened my door. Then they dragged me out of the truck."

"They?"

"Yes."

Michelle placed her hand over her heart, as if that motion could stop it from pounding. "Can you describe them?"

"Not really. Voices more than anything else." He closed his eyes, trying to force the memory. "Just like that, it's gone."

She rubbed his back. "That's okay. It'll come back in time."

"I just hate when it seems so real, then it fades away before I can really visualize it."

Michelle nodded. "I know, honey." She lay against him, hating herself for being weak. She had fallen in love with him all over again. But she had never stopped loving him in the first place.

Brad kissed her forehead. "Thank you for listening. I hope I didn't scare the children."

She could feel the rapid beating of his heart. "No, you didn't. They are downstairs." She didn't want to move from that spot. "We're having breakfast. Are you hungry?"

"My head is hurting. Do you mind if I stay in bed a little longer?"

"I don't mind." She stood and faced him. "I'll get you some water." She hurried out of the room.

In the bathroom, Michelle splashed cold water on her face and gave herself a little lecture. "Get a hold of those hormones, girl. He looks sexy only because he doesn't remember what happened to the marriage. Once his memory returns, he'll be neglecting you like always." Using bitter memory as a shield, she returned to Brad's room with the water.

"Here you go."

Brad nodded and took the medication and water. "Thanks, Michelle."

"I'll bring you something to eat once I have the kids settled."

"Okay."

Michelle left, quietly closing the door. She hoped his nightmares would not get any worse. Maybe he just needed stronger medication.

Back in the kitchen, she looked distractedly at the kids' clean plates. "I see you guys finished eating."

"How's Brad?" Jeremy asked.

"He was having a nightmare or a vision of some kind. He's sleeping." She sat at the table and poured a cup of coffee. "This is a lot harder than I thought it would be."

Jeremy sat next to her. "Look, Shell, if this has become too much for you, we could hire a nurse or aide."

Before responding, Michelle sent the kids to watch TV. "But don't go upstairs. Honey is sleeping."

"Okay, Mummy," Peri said, taking her younger brother's hand and leading him out of the kitchen.

The kids out of earshot, she asked her brother. "What would a nurse do? Watch Brad sleep? I just don't see what good it would do."

Seeing the fatigue in her face and hearing it in her voice, a concerned Jeremy promised not to be gone long. "I just have a quick meeting with a client. I think you need some girl time. Not mommy time, just the girls."

"I was hoping for a workout today."

"Great. I'll come home early, and you can take off for a while."

Maybe that was exactly what she needed: some time with other women, and maybe some good old male bashing. "Thanks, Jeremy."

With the kids settled in for their nap, Michelle had planned to take a quick nap, too. But it was not to be; someone was the front door.

"Mrs. Killarney?"

"Yes?" A tall, muscular man stood in the doorway.

"I'm the therapist, Joel Hampton." He unclipped his ID badge and presented it to her. "Our firm was retained by a Mel Killarney."

Mel had said she was hiring a therapist to help Brad, Michelle remembered. She didn't know he would arrive so soon.

Something about him, about the way he filled out his polo shirt, didn't sit well with Michelle. He looked more like a stereotypical wiseguy than a therapist. Michelle handed him back his ID. "Who did you say referred you?"

"Mel Killarney."

Michelle's instincts told her something was definitely off about this guy. "Let me see your ID again?"

Hampton had the nerve to look inconvenienced. "I do have other patients today."

"My father sent you," Michelle baited him. "He was supposed to send a woman."

"Sorry ma'am. Mr. Killarney didn't specify when he made the appointment."

Michelle stuck her hand out for the ID, but Hampton still didn't comply with her request. "I'm going to call your office and get all this straightened out."

Hampton shifted his weight from one foot to another. "You know, maybe I have the wrong Killarney. I'll be right back." He went back to his car.

Michelle closed the front door and locked it just as she heard a car taking off at warp speed. She looked out the front window and saw the therapist speeding down the road.

"Well, I guess that's settled. We're in real trouble." She walked upstairs to check on everyone. Peri was sound asleep, but Preston wasn't in his bed. Michelle didn't panic; she knew exactly where her son was. He had the habit of going to her bedroom and sleeping in her bed when she wasn't near. She opened her bedroom door and there was her little man. Sound asleep in the middle of her king-sized bed.

She knocked on Brad's door.

"Come in."

He was lying across the bed, staring at the ceiling. "Who was at the door?" He sat up and faced her.

"The therapist, or I guess it was the therapist."

"Huh?"

"He said he was a therapist, but he said Mel was a man."

Brad chuckled, then rubbed his side. Those ribs were still bothering him. "Oh."

"I'm going to give your sister a piece of my mind for hiring that moron."

"You didn't let him in the house, did you? You did check him out?"

Michelle sat on the bed. "Yes. Your sister wouldn't have hired someone without giving me a dossier on their entire life. Mel didn't say she'd hired anyone yet."

"Oh." He wanted to talk to her. "Where are the kids?"

"They're taking a nap."

He noticed the lines of fatigue around her eyes and mouth. No wonder, he thought; the strain of playing nursemaid to him, as well as dealing with the children, was probably wearing her down. "Why don't you take a nap?"

"Do I really look that bad? Gee, thanks." She yawned again.

"No, you look beautiful, as always," he told her honestly. "You're up early with the kids, then you're waiting on me. You could probably use some rest."

"You're the second person to say that to me today. I must really look bad. I don't have time for a nap. Anyway, Jeremy isn't home."

"What does Jeremy not being here have to do with anything? You could take a nap while the kids are asleep."

Not answering, Michelle quickly averted her eyes. He knew in an instant what she didn't say: since he didn't know who his enemies were, she couldn't leave him in charge of the children. For some reason, that hurt.

He moved over in the bed. "How about a compromise?"

Michelle gave him a look that said she knew he was up to no good. He struggled to keep his voice even.

"You lie here and take a thirty-minute nap. I promise to wake you if I hear so much as a footstep. I'll even go lock the front door," he offered.

"It's already locked. I must really be tired, because that compromise sounds good." Kicking off her shoes, she got into the bed with him.

He was pleased with his small victory. At first, she lay on the very edge of the bed, so their bodies wouldn't touch. She looked so uncomfortable. He pulled her closer to his body, so that they were lying her back to his front. "Doesn't that feel better? I know it makes me feel better." He draped his arm across her, making sure she stayed in place.

"You're awful."

"I hope so. Now go to sleep."

Something touching Michelle roused her from of a restful sleep. It was a finger; actually, fingers. She opened her eyes and yawned, and realized she was in Brad's room. In Brad's bed. Under the covers.

"Hey, I think I hear something." Brad smiled at her. "You snore."

"I do not."

"Yes, you do. Loudly, I might add."

She sat up. "I must have been really tired. How long was I out?"

"About an hour."

"Oh, my goodness." She jumped out of bed, slipped on her shoes, and ran out the door—and into Jeremy.

He smiled. "I just got home. Sorry the meeting took longer than I thought. You look a lot better."

"I'm so sick of everyone saying how tired I look."

Jeremy patted her shoulder. "Michelle, what's wrong with you? You're acting a little weird."

She motioned for her brother to follow her downstairs to the den. "The therapist Mel hired for Brad was here today, but he gave me a weird feeling. I think I scared him away when I wanted to check with his company. He thought Mel was a man."

"Yes, well, I know to trust your feelings when it comes to things like that."

"Thanks, Jeremy. I'm going to tell Mel that he really doesn't need a therapist. I don't like the thought of strangers coming in the house. I thought I would be able to do it for his sake, but I can't."

"I knew it." He smiled smugly. "Why don't you finish your nap? I'll take care of the kids and Brad."

"You got a deal," Michelle said, heading back upstairs.

When she woke again her bedroom was dark and the house was quiet, but then the phone rang. It was Mel.

"Your therapist sucked," Michelle informed her.

"What are you talking about?"

"The therapist you hired showed up today. But he thought you were a man. He gave me a bad vibe. I didn't like him."

"Michelle, you're not making any sense. That is why I'm calling—about the therapist."

"What are you talking about, Mel?"

"I called to tell you that the therapist will be there next Monday."

"They know he's here," Michelle said, voicing her fear out loud. "Some guy showed up today, claiming he was a rehab therapist, but he didn't act like a therapist."

Melody sighed. "If they know he's there with you, they must think he knows something."

"Yeah, and they must be watching the house. The therapist showed up while Jeremy was out with a client."

"I don't want anything to happen to you or the kids. I'll try to find some other place for him to recover," Mel said.

Michelle knew that wasn't possible. "Look, Mel, I know this isn't what any of us planned on, but now we've got to do what's best for Brad. Personally, I think he'll do better without strangers coming in and out of the house."

"I guess you know best. I'll cancel the therapist. What about your safety?"

"Now that I know what I'm up against, I can be on the lookout."

CHAPTER 14

"Where are you going?" Brad asked.

"I'm going to the gym and then out with some friends. I won't be gone long," she promised. She felt awful that he looked so lost. He actually looked frightened.

Michelle assured Brad that he would be all right. "Don't worry, Jeremy will be here with you and the kids. You'll be safe."

"I'm not worried about me. I'm worried about you. Who'll protect you?" He was directly in front of her, blocking her way to the door. "I think I should go with you."

"No, you stay here and rest. I'll be fine."

Brad said nothing. He just looked at her with those vacant eyes that somehow evoked her feelings for him and her need to keep him safe. Jeremy intervened just in time.

"Brad, she'll be just fine. Besides, I plan to watch the baseball game on TV after the kids go to bed. Please don't make me watch by myself?"

Ignoring Jeremy, Brad focused on Michelle, a worried look on his face.

"I'll call when I get to the gym. Would that make you feel better?" Michelle asked, picking up her gym bag and a change of clothes.

"Okay, but I'll wait up for you," he said with an air of authority, sounding very much like the old, stubborn and pigheaded Brad.

"No, it might be late when I get home."

He shook his head. "It doesn't matter," he said, leaning down and kissing her.

Michelle knees buckled when his tongue touched hers. Without reservation, she curled hers around his in the most delicious game of tug-of-war. He might sound like the old Brad, but he sure didn't kiss like the old Brad. She was in so much trouble.

Jeremy cleared his throat, and slowly they ended the kiss. "I think you'd better let her go, Brad, or we'll never get rid of her."

Michelle looked at her brother, smiled at Brad, and left the house for the evening.

Michelle relaxed as soon as she entered the gym. Her friend Pam was already on the treadmill. "Hey, Pam, sorry I'm late."

"It's okay, girl. I just got here myself."

Minutes after joining her friend on the treadmill, she heard her name over the loudspeaker.

"Michelle Killarney, telephone at the front desk."

She almost tripped in her rush to get off the treadmill. "I hope it's nothing bad," Pam said. "Do you want me to come with you?"

"No, but thanks. I'm sure it's just my kids or something."

"I'm Michelle Killarney," she told the front-desk receptionist. The young man smiled and handed her the phone. "He sounded kind of worried."

Oops! She had forgotten she was supposed to call Brad. Inhaling deeply, Michelle took the phone. "Hello."

"You didn't call," Brad whined. "You said you would call." "Why didn't you call?" he asked worriedly.

She giggled. "Brad, I just got here. I was talking to my friend and it just slipped my mind. I'm sorry. Did you take your medicine?"

"Yes. Call when you leave the gym." Then he cut the connection.

Pam was power walking on the machine when Michelle returned. "I'll never catch up with you," she said, hopping on the treadmill.

"That's okay. I'll slow down a little," Pam replied. "Is everything okay?"

"Not really."

"Would you like to talk about it?"

"It would take too long; it's way too complicated."

Pam laughed. "A man must be involved."

"Worse. My husband."

"I thought you guys were separated."

"That's why it's so damn complicated." Michelle punched the button to speed up the tempo. "It was going pretty good, but then the bottom dropped out of everything."

Pam nodded. "Okay, you have to tell me."

Pam was the closest thing Michelle had to a friend, since she'd only been back in the States a few months and her mother was thousands of miles away at the moment. "Well, Brad was badly beaten and has lost his memory. He has selective amnesia. He's been staying at the house with me and the kids. But there are people after him, and he doesn't even know why they want to kill him. His sister thought being around the kids would speed up his recovery, but it hasn't really. But this Brad is so different from the Brad I knew. That's who called. I promised to call him, and I forgot."

Pam shook her head sympathetically. "Yes, I see why it's complicated. But do you regret taking him in and helping him?"

"No, I guess not." Retreating a bit she added, "That came out wrong. I don't mind helping him. It's just that…" she began, her sentence drifting off.

"You're falling in love with him again. It's easy to do. He's vulnerable; you're vulnerable. With his memory gone, he's a different person."

"Thanks, Pam. It's nice to have someone to talk to about it. How's your situation?"

"About like yours," Pam revealed. "I thought once I came back home, everything would be fine. I would have the job I always wanted, and the kids would be okay. But I really miss him. More than I thought. I called him and we talked, and he misses us, too. He's coming to visit in a few weeks."

"What are you hoping for?"

"I guess I'm just hoping for a little sanity. We'll figure out the location later. I guess it boils down to the dream job not being what I really wanted after all these years. I wanted my husband." She chuckled. "Go figure. I was so career-driven all those years. Now look at me, ready to quit my job and move back to Japan, if that is what it takes."

Their workout on the treadmill finished, they headed for the showers and Michelle began her ritual of cleaning the shower. "I'm sorry, Pam. I have this thing about using public showers."

"We could have gone to my house or something. You don't have to do all that just to take a shower," she said as Michelle sprayed the tiled walls with Lysol.

Michelle continued spraying. "I know, but I need to conquer my fear. Besides, if I had gone home, I would have ended up staying with Brad and the kids out of guilt." She sprayed the walls once more and then stepped inside the small stall.

"Wish me luck," she said.

As she dressed for the evening, Michelle felt proud of herself. She had conquered one of her biggest fears. She had taken a shower in a public place. She didn't think she would do it again, but it was good to know that she could if she had to. The ringing of her cellphone ended her moment of triumph.

"Hello."

"When are you coming home?" Brad asked in a small voice, sounding like a frightened child.

"We had this discussion."

"I know." His voice sounded slightly muffled. Was he in bed?

"What are you doing?" Michelle asked, slipping on her slacks. "Did you take your medication?"

"Why do you keep asking me that? I think I can remember to take a pill."

Michelle knew she had probably hurt his feelings. "I'm sorry, I just wanted to make sure you're okay. I won't ask you again."

Relenting, he said, "I took one of my pills. I'm waiting up for you, so I can't take the others."

"I don't want you waiting up for me. I'll wake you when I come home. Promise."

"Okay. I'll see you later."

"Goodnight." Michelle closed her phone, pressing it against her chest. "I'm in so much trouble."

Pam sat by her on the wooden bench. "No, girl, you're just trying to fight the inevitable. It won't work. I'm here to tell you. You can fight it, but it won't help. Ready?"

"Yes. I need some girl time."

It was after two in the morning when Michelle got home. Trying to be as quiet as possible, she headed for the kitchen. Brad was at the table, drinking coffee.

"Brad, what are you doing up?"

"I was waiting for you. Why are you so late?"

"Why are you worried? I told you I was going out with a friend." Feeling a hunger pang or two, Michelle made herself a sandwich. She then sat at the table and made a stab at conversation. "Did you get any sleep tonight?" she asked lightly.

"Yes, a little bit. But when you weren't home after midnight, I got worried. And your cellphone was turned off."

"I turned it off when we went into the club."

"Club?"

"Yes, Pam and I went to a jazz club. It was nice. I had forgotten what is was like to be in the company of adults."

Brad leaned back in his chair, gazing at her uneasily. "Yeah, or when your husband doesn't remember anything about our previous life." He stood abruptly, knocking the chair over.

After righting the chair, he said testily. "Goodnight. I just wanted to make sure you were okay." He strode from the kitchen without another word.

Michelle tried to make sense of what had just happened. Brad was upset. She didn't think she had insulted him. Maybe because he couldn't reach her he had convinced himself something had happened to her.

The more she thought about it, the madder she got. How dare he be upset because he couldn't find her at the very moment he wanted to find her! Her brother wasn't worried, so why was Brad? She finished her sandwich, cleaned up the kitchen, and then went upstairs, still seething.

Before going to her room, Michelle checked on the kids. Peri was cuddling her teddy bear. Preston was sleeping, looking like the energy zapper that he was. The cover had been kicked off his small body and was practically off the bed. As she left the room, she swore she wasn't going to do it. She was not going to check on Brad.

But she found herself walking down the hall to the last bedroom. She quietly opened the door and walked over to the bed. He was awake and watching her.

"What are you doing awake?"

He sat up and turned on the lamp. "I couldn't sleep. I was debating going back downstairs and apologizing for my rude behavior. I had no right being mad at you. You deserve some time off." He moved over in the bed. "Sit down."

"I'd better not." But still she stood near the bed. She had only to bend her knees and she would be sitting.

"I'm not going to try anything. I just wanted to know about the jazz club," he said, patting the space between them. "Come on, I won't bite."

"How do you know I won't?" she asked, taking off her shoes and crawling in the bed. "How do you know I won't take advantage of you?"

"Because I feel that if something did happen, it would be because we both want it to, not because anyone was trying to play seducer, right?"

Michelle stretched out against him. "I'm just going to lie here a minute. I don't want the kids to see me like this."

Brad let the remark go. "How was the jazz club?"

"It was nice. It's called Nostalgia, and the atmosphere is very cozy. I think Pam and I were the only women there without dates."

"Do I like jazz?" Brad asked, pulling the cover over her.

"Sometimes. It usually depended on your mood. You mostly listened to talk radio. You were very involved with your career, so we really didn't go out that much unless it was related to your job."

"Obviously, I neglected my family in the process. Well, I'll change that when I go back to work. My family should come before my job, not vice versa." He moved closer, until he was nearly on top of her. "Michelle, when I recover, I will make all this up to you and the kids."

"Brad, it wasn't all your fault. I should have said something years ago. Instead I let it build up until I exploded."

"Would I have listened?"

Michelle didn't want to answer that question. It would only upset him.

"Your silence tells me what I need to know. When I'm better, we'll go dancing."

Michelle couldn't help laughing at that promise. "You don't dance. As a matter of fact, you hate to dance. When we did go out, I'd always had to dance with someone else."

The fact that they were so close was not lost on Brad. He leaned over and kissed her, his tongue pushing her lips apart. "You mean I was stupid enough to let you dance with another man?"

Michelle moaned. The roughness of his morning beard against he her soft skin was doing dangerous things to her hormones. He kissed her neck, waiting for her answer. "Usually I would only get to dance a couple of times before…."

Brad stopped smothering her neck in kisses and asked, "Before what?"

She hoped he would stop now while she still had enough willpower to leave. "Before you got in a snit."

He eased his large body on top of hers. He kissed her deeply, his body gently moving against hers. "Well, I promise from now on, I will be the only partner you're going to have, and I'm not just talking about dancing."

Michelle opened her mouth to tell Brad it was much too early for those kinds of declarations, but she wasn't given the chance. He took her mouth in a gentle, but powerful kiss that sent her hormones on high alert. He pulled her closer to him so that now they were body to body. His tongue mated with hers with a hunger that shocked

Michelle. If she thought his earlier kiss was the bomb, this one was off the chain.

When they finally came up for air, Michelle asked between ragged breaths. "Are you okay? We really shouldn't be doing this, Brad. Your ribs are bruised."

"My ribs are fine. The only pain I feel is the pain you're causing." He nibbled on her neck, while his hands roamed under the front of her blouse. Unsnapping the clasps with precision, Brad quickly divested her of it and her bra. He kissed her throat, nipped at her collarbone and moved lower to her breasts.

His tongue glided easily over the areole of her breast before he took it in his mouth and began to suckle. He was gentle but firm, driving Michelle out of her mind.

She pulled at his pajama top, wanting to feel the heat of his naked body. He shrugged out of it, without breaking contact.

Michelle caressed his back, as he moved to the other breast. Her body was on fire; suddenly her slacks were too hot, her underwear was too hot, and she thought she was getting ready to go up into an inferno.

Brad must have been reading her mind or her hormones. His deft hands unbuttoned the slacks and slid them down her legs. He stopped his ministration to her breast to slip off the pajama bottoms. He was naked from head to toe and looked like a Greek god dipped in chocolate.

He pulled her in his arms and kissed her again. His kisses had a steady southerly path as he kissed her neck, breasts, and stomach. Michelle held her breath as he took off her lacey panties.

He kissed her navel and the area below of her stomach, his warm breath tickling her center. His kisses moved lower still as he parted her womanly folds with his fingers and kissed her there. His tongued delved inside and sent her on a journey to the stars. But she wanted him to join her. "Brad, please."

He didn't stop. He increased his tempo and moved deeper inside her, making the ceiling move counter-clockwise and spin out of control.

When she came back down to earth, Brad was waiting for her. He moved on top of her and kissed her. Michelle wrapped her arms around him tightly, as if she thought he might fly away.

Brad untangled himself from her grasp and held her arms away from her body. Michelle didn't recognize this Brad. Brad was never like this in bed, never this amorous.

He let her hands go, but not before he kissed the stuffing out of her. While she was recuperating from that, he entered her to the hilt. He pulled back almost completely out of her, then he surged forward. He wrapped his arms around her and he buried his face in her neck as he repeated the motion slowly until she could catch up with him. As he increased the speed of his hard thrusts, she hung on for the ride of her life.

"Damn." They said in unison as they climaxed seconds apart. "Damn," Brad said again before they both succumbed to sleep.

CHAPTER 15

Jeremy was taking a chance. He had brought Brad home, hoping for, maybe even expecting, some sign of recognition.

As soon as they entered the apartment, Peri and Preston went straight to the living room. But Brad stopped in the hall, showing no sign of remembering the place. "Do you remember living here?"

"No," Brad said, "I don't. Are you sure I lived here? It doesn't feel like it. When I went to Michelle's house, I felt something. I haven't sensed or seen anything familiar here."

Jeremy chose his words carefully. He didn't want to say or do anything that would send Brad into some kind of fit. "Well, this is your place, man. You have only been living here a few months. Maybe that's why you don't feel anything."

"Where did I live before? I keep seeing a place with appliances in strange places. You know, like the washing machine was in the kitchen. The appliances were small, too. It's raining, but the place has a good feel. Michelle looks pregnant. How long ago was that?"

Jeremy realized this might be a mistake. "About two years. You got a job promotion right about the time Michelle found out she was pregnant with Preston. When you guys moved across the Atlantic, she was about three months pregnant."

"So Preston was born in London."

Jeremy's heart was pounding, as he hadn't mentioned where overseas they had moved. "Yes, he was born there."

"I can see it," Brad said, smiling and crying at the same time. "Michelle and I are at a dinner party, and she starts having stomach cramps. He was a month early."

Jeremy didn't want to cry, but the tears came anyway. "That's right, man." He then directed Brad to the bedroom down the hall.

Jeremy started looking around as soon as Brad left the room. He checked the answering machine first. All the messages were from the operations president and left on the night of the attack. The last message was about an hour before he was probably attacked.

Brad reappeared with a bag of clothes. "I think I have everything I need."

Jeremy thought Brad was right. This place did have a bad feel to it. The apartment felt empty, and cold. He called the kids and they left.

Later that afternoon, enjoying some additional quiet time, Michelle had just closed her eyes for a nice nap when the phone rang. "Who is it?" She wondered, reaching for the phone.

"Hello," she mumbled.

"Mrs. Killarney?"

"Yes?"

"This is Officer Jones from the police department," he said in his formal cop voice. "I was calling to let you know that we're ready to release your husband's truck."

"Really? I thought it would be weeks."

"No, the investigators went over it with a fine-toothed comb and found very little in the way of clues. The only blood we found was your husband's."

"Oh?"

"Do you and your husband want to pick it up? Or I can pull a few strings and have it driven to your house."

"That would be great. Brad isn't here right now. He'll be back later this afternoon. Would it be possible to bring it then?" She also thought if Brad saw his favorite toy, it might jog his memory of that night. But if she was wrong, he could possibly have a relapse back to those comatose days in the hospital.

"We'll bring it about five," the sergeant promised.

Michelle settled for a quick nap before the gang returned.

Hearing voices, Michelle knew her private time was over and went downstairs to greet her returning family. She saw immediately that Brad didn't look right. His eyes looked dull and tired.

"What's wrong?" she asked.

"Migraine," he said softly, rubbing his right temple.

Michelle put her arm around him, leading him to the stairs. "You should go take your medication. You probably just moved around too much today. Go ahead. I'll be right up."

Brad nodded and went upstairs. Michelle marched over to her brother, who was holding a bag of clothes. She looked down at the kids.

After she made sure the kids were settled, Michelle went to Brad's room. She knocked on the door, and she heard him mumble something. After she entering the room, she got the feeling that this was much worse than his usual headaches. He was sitting on the bed, holding his head.

"Brad, did you take the medicine?"

"Yes," he whispered.

"I can call the doctor to see if he can prescribe something else. We can go to the ER." She didn't know what else to do.

"No," he whispered. "I'll just ride it out. Once the medicine gets into my system, I'm sure I'll be fine." He took off his shoes and slipped under the covers.

"I'll check on you later. If you don't feel better in thirty minutes, we're going to the ER."

Now she had to find out what had happened at lunch. Jeremy was staring at the computer screen when she entered the den. Peri and Preston were engrossed in a movie playing on the small DVD player. Michelle sat in chair near the desk. At first, she thought he was ignoring her, but then on closer inspection she could see that he was studying something on the screen.

"Jeremy, what are you doing?"

He didn't take his eyes off the screen. "I'm searching Brad's phone records."

"I know I'm only his wife, but why?"

Finally, he looked at her. "Well, when we were at his apartment, it looked like someone had been in it. You know, searching for something. When I went there the day after Frank was killed, the apartment was as neat as a pin. This time things were thrown about. I listened to the messages on his answering machine. He had four messages from the operations president. I know Brad is vice president of investments, but I don't think the operations president would have any reason to call him at home."

"I don't know the operations president, but I know there's been some restructuring in that section of the company. When we were in London, some of the top execs did call him at home."

"Four times in one night?" Jeremy asked incredulously.

"No. That does seem a little excessive. What did the messages say?"

"Well, the first one was about a meeting with Frank the night he was attacked. The second one told him to bring the report with him, and the third asked if he could come alone. The fourth message was the really odd one. It said to make sure the report was signed with no questions."

Michelle shuddered, not liking what she was thinking. "I know he was having misgivings about that report. Alex and I found it, but Brad does the preliminary report in a code he designed and only he understands. So whatever he found out is lost until he gets his memory back."

Jeremy nodded, still pondering the phone bill. "I see a phone number, it has to be the operations president's number."

"That won't help us. All it proves is that Brad called him and they were in contact, but he could say it was work-related." Michelle wished something would jump out at them so they would know what happened. "What happened at while you were out?"

He leaned back in the chair. "Well, he started remembering more things about London. He realized Preston was born there. He could remember when you went into labor at the dinner party a month early. Personally, I think the complete return of his memory is just around the corner."

Michelle thought that, too. "Yeah, then maybe some of the riddles will be solved. I would like to know how he got to the hospital. When he was left for dead, why weren't his wallet, his PDA, or his cellphone taken if it was a robbery?"

He inspected his sister's face. "I don't think it was robbery."

"I don't either. Or it seems they would have taken the Rover, since the keys were still in it. The police are bringing his truck at five, in about another hour. I'm hoping it may shake something in his head, but after the day he's already had, I'm having second thoughts." She hoped they wouldn't have to spend the night in the emergency room.

"It should be okay. His headache will have disappeared by then. They only appear when he has a breakthrough of some kind."

"I have noticed that," Michelle agreed. "Or if he's trying to force a memory." Sighing, she said, "I just wish this was over, and things were back to normal."

"You had so-called normal and you hated it. You know you like this. It's keeping you on your toes."

She hated to admit it, and wished they weren't in this predicament, but she did like the fact that she had to stay focused and didn't have time to dwell on having just slept with Brad the night before, and that it was the best lovemaking session she'd ever spent with him.

An hour later, she checked on Brad. He was sound asleep and looked like he'd probably be asleep until dinnertime. Plenty of time to call his sister, she thought. She closed the door to his room and walked downstairs.

CHAPTER 16

A little after five, Michelle opened the front door with Jeremy at her side.

"Hello, Dryson. I really appreciate you bringing the truck," she said, watching his partner park an unmarked vehicle behind Brad's SUV.

Dryson was dressed in his blue police uniform. "You're welcome. I'm off duty, so I just got a fellow officer to follow me here. Could I ask your husband a few questions, off the record, of course?" he asked, taking a notepad out of his pocket.

"You can try," Michelle warned, "but he has amnesia. He doesn't remember anything about that night. I, myself, was hoping the truck would bring back some memories, but he has a headache."

Dryson frowned. "That's too bad, but I'd still like to try," he said, just as his partner walked up. Michelle invited the two cops inside.

"I realize how much you're going out of the way for me, uh, us. I want to help you anyway that I can." She led the men into the living room and they took a seat on the sofa.

"Thanks, we could use all the help we can get on this one," Dryson said. "That's why we're here unofficially. This case is weird from all angles. Nobody cares about this guy, not his current wife, not the ex-wife, not any of his kids. His body is still at the morgue. No one will come forward to claim it, let alone give the poor guy a funeral."

Michelle felt sorry for Frank. Everyone has the right to a decent funeral. "What happens if no one claims the body?"

Jeremy shot her a look that almost made her want to take the question back. "Surely you're not feeling sorry for that guy?"

She shook her head. Although Frank was the reason for her finally blowing her top at Brad, she still felt sorry for him. "No," she lied. "It's just sad that no one wants to claim his body and give him a decent burial. It's been over a week."

Dryson listened to the siblings' tense exchange for a minute and then answered Michelle's question. "Well, usually in cases like these— which are usually the homeless, not a high-powered executive who has a family and high-dollar insurance policy—after ten days, the county will bury the deceased at no cost."

That sent an icy chill down Michelle's spine. "That's weird about his family," she said. "He was an executive at Herrington Global and I know he has insurance. Who's his beneficiary?"

"Shell, what are you thinking?" Jeremy asked.

Dryson cocked his head skeptically. "I think I'm with Jeremy on this one, Michelle. What's going on in your head?"

Michelle stared at the three men looking at her in utter male confusion. "Well, I was thinking that if his beneficiary knew that the county would bury him anyway, he or she might just let that happen and keep all the cash. I know it sounds cold, but depending on someone's financial situation, it could happen," she insisted.

Conceding that she had a point, Dryson jotted down a few quick notes. "Well, I'll check on that detail when I get back to the station. I'm sure someone has already looked into it, but you've piqued my curiosity." Dryson gazed at her. "Do you think your husband is ready to look at the truck?"

Jeremy rose, saying to his sister, "I'll get him."

"Okay." When Jeremy left the room, she checked on the children. They were still watching cartoons. She then met Brad at the foot of the stairs.

He smiled and took her hand. "Jeremy said the police wanted to talk with me."

"Yes, they do. They also brought your truck here. It's outside. You've had one incredible day. Do you feel up to it?"

Brad said, "Yes, maybe it will help me." He walked into the living room and extended his hand to the police officers. "I'm Brad Killarney."

"Brad, this is Sergeant Dryson Jones, and this is Officer Drew Hall. Dryson is an old friend of the family," Michelle volunteered.

Dryson cleared his throat and began. "Mr. Killarney, I realize your memory of the things that happened to you is still a little foggy, but if you could look at your vehicle, maybe something could come crashing back to you."

Brad nodded, still holding Michelle's hand. "Sure, no problem. Ready?"

"Yes," she said, hoping this experiment wouldn't slap her in the face.

Trying to calm down, he took a deep breath, as he opened the front door. There it was. His baby. Striding toward the truck, he instinctively looked for dents or other damage. Dryson followed him as he took a closer look. "Where was my truck found?" he asked, opening the driver-side door.

"It was found in Herrington's parking garage. The security guard reported it when it hadn't been moved for two days."

Brad was listening, but he was also trying to figure out how various events were tied together. "Michelle said I walked into Kennedy Memorial Hospital Thursday night. How did I get from work to the hospital?"

"Yeah, we'd like to know that, too," Dryson said, acknowledging the police had no leads or clues. "If you walked to the hospital, someone should have seen you. It's ten miles from Herrington Global to Kennedy Memorial Hospital. And why that particular hospital? Yet there are no reports of a man walking around bloodied and almost unconscious."

"But the hospital said I walked in," Brad reminded Dryson. He really didn't like the man, probably because Michelle was flashing that irresistible smile at him.

"That's what the emergency receptionist is telling us."

Dryson scribbled something down and then extended his hand to Brad. "Thank you, Mr. Killarney. I'll be in touch. Will you still be here at Michelle's?" he asked, smiling at her as she moved next to Brad.

"Yes, he'll be here," she said quickly. "Until his memory has completely returned."

"I'll be here regardless," Brad clarified for both Michelle and the officer. "I'm not going anywhere without my family."

"Okay. I'll be in touch." He and his partner got into their car and drove off.

Together, both Brad and Michelle searched the truck thoroughly. He sat in the driver's seat and closed his eyes, trying to recreate his last clear memory.

In his mind, the scene unfolded slowly. He was sitting in his truck, double-checking his PDA for the time of the meeting with Frank. He had called Frank on his cellphone and discovered Frank had to cancel the meeting. Then the scene became fuzzy and faded away.

"Brad?" Michelle gently touched his arm. "You know it doesn't do you any good to force the memory."

"I know, but I could see a little more this time. Frank had to cancel the meeting. I never saw him. But I can't see who pulled me out of the truck." He wished he knew what kind of trouble was stalking him.

"Did you call Frank, or did he call you?" Michelle opened the glove compartment.

"I called him. I remember that very clearly. He sounded very distracted. I thought maybe he had a woman up there and didn't want me in the building. He told me not to come up."

Michelle gasped. "What exactly did he say?"

Brad tried to recall Frank's exact words, but another migraine was making itself known. The best he could manage was, "He said something like, 'Don't come on the property. I'll call you when it's safe.' "

"Didn't that strike you as odd?"

"At that moment I was too pissed to fully grasp what he was saying. The next thing I know, my door was opening and I was being dragged out of the truck."

"Instead of this becoming clearer, it's becoming more murky," Michelle whispered, her perfectly arched eyebrows knitted, her fingers restless.

A memory from another time and place suddenly came to Brad. "Do you remember when we got this truck?"

"Yes," Michelle answered.

He caressed the steering wheel. "Remember how we christened it?"

Michelle could feel her face blushing. "Yes, I remember. Preston was five months old. Mom was visiting, and she made us go out for dinner," she added wistfully.

"Then what happened?" He wanted her to say it out loud.

"We went for a drive and somehow you found this deserted road by the house."

She was beautiful when she had that dreamy look in her eyes. "You attacked me. I never had a chance," he teased.

"Talk about selective amnesia," she shot back at him. "I'm sorry, I didn't mean…." She stopped in midsentence, embarrassed.

Reaching across the console, he took her hand and kissed it. "Michelle, I know you didn't mean anything by it. It's the truth. How about finishing the story?"

"We parked across from my favorite park in London. It was the first time we had been out alone since I had Preston."

"Why was that?"

"You were working unbelievable hours, and every time I brought up the subject of taking some time off, it started a fight. So I stopped asking."

"Oh, Michelle," Brad said, his voice choking with self-reproach. "I was a jerk," he said, as realization dawned. "I see why you left me."

"It was my fault, too. I should have spoken up, but I just kept it inside, letting the resentment grow."

"Continue the story."

She looked around the truck's interior. "You know maybe we should put this in the garage, so whoever is looking for you won't see it."

At that moment, he didn't care one bit about the truck. He wanted her to finish the story. "Continue."

"You just aren't going to let it go, are you?" she said, smiling. "Anyway, the evening was beautiful. We went to my favorite Italian restaurant in London. Then we went to a bar for a drink, something we hadn't done in ages. That's when you got the bright idea for a drive by the park." Her voice grew soft. "I thought we were just going to take a quick drive and go home."

"We didn't?" He pretended ignorance.

"You know, I'm onto your little game. No, we didn't go home. We parked facing the Thames River. You had this great idea that if the seats were reclined we could watch the moon through the sunroof."

"I remember you loved star-gazing."

"Yes. I still do. I can't believe you remember that. We gazed at the stars and held hands. I loved you so much that night for doing something I knew you thought was boring."

She used the past tense of love. Did that mean that she didn't love him now? What had happened to make them lose that feeling? "Do you love me now?" He hoped against hope that she still did.

"Didn't we make love last night, I mean, this morning?"

"Yes, but you didn't answer my question."

She laughed, not exactly the response he was expecting. "You know if you had asked me that a month ago, I would have said yes with hesitation."

"And now?" He didn't know how to pick up the pieces, especially when he didn't know what the pieces were.

"Yes, without any doubt." She lowered her head and spoke in a whisper. "More and more each day. I fall in love with you more and more each day."

"I love you, Michelle."

"I think we should wait until your memory has returned before you make such declarations."

What was in their past that she wasn't telling him? He was sure whatever it was could be fixed. He would give certainly it his best shot. "You were telling me how you attacked me when I was looking at the stars."

CHAPTER 17

Monday morning, Michelle sat with Brad in the waiting room at the Family Medical Practice in Arlington. By the greatest stroke of luck, earlier that morning, Brad's doctor had called wanting an update on his progress. After Michelle informed him that Brad was having migraines, he told her to bring Brad right away.

Dressed in slacks and a button-down shirt, Brad was attracting attention from some of the women in the waiting area. He barely noticed, as his mind was on the underlying cause of his recurring headaches.

Michelle tried to repress the emotions surging through her heart. She wanted to reassure him, but didn't know what she was up against. "I'm sure this won't take long," she said, noticing his fidgeting.

"Hopefully. You know this is the first time we've been out alone since I've been with you. I love being with the kids, but this is nice, too."

"You're right. I think we should celebrate," Michelle said. "After we finish here, why don't we have lunch before we go back to the house?"

"That sounds good," Brad readily agreed. He kissed her on the cheek. "What about my job?"

"What do you mean?"

He briefly flashed those pearly whites, taking her back to when they first met. "I mean, when am I expected back at work? I'm feeling idle, and I know I shouldn't."

Michelle sighed. That question was not good news. The old Brad was on his way back. Darn it. "Your employers know that you're incapacitated right now and not able to do your job. You're on medical leave and under the doctor's care. I know you miss your job, but you can't go back to work until the doctor releases you, anyway."

He acted as if none of what she just said had sunk in. "Maybe he'll notice how well I'm doing and will let me go back to work."

Not with those headaches, Michelle thought, and not with your memory loss. "Yes, you were always very focused on your career." She watched him rubbing his forehead and saw the tears welling up. The migraines must be excruciating; still he was anxious to go back to work. Typical Brad.

"Maybe I'm not as ready as I thought. My vision is blurring. I can barely see the TV in the corner."

What else could go wrong? Michelle wondered. The thirty-six-inch TV was only about twenty feet away. If Brad couldn't see it clearly, what could that mean? "How blurry?"

"I'm seeing spots dancing around. Sometimes they're little, sometimes big. This always happens when I have migraines."

And the migraines only occurred when he remembered an event from the past, particular something painful. Maybe yesterday was too much, and now he was paying the price. "I'm sure the doctor will give you something."

They waited an eternity before his name was finally called. He grinned at Michelle. "A little relief may be in sight," he said hopefully. "Come on."

She took his hand and they walked to the doctor's private office. He met them in the hall. "Brad, go into the first examination room. I'll be right there."

Michelle started to follow Brad down the hallway, but the doctor motioned her to walk with him around the corner, frightening Michelle to death.

"What about these migraines?" the doctor whispered. He had a serious doctor look on his face.

"He started having them a few days ago. Whenever he remembered—or tried to remember—he would get these terrible headaches."

"Well, it could be good news. I'll need to run a few tests to be sure."

"What do you mean?"

"It could mean that the complete return of his memory is just around the corner. Or it could mean that he has some permanent brain damage."

In the examination room, Michelle sat in the chair nearest the table on which Brad was sitting. Brad's face wore a tight little smile.

"I was beginning to wonder what happened to you."

"I was talking to the doctor," she said, patting his knee. "You'll be fine." Who was she trying to reassure?

She listened carefully to the doctor's questions and tried to assess Brad's reaction to each one.

"Michelle tells me you're having some severe headaches. Why don't you tell me what you're feeling?"

"They're like splitting headaches, only about twenty times worse," he explained. "It feels like someone is hitting my head with a sledge-hammer and an ax. The pain is so intense I have to close my eyes against the light."

The doctor stood and began examining Brad. "Now I'm going to shine a light into your eye," he warned.

Brad reached for Michelle's hand, and she instantly felt his fear and anxiety. He gripped her hand more tightly as the pain became more intense. His vise-like grip became almost unbearable.

Despite his pain, he sensed her extreme discomfort. "Sorry," he mumbled through his clenched teeth. As he enclosed his large hand around hers, she felt his fear. He gripped her hand more tightly as the pain took over his body.

Michelle's attention was fixed on the doctor, who was now sitting on his stool and making notes on Brad's chart.

"Brad, I'm going to need to run some tests," the doctor said, opening the door and motioning for them to follow. They walked down another hall to the testing area. "When they have completed the test, come back to the waiting area." Then he was gone.

Michelle said okay and sat down. Brad was a bundle of nervous energy, pacing the small waiting area. After his umpteenth round trip, she couldn't take it anymore.

"Brad, will you please sit down? They will call you when they're ready for you."

"All right." He stopped pacing. "But why do I have to take tests? I thought you said he would just give me more medication."

She didn't want to tell him exactly what the doctor had said, but she wanted him to know why the tests were necessary. "Because the doctor wants to make sure there is no brain damage. With your headaches occurring more frequently lately, he thinks full recovery may be just around the corner."

Brad looked a little relieved. "Well, at least that's something."

By the time they had left the doctor's office, they had gotten the news that Brad didn't have any brain damage. He was given another prescription for the migraines, and then they went to a nearby restaurant for lunch.

The restaurant's atmosphere was quiet and restful. Her only worry was the fact that Brad was staring blankly at the menu. He couldn't remember what he liked.

Michelle cleared her throat. "What are you having? I'm having the baked chicken. You're probably having the salmon. That was your favorite."

"No, I think I'll have the chicken. Thank you."

"For what?"

He smiled. "You knew I was having a hard time with the menu. I couldn't decide, and you hinted. Thank you for not making me feel stupid."

If he was going to continue saying things like that, heaven help her. "You're welcome."

After the waiter took their order, Brad scanned the room. His gazed lingered on a blond-haired gentleman and a black man sitting at a corner table.

Whispering, Michelle asked, "Do you know them?"

He shook his head. "No, I don't think so."

"Why are you staring at them?"

"Because they've been staring at us. I thought maybe it was someone you knew and I didn't."

"You thought it was a boyfriend I forgot to tell you about?" She laughed, seeing the expression on his face.

"Well, you never know. You're very attractive. Anyway, they're walking over here."

Thoughts of gunfire ran through Michelle's mind. She looked for the nearest exit. She took out her cellphone and dialed nine then the one, but not the last digit of the emergency number. Just in case, she thought.

The two men approached the table. "Excuse me, but are you Brad Killarney, from London? You know, the Backstreet Boys, the rugby team?"

Brad looked at the men blankly. Then, as if a light bulb had gone on, he smiled broadly. "Niles and Porter. What are you blokes doing in Texas all the way from Holland Park?"

Niles spoke for the pair. "We had a business meeting in Dallas. A few guys told us to check out Arlington for some authentic English food at the Fox and Hound. We couldn't find it, so decided to stop here. Why is it Americans are always assuming that the English can only eat English cooking? We're in the United States."

Brad could relate to their experience. "Yeah, the same thing happened to us when we first moved to England. People were always telling us that McDonald's was down the street, whether we asked or not."

Brad invited the men to join them. Niles declined, saying, "I'm sorry, but we're on our way to another bloody meeting in Dallas." He scribbled a number on his business card. "Here's the number for our hotel. It would be brilliant if we could have a night out or something before we head home." He handed the card to Brad, and then noticed Michelle. "I see your beautiful wife is as quiet as always. It was great seeing you both. It's been the best thing about coming to this hot place. Cheers."

Brad had been pleasantly surprised to see the two Londoners. "Man, I can't believe seeing those guys. I really miss them."

Michelle's eyes watered. "Brad, what do you remember about them?" Was it just a fluke he remembered their names and the thing about McDonald's? she asked herself.

"Oh, I remember playing rugby with them and going to the pub afterwards for a pint of bitter. I remember you rubbing my back with something awful-smelling. I would swear that was the last time I was gonna play, and I would be back out there the next Sunday." She hadn't seen him this animated in a long while.

As the waiter placed their food on the table, Michelle tried to find meaning in the recollections ignited by Brad's rugby buddies.

Maybe they had been happy and hadn't realized it. Some of her fondest memories were also tied to their time in England—until Frank Sims showed up and brought everything to a boil. But England was also where she had been her unhappiest. Brad had begun working so much that Michelle started to feel neglected.

"What's wrong, honey?" Brad asked, cutting his chicken with a steak knife.

"Just thinking."

Later that evening, Brad was asleep, thanks to his new medicine. Jeremy had taken the kids for the afternoon and they were still out. She had at least a two-hour window of solitude, just enough for her make a grocery list, pay bills online and make a menu for the rest of week. The phone rang as she reached for a pen and paper.

"I just wanted to know how Bradley is?"

"Mom?" Michelle sat up. It was Brad's mother. "I thought you were in Hong Kong?"

She laughed. "We are, dear. Melody has been keeping us up to date on his condition with phone calls, but I wanted to hear my son's voice for myself."

"He's sleeping right now. He went to the doctor this morning, and he gave Brad some new medication. It knocked him out."

"Is he all right?"

"He hasn't regained all of his memory yet, but the doctor is very hopeful that he will soon. Don't worry, Mom."

"We were thinking of coming to Texas instead of back to Boston. Is that okay?"

"Sure," Michelle said quietly.

Brad's mother laughed. "I know you guys are separated. I think it was very nice of you to take him in when Mel had to leave. How are your parents?"

"They are on a seniors' cruise and will be back next Monday." That would mean a whole new set of problems when her mother returned home and found Brad in her house, recuperating.

"I guess we all had the same idea for vacations. These senior citizen vacations are wonderful. They do everything for you. Here's our number at the hotel. We're fifteen hours ahead of you. We will be at this hotel until tomorrow, about three our time."

Michelle calculated the time difference. "It's five o'clock in the morning there. You know, I can wake him. He may be a little groggy."

"No. No. It's okay. Just tell him I love him and to call me."

"Okay, Mom," Michelle promised.

Brad lay awake in his bed, thinking about the day's events.

Seeing Niles and Porter brought back more than memories of London. But he wasn't ready to tell her yet. He wanted her tied to him so securely that she wouldn't care about their past and would want to build a future together as badly as he did.

He wasn't completely healed. That he knew. His bruised ribs still gave him fits, not as bad as last week, but they still hurt when he laughed too hard. But after seeing his London friends a few more details made sense. But he still couldn't remember who dragged him out of the truck or why. He wasn't clear about the details of their separation, but knew somehow that it had something to do with Frank.

Michelle had gotten a funny expression on her face when she mentioned his name.

He needed to talk to someone. Alex Cole's pale face came to mind. They had been friends since college. He was the kids' godfather, best man at the wedding, and Brad's sounding board. Yes, full recovery was just around the corner. But he didn't have a phone in his room.

How could he call his friend and not give anything away?

CHAPTER 18

Brad watched Michelle read to the kids on the couch. Peri and Preston seemed engrossed in the classic tale of determination, perseverance, and winning. He hoped his little game of deception didn't blow up in his face as so many things had lately.

He rose from the love seat. "My head is starting to hurt. I think I'll take a nap."

Michelle looked up from the book and nodded. "Good. I can get you some water for your medication."

"Michelle, you don't have to wait on me hand and foot. It's not like..." He had almost given himself away. He almost said it's not like when he sprained his ankle when they were married. "It's not like I can't take care of myself. I'm not some cripple. I just can't remember."

He hated when she gave him the sympathy look. But he would take that up with her later. He wanted her to treat him like he was all man.

"I know that, Brad. I was just trying to help," she said softly.

Now he had hurt her feelings. She had done everything in her power to make his recovery as smooth as possible, and what did he do? He hurt her feelings. He felt awful for that. "I'm sorry, Michelle. You know I appreciate everything you do for me."

"I guess we're both trying too hard." She resumed reading the story to the kids, dismissing him from the room.

Brad went upstairs to his room, but his medication wasn't in the usual place. Actually, none of his pills were where they should have been. Had someone been in his room?

He opened the drawer to the nightstand and laughed. Michelle probably moved them so the kids wouldn't find them. She always thought of the kids first.

Michelle finished reading to the children as she listened for sounds of Brad upstairs. The glazed look in his eyes was gone. His eyes looked normal. It could have just been her wishful thinking, she reminded herself. If she went through with the next phase of her plan, she would soon know if Brad was better or not.

She reached for the cordless phone on the table and dialed Alex. He was happy to hear Brad was doing better.

"I think something is going on with him. Why don't you come over and talk to him? Maybe he'll tell you."

Alex hesitated, but finally gave in. "All right, Michelle, I'll come over, but I'll leave if he starts freaking out."

"You're his best friend in this world. Why would he freak out?"

"You're his wife, and he freaked out when you told him who you were," Alex reminded her. "He might have blocked me out of his memory, since we both work at Herrington, and this is where all the trouble started."

"About that…" Michelle hedged carefully. Alex would be a tough sell, if he didn't want to cooperate with her. She needed his help in solving the riddle of Frank's death. "I was wondering if you could bring that report with you and maybe show it to him. Maybe it will jog his memory. You know, when we ran into two of his old friends from London, he remembered them the instant he heard them speak. I'm sure once you start talking to him, he's going to remember you just as he remembered those guys."

Alex laughed. "Shell, you don't have to spin me some story just to come see Brad. I just don't want to upset him and be the cause of a relapse, or worse."

She had thought about that. She didn't want to have to explain to Melody why her brother had suffered a setback when he was doing so well. But she had to take a chance, so she pressed on. "He saw his car, and all he remembered was the time we went out in London."

"The time at the park?"

"How do you know about that?" She could feel her face flushing. She was probably a lovely shade of red.

"Because he said it was the best sex ever," Alex said truthfully, feeling no embarrassment discussing something so intimate with her.

"He could tell you, but not me? Typical. I didn't really find out how he felt about it until a few days ago. Why is he so reticent about displaying any emotion?"

Alex defended his friend. "He *told* you. You just said so."

"No, Alex. Amnesia Brad told me. Amnesia Brad likes to cuddle in bed and make promises about the future. Brad didn't."

"Sounds like Amnesia Brad is getting further than Brad ever could," Alex said accusingly.

She didn't like the tone in Alex's voice; it was almost as if she was cheating on Brad with Brad. "What are you trying not to say, Alex?"

"It just seems as if you're giving Amnesia Brad a break, whereas you were making Brad jump through all kind of hoops just to take you out to dinner. He will regain his memory, then what? You're going to throw him out just because he doesn't cuddle with you or isn't at home as much as you think he should be?"

Michelle softened her voice; she didn't want to yell in front of the children. "Alexander Everhart Cole," she said very slowly, "I want Brad to get well just as much as you do. I realize that Brad will always be Brad. He's the man I love, but since his memory loss, he's a different man, a caring man. It would just be wonderful if he could keep that little characteristic when his memory returns."

"So is there a chance of reconciliation?"

Michelle laughed. "You baited me. You rat! I don't know. We'll see how Brad is."

"You love him, he loves you. What's the problem?"

"Alex, it would take too long to tell you."

"I think, Michelle Killarney, that you're avoiding the issue. How about I come over for dinner? I haven't seen my godchildren in weeks."

"When did you see them? Oh, of course, when Brad had them," Michelle guessed.

"You think your husband could take care of two hyperactive kids for two whole days by himself? Of course I helped him. But that's our secret, okay?"

"All right. I won't tell Brad you ratted on him. Just come for dinner and you can judge for yourself how he's doing. We usually eat about seven."

It was nearly time for dinner when Brad woke up. He hadn't wanted to sleep that long, but he did have the most wonderful dream. He and Michelle were together. It was early in their marriage. They were packing. Why? Then the dream became a nightmare. They were separating.

He had to find out what happened between them. He couldn't imagine anything worse than being without her. Not seeing her smile, or how she interacted with the children. Most of all, how patient she was had been with him when he crashed into a mental brick wall and couldn't remember anything.

Alex's face popped into his mind's eye again. He had to find a way to call him after dinner. Maybe Alex could enlighten him. If he knew Alex Cole, and he did, he probably already had a plan to get them back together.

Downstairs, Brad found Michelle setting the table. But she was setting it for six instead of five. Maybe Jeremy was bringing a date.

"Hi there. How was your nap?"

"Want to help me set the table?"

He followed her to the kitchen. "Is someone coming to dinner?"

She looked at him with eyes that were obviously hiding something. "Alex Cole will be joining us for dinner. Does that name sound familiar?" she asked innocently.

Brad put on a clueless expression. "No. No, I don't think so. Who is he?" He went back to the dining room and finished setting the table.

Michelle was laughing lightly as placed the salad on the table. "You know, I've watched you set the table for the last week, but it knocks me over every time."

"I like helping you. What's wrong with that?" But he knew what she meant. He had never helped with the everyday domestic aspects of marriage. He had left all those things to her. No wonder she wanted a divorce. "I'll help out as much as you want me to. All you have to do is ask."

Michelle was placing the baked chicken on a platter when the doorbell sounded. "Can you get the door, Brad?"

"How am I supposed to know him?"

"Oh, that's right. I'll get it, and you can put this on the table." She handed the platter to him.

He was pleased with himself; he had played that well. It was as if she knew he needed to talk to Alex. Maybe his medicine was a truth serum. Or had he talked in his sleep? He started bringing the rest of the side dishes to the table.

Alex walked into the dining room alone; he was dressed in a suit. He stared at Brad cautiously. "Hi, Brad. Remember me? We work together." He sat down at the table.

Why was Alex speaking to him like he was mentally challenged? Of course, no one knew he had regained most of his memory, so they still treated him like an invalid.

"I'm sorry, I don't know you," Brad lied. He hoped he could keep a straight face and not give away the game. "Where's Michelle?"

"She went to get the kids."

"So are you a friend of Michelle's?" Brad asked his best friend since college.

"I am now. Actually, I'm your friend. We met at Boston University. In economics. Remember Professor Edmonton?"

Brad grinned. He couldn't fake not remembering Edmonton. "The guy with the comb-over? I got a B in that class. He ruined my GPA," he griped.

145

Alex couldn't believe what he was hearing. "Man, that was over twenty-five years ago. Let it go. It's just made you more human—having a 3.98 GPA versus that 4.0 you were always throwing in everyone's face."

"Don't tell me he's going on about the only B he got in his college career again," Michelle asked, as she and the kids came to the table.

"Uncle Alex!" Peri jumped onto Alex's lap and kissed him on the cheek. "I missed you."

Alex hugged her. "I missed you, too. I bet you've been running your mom ragged."

Peri slid from his lap and went to her usual customary seat. Preston went to Michelle for help getting into his high-chair.

"Thank you for setting the table, Brad."

Before he could answer, Alex exclaimed, "Bradley Huntington Killarney set a dinner table? I don't believe it."

"I'll have you know I set the table all the time," Brad boasted as Jeremy took a seat at the table.

Michelle winked at him, sending his heartbeat into overdrive. "He helps all the time, Alex. Okay, Alex, did you wash your hands?"

After dinner, Michelle suggested Alex and Brad talk in the den while she got the kids ready for bed. Claiming fatigue, Jeremy said he was going to bed early.

Alex followed Brad into the den and closed the door. Brad faced his longtime friend, ready to confess, but Alex beat him to it.

"Okay, Brad, I know."

"What?"

"That you can remember more than you're letting on."

"I have no idea what you're talking about."

Alex leaned back in his chair. "Oh, come off it. I think you know exactly what I'm saying. I could tell by the way you chose your words before you spoke. So how long?"

He gave up, knowing Alex would no doubt tell Michelle, and she would toss him out on his ass for using her. "You're going to tell her, aren't you?"

"No, I'm not telling her. But I want to know what happened?"

"That's just it; I don't know for sure. We ran into some friends from London and a lot came back to me. But I still don't remember the night I got attacked or why Michelle and I are separated. Do you know?"

Alex's expression confirmed what Brad had surmised and feared: the break-up was his fault. His next words left no doubt. "Yes, I do know why, but I'm not going to tell you. You need to find out on your own. But I will say this: I love Michelle, mostly because she's your wife; and I love you like a brother. But since you've been sick, she's been relentlessly trying to find out what happened to you that night. You know, there's still the fact that three million dollars is missing, and it's from your department. I know you had nothing to do with it, but with Frank dead and no clues as to who did him in, you're the person most likely to be suspected. Michelle is trying to clear your name. I know she loves you. She wouldn't be searching your office for clues if she didn't. But if you're going to use this to try to manipulate her into taking you back, then, yes, I will tell her. I will not let you hurt her a second time."

Brad searched Alex's face for some sign of humor. Alex didn't take anything too seriously. Except for Michelle, apparently. "I'm not going to hurt her, Alex. But if I didn't know better, I would think you have some personal stake in this."

Alex laughed. "Yes, I do. You, her, my godchildren. You all are the closest thing I have to a family. Why do you think I was so happy when you came back to the States? Why do you think I was flying to London to see you guys every couple of months? You didn't think it was for the food, did you?"

Brad shook his head. He was an idiot. "Sorry, man. I thought you had a little something on the side in London. I thought you just didn't want me to know who it was. I guess I must have been neglecting or taking for granted everyone who made my life worth living." He extended his hand to Alex. "Forgive me?"

Alex nodded his okay. "Man, you've changed a lot. I see what Michelle is talking about now."

He knew it, too. Every time he touched her, she would almost jump out of her skin. She wasn't used to him being a loving husband. "I know

I have a lot to answer for. I don't know where my head was before, but it's like I'm starting over with her."

"I know, but you were in the hospital when she found you. Maybe that's it. She can't move past how badly injured you were just a little while ago."

"I want her to treat me like a man. Her husband, not a damn invalid. She won't even let me drive. My truck is in the garage. She has the keys." He smiled, remembering how she had wrestled him on the bed and extracted the keys from his pocket, and then left the room before any serious foreplay could ensue.

"You're just going to have to prove to her that you're able to drive. But that's going to be a hard sell." Alex reached inside his jacket pocket and pulled out some papers. "Look at these and tell me what they mean." He handed them over to Brad. "No one can make heads or tails."

Brad studied the papers, but it didn't make any sense. It looked like something Preston could have scribbled. Maybe he was getting a headache. He handed the paper back to Alex. "Sorry, but this looks like gibberish."

"Well, it was worth a try. Why don't you keep this? Maybe in a few days it will make sense to you, and then you can tell me what it means."

Brad took the papers and examined them again. "What is it, anyway? Looks like a code of some sort."

"Yes, it is. Yours. No one else knows what it means."

"Why would I use a code?"

"You always did. You were working on the quarterly report when all this happened. Whenever you worked on something of that magnitude, you would make up some kind of code until you could verify all the funds in the accounts."

Brad placed the paper on the desk. He had a feeling that once he deciphered the code, he would have the answer to why he and the woman he loved slept in separate bedrooms.

CHAPTER 19

Michelle was in her bed, reading to the children. Brad and Alex were still downstairs talking. When she had gone to check on them, they had stopped talking the minute she entered the den. Thinking she interrupted some serious man talk, she apologized and left, but her temper rose when she heard them laughing, reminding her of a typical Alex Cole visit. "What was I thinking, inviting that man into my house?" she muttered to herself.

"Mummy, you stopped reading," Peri chirped.

Michelle looked down at the book. "Oh, sorry, baby. Mommy's mind was wandering." She resumed reading.

"Mummy?"

"Yes, Peri."

"When Daddy's headaches go away, will he live with us like before?"

That was the question of the day. "I don't know. He might have other ideas. We will just have to wait and see. Don't you like living with Grandma and PaPa?"

"Yes, but I like Daddy now. He's fun. He makes breakfast and he plays with us. Before he didn't. Why can't we have both?"

Why couldn't they? Peri made it sound so simple. They could all live together under one roof, right? Not as long as Emily Shaw was under that roof. Brad would never agree to it, anyway. He liked being king of the castle.

But it would be nice. Michelle could be with her parents in their golden years, and they could enjoy their only grandchildren.

"Mummy, why?"

"I don't know."

Peri yawned. "I think I'm ready to go to bed." She scooted off the bed and walked to the door.

Michelle felt a trick being pulled, but she couldn't imagine her four-year-old daughter was trying to manipulate her own mother—until she spoke.

"Can I say goodnight to Daddy?"

"He's still talking to Uncle Alex downstairs. I'll make sure he comes and says goodnight to you."

Peri nodded.

"Come on, Preston." Michelle picked up her son. "It's time for bed." He was almost asleep.

"Are the kids already in bed?" Brad asked as she walked out of Preston's room.

"Yes, thank goodness. Peri tried to wait up for you, but she fell asleep."

He nodded and headed to Peri's room. Michelle was beginning to think as her daughter had observed earlier. Brad was a much better person now. He spent time with his children, and was not always concerned about the next big thing. They acted like a family. They sat down to dinner and there was not one word about the latest prospectus or the next hot business deal.

She had nothing against him being focused about his career; that was what attracted her to him six years ago. They were both career-driven; she just put hers on hold to stay with the children. Brad had to realize that he could have both. Okay, so he couldn't remember much, but at least his feelings weren't hiding behind some stupid male stereo-type.

She went to her room and dialed Mel's cellphone number. "Hey, Mel. How are you?"

"Oh, my God. What's wrong with Brad? Is he in the hospital?"

Michelle laughed. "Calm down. I just wanted to ask you a few questions about Brad's clothes."

"What? Does he need more clothes?"

"No, Mel. Concentrate. Remember when Brad was released from the hospital?"

"Yes."

"Did you get the clothes he had on when he stumbled into the hospital?"

Mel answered quickly. "No, Michelle. You know, that was strange. The nurse told me his clothes were taken by the police."

"Rats!"

"What is it?"

"I was hoping to look through his clothes for any kind of clues," said Michelle.

"I can't figure out why he would go to that hospital when he would have had to pass at least two to get there," Mel added.

"I think someone picked him up."

Mel gasped. "You think someone saw him walking covered with blood and gave him a ride to the hospital, but let him walk in on his own?"

"Yes, I think it was someone who knew him and knew which hospital was on his insurance."

"But if someone comes to the emergency room all bloodied, they have to treat them," Mel interjected.

Michelle agreed. "But there was never any talk of transferring him to the county hospital because he didn't have insurance. Did they give you a bill when he was released?"

"You know, come to think of it, when I offered my credit card, the nurse told me his insurance would cover his care."

"So," Michelle asked, "how did they know? No one asked me anything about insurance."

Michelle had finished her bath and was getting ready for bed when Brad knocked on her door. She tightened her bathrobe around her body as if it were armor and said, "Come in."

Brad came in, already dressed for bed in midnight blue silk pajamas. He usually slept in boxers and nothing else. Or he used to. "I wanted to say goodnight." He walked further into the room and closed the door. "You take a long bath, huh?"

"Yes, I always take at least an hour in the bathtub. You actually timed me once."

He sat on the bed beside her. "Why would I do something like that?"

"You said I took too long in the bathtub. Once, Peri woke up and you had to take care of her." She remembered that well. It was one of their better shouting matches.

He looked away. "I was awful. What did you do?"

"I still take baths," she laughed.

"That means I lost that one?"

"Yes, it does."

He slowly reached out to gently touch her cheek with the back of his hand, rubbing her skin. "Your skin is so soft and you smell great. I vote for the bath no matter how long it takes." His lips grazed hers in a light kiss, waking Michelle's sleeping hormones.

"Thanks for having Alex over for dinner. It was a real help. He filled in some of the blanks for me. Not all, but some. He made me realize I had been shutting out the people who loved me the most of all, in the name of work."

Michelle couldn't hold back the tears. "Yes, the last few years, you had become completely focused on your career. Your goal was to be vice president of investments, which is what you were before...all this happened."

Brad brushed her tears away. "I must have had a reason."

"Yes, but it wasn't a good one in my opinion."

Brad said nothing, as if he knew how much he had hurt her in the past. "Would you mind if I slept in here with you?"

What could she say? Maybe too many doors had opened for him too soon, and he was mentally exhausted and didn't want to be alone? She did miss the feeling of security. "You can sleep in here, but I have to put on my nightgown. I'll be right back." She walked to the bathroom, closing the door behind her.

She quickly changed into her silk nightshirt, brushed her hair, and brushed her teeth again. What was she doing? Maybe she just needed comforting. Maybe she just wanted proof that the last couple of weeks hadn't been a dream. Maybe Brad really wanted the family back together again as much as she did. And maybe she should stop staring at herself in the mirror and go face the man.

When she came out of the bathroom, Brad was already in her bed, looking like he belonged there. He was on her side of course; he always had to be near the phone. He was waiting for her.

"The kids are fine," he told her. "I checked on them before coming in."

She got into bed, and expected him to fall asleep as soon as the lights were out. He didn't. He pulled her back against his front and wrapped a strong arm around her. He wanted to talk. Their feet were doing a lovers' mating dance, and he wanted to talk. "What are we doing tomorrow?" He kissed her neck as she relaxed and enjoyed the sensation of his lips against her skin.

He said we. Michele couldn't think ahead ten minutes, let alone a whole day. She wanted him to continue kissing her. "I don't know. I have class tomorrow night. Why don't you and Alex do some male bonding? It might do you some good. You've been here for the last two weeks. "You might want to get out and have some fun."

"I'm having fun right here with you and the kids. I would like to see Niles and Porter before they head back to England. I thought maybe we could have dinner out or something."

"I think it's better if we invite them here. We still don't know who's after you, or why." She took deep breaths to calm herself.

He turned her so she could face him. She could see him in the dimly lit room. He kissed her mouth with a forceful pressure that Michelle matched. He moved his head to the left, she accommodated him by moving to the right. They were both panting when they came up for air. "Okay. I'll call them tomorrow." He unbuttoned her nightshirt and helped her out of it. "Now for more important matters," he muttered against her breast as he took one hard nipple in his mouth.

Michelle's back arched at the intense pleasure. Her head moved from side to side against her pillow. Blindly she reached for Brad, enjoying the feel of her husband's mouth on her skin. She groped at his pajama top, almost ripping it from her husband's body.

"Take it off, Brad. I have to feel your skin," she moaned.

Wanting to please his wife, he tore the silk pajama top from his body, while still suckling her breast.

He moved lower to her stomach leaving a trail of fire along the way past her navel. He ripped her lacey panties in his haste to get them off. "Sorry, baby. See what you do to me?"

Michelle knew exactly what she did to him; he was doing the same thing to her. But tonight, she wasn't going down without driving him out of his mind.

Michelle's eyes opened wide when she felt something move against her. Then she heard something move behind her. Brad. He shifted his position and snuggled closer to her. She was enjoying the feeling of comfort. She closed her eyes as his hands move along her hips.

She had just rocked his world, and now they were both spent.

She should have dropped into an exhausted sleep, but she didn't. Her mind was darting from one thing to another. She needed to talk to Alex so she could compare notes with him about what Brad had talked about. She needed to talk to Dryson. She also wanted to check out the buildings from Herrington to Kennedy Memorial. Maybe someone would remember seeing Brad walking down the road. But how could she find a way to do a little snooping without Brad in tow?

His hands tightened around her waist. Maybe he was just dreaming, she thought. But his grip became tighter, and his breathing had become heavy.

"Stay away or I will kill him," he said through gritted teeth.

His hands were suddenly around her throat. He was choking her. With all his manly strength, he was choking her.

"Tell your men to stay away from me, or I'm killing this bastard."

Michelle gasped for air. "Brad," she called.

"You stay away from my wife or you will be sorry."

"B-r-a-d, Brad!" Michelle sputtered. If she could wake him, he would let her go. But she didn't have enough strength, and the room was starting to fade away. She would have to kick him.

She called his name one more time. "Brad." He didn't relinquish his grip on her throat. She closed her eyes, and kicked him with all the strength she could muster. Then he let her go.

She thought he would have woke up, but he turned on his side, still asleep.

Gasping for air, Michelle switched on the lamp on the night table. She wondered where that episode had come from. Could he now remember more from that night? And could he fill in some of the blank spaces?

"Hey, what are you doing up?" Brad turned over, facing her. Yawning, he acted as if he had been sound asleep the entire night.

"You don't remember anything?"

He sat up. "No. What are you talking about?"

She hoped telling him wouldn't cause a setback. "A few minutes ago, you tried to choke me."

He held his head in his hands. "Oh, no, I thought it was over. I'm sorry. I hope I didn't hurt you."

Michelle coughed hoarsely. "What do you mean? You've had these dreams before?"

"More like a vision. Someone is attacking me, but somehow I get the upper hand and I have him at a disadvantage. I threaten the other men, and they pull back."

Michelle coughed again. "You said, 'Don't come near my wife.' "

He shook his head. "That's new."

"How do you know that?"

"Jeremy told me that he heard me one night. Then the next night he recorded me and let me hear it. It was awful. I was being attacked. I tried to figure out when it was, but I couldn't." He got up and began putting on his pajamas.

"Brad, what are you doing?"

"I can't stay in here with you when I'm choking you in my sleep. You're not safe." He headed for the door. "I love you and don't want you to be at risk. Until I can figure out what this is, I can't be trusted." He left the room.

She was near her wit's end. What else could possibly go wrong?

Brad didn't come down for breakfast the next morning. Michelle knew he was embarrassed about last night and wanted to ease his despair. But she couldn't leave the kids unattended; she knew she would have to wait. After Jeremy came in the kitchen and she had fed the kids breakfast, she went upstairs to Brad's room.

"Brad." She knocked on the door as she turned the knob. The door was locked. "Brad, it wasn't your fault."

"Michelle, I just need to be alone."

"Please," she whispered.

Silence. Then she heard him come to the door and unlock it. He opened the door only part way.

"Brad, I would like to talk to you."

He wasn't going to let her inside. "Talk."

"Please let me come inside."

He let out a resigned breath, then opened the door all the way.

Michelle sat on his bed and motioned for him to sit beside her. She knew she would have to be crafty to get him to open up. Brad didn't like talking about anything emotional, another sign the old Brad was returning. Her throat still felt raw from the night before. "Brad, if you don't talk about it, it will only eat you up inside. I know you're hurting."

He sat beside her, but remained silent.

She reached out for her husband, wrapping her arms around him. "Brad, I know you wouldn't hurt me physically. I think you were reliving the night you were attacked."

He hugged her back. "Thank you. I really needed to hear that. I was wondering what kind of man was I if I would harm you."

She thought about it. "You're a good man, Brad. Sometimes you act first and ask questions later, but your heart is in the right place." She kissed him on the cheek. "You can come down for breakfast. Jeremy is going to eat all the food if you don't hurry."

"No, I've got some thinking to do. I'll be down later."

"Well, the kids and I are going to the park, and then we're going shopping. Jeremy will be here all day. If you need him to take you somewhere, he will." She rose to leave.

"When do you think I'll be able to drive alone?"

"When you can tell me what happened that night." She opened the door. "And if you're thinking you can convince Jeremy to let you drive, he has specific instructions not to. He also has no idea where your keys are."

CHAPTER 20

In the park, Michelle kept a wary, watchful eye on her playing children. She was also scrolling through Brad's Palm Pilot, checking the calendar. She didn't know what she'd find, but she still hoped.

True to form, Brad made a memo of everything. She checked the calendar two weeks before Frank's death. She punched the screen with her finger to bring up the details of the meeting. There it was before her. Good old Brad. She'd never complain about him being anal again. It told her exactly what the details were about the meeting.

She let the kids have McDonald's for lunch, and then they headed to Herrington Global for a little research.

Brad stayed in his room for as long as he could stand it. Michelle and the kids were gone. That he was glad of. He couldn't face them right now. He went downstairs to fix some lunch.

He walked into the kitchen and found Jeremy at the table having coffee. "Hey, how do you feel? Michelle will probably be out all day. She said not to worry."

Brad was too embarrassed to face his brother-in-law. "Did she say why she was going to be out all day? Was it because of…" He couldn't say the dreaded words.

Jeremy stood and pulled a chair out. "Sit, Brad," he said, pointing to the chair. "I know about last night. Shell can't hold water, especially if something is bothering her. You're just working through your amnesia. I think it's a suppressed memory from the night you got attacked."

Brad rubbed the side of his head. "Then why was I choking my wife?"

"I don't know. That does seem strange. Unless…" Jeremy was guessing. "Unless her life was being threatened."

"So I choke her to save her. Nice try, Jerry."

Jeremy stared at him with a puzzled look on his face. Brad realized instantly that he had misspoken. Jerry was the family nickname for Jeremy. Few people outside of the family called him that. Jeremy's next words confirmed it.

"Why did you call me that? Jerry?"

Brad shrugged. "I don't know. It seemed right. You don't like it?"

"No, but you used to call me that and you haven't in a while. Maybe your answer to the nightmares will come to you soon."

The doorbell sounded, saving Brad from having to respond. "I'm not expecting anyone," Jeremy said. "Do you know if Michelle was?"

Brad shook his head. Jeremy started from the door, saying over his shoulder, "I'll be right back. If I'm not back in five minutes, dial 911."

Brad nodded obediently. He hated being treated like a child, but that would end soon.

Soon Jeremy returned almost immediately. "It's your boss."

Brad was confused. "I thought he was dead."

"Well then, your boss's boss. He's in the living room."

Brad didn't know the man, had never seen him. He felt uneasy about being alone with a stranger. "Jeremy, would you mind..." His voice trailed off. He hated being needy; only weak people were needy, and he wasn't weak.

"Yeah, I'll go with you."

Brad relaxed and walked into the living room. The man on the couch wore a very expensive suit that had some kind of emblem on the jacket pocket. His chestnut brown hair was combed straight back, and his pale, smiling face wasn't familiar to Brad. He stood and extended his hand as Brad neared the couch.

"It's good to see you up and about, Brad," he said in a Scottish brogue.

Brad couldn't place the man to save his life.

"My name is Conrad Jameson. I'm the president of operations at Herrington Global. I know this is probably gibberish to you, but I'll try to explain. The company has four tiers of management: public relations, marketing, investment, and operations. Operations oversees the entire company. That's why I'm your boss."

"My boss? I don't understand."

"I'm here in an official capacity. I want to offer you the job of president of investments; when you're able to return to work, of course."

Brad was dumbfounded. "What about the report? The missing money?"

"The board of directors doesn't hold you accountable for that. The audit found that the problem has been going on for the last year. The board elected to replace the missing money so that the investors won't have to absorb the loss."

Brad nodded, even though he didn't fully understand.

But Jameson continued speaking. "There will be a raise and other incentives. You know, the usual—stock options, vacation, a handsome annual bonus, and a larger expense account."

"Could I think about it? I'll need to discuss it with Michelle."

Jameson coughed. "Sure. You can discuss it with her. I was under the impression you were getting a divorce."

"No. We were separated but are working it out. Where did you hear I was getting a divorce?"

Jameson shifted uneasily. "Frank mentioned it when I spoke with him before his death."

The conversation was making Brad feel anxious. Michelle would be happy about the promotion. At least, he hoped so. It would give them more money for the college funds and they could buy their own house, instead of living with her parents.

But he also knew that Michelle was living with her parents for another reason. It had nothing to do with money. Even without his salary, Michelle could well afford a large home if she so chose.

The thought of living under the same roof as Emily Shaw was incentive enough to accept the promotion.

Jameson was droning on. "I understand you haven't been released by the doctor yet. The job, if you want it, will be waiting for you." He rose to leave, extending his hand to Brad and handing him his business card. "I will be in touch."

Brad followed him to the front door. "As soon as I make a decision, I will let you know." He shut the door behind the strange, unsettling man. He returned to the living room and placed the card on the table.

Jeremy smiled faintly. "That promotion sounds pretty good. President. Shell is going to freak."

Brad didn't hear the doubt in his brother-in-law's voice. "Yeah, I think she'll be pleased. Maybe this will be the deciding factor about us getting back together."

Jeremy wasn't smiling. "Maybe."

That one word told Brad he still had a lot of work to do.

Michelle walked into Herrington Global and headed for Alex's office, but first she stopped at Brad's secretary's desk.

Michelle saw the unspoken concern in Mary's expression. She knew Mary wanted to know about Brad's progress, and she wanted to reassure her.

"Mary, he's doing well. Why don't you come and see him?"

But Mary declined. "I know he doesn't remember a lot of things. I don't want to give him a shock. I just wanted to know if he's all right. He's been through so much."

There was something in Mary's demeanor that wasn't right. "Yes, we all have. Anyway, he's getting better and remembering more each day. The kids are enjoying him being at home."

Mary smiled her motherly smile at Michelle. "Any hope of a reconciliation?"

Michelle always found herself wanting to please Mary. "Maybe."

Mary leaned back in her chair, smiling. "Well that sounds like a yes to me. Look at you, all relaxed and glowing. Just like a woman in love. I know you're here to see Alex. Why don't you let the kids stay with me while you talk to Alex? I'm sure it's something that little ears shouldn't hear anyway." She let Preston climb up on her lap. "They'll be fine."

Michelle nodded. "Okay, then. Be good, guys. I'll be right back." Michelle walked to Alex's office down the hall.

After she was seated, she got right down the business. "Did Brad say anything important last night?"

He hedged, trying to collect his thoughts. "Yes and no."

She crossed her arms in front of her chest. "Please explain."

"I showed him a few pages of the report that we found. He couldn't make heads of tails out of it. He said it looked like something Preston could have done. But I left it with him. You know, to give him something to focus on. Speaking of, where is he?"

"He's at home. He had kind of a setback this morning."

"Explain," said Alex.

"Well, he came into my room last night and asked me if he could sleep with me. I figured he had too many visions and just wouldn't want to be alone."

Alex did as he was told. "Okay, continue. I don't see the problem. So he didn't want to sleep alone. That doesn't sound like a setback to me. He sounds human."

"I know, Alex. Over in the night he was having a bad dream and he ended up choking me. After I managed to wake him and told him what he did, he went to his room. He was ashamed."

"Why did he choke you?"

Michelle wished she knew. "When he was having the dream, he told whomever he was fighting not to hurt me."

Alex whistled. "Man, this is getting so weird. You weren't there when he was attacked. You were nowhere in sight."

"I know. Do you think whoever attacked him had threatened to come after me? I can't figure out why."

"Me neither."

"Brad feels really bad about what happened last night. He wouldn't come down for breakfast. I just wish I knew what to do to make him feel better. Any ideas?"

"Well, you aren't going to like this."

"What?" she asked suspiciously.

"You'll have to persuade him to sleep with you again until either he goes through the whole dream or he stops having them."

"You were right. I don't like your idea. It's boneheaded. One of those get-back-on-the-horse-again ideas. What if he chokes me again and I can't stop him?"

Alex smiled. She didn't like the way his lips turned upward. It was sneaky. "I'd leave my door unlocked if I were you."

"I don't think I could get Brad to sleep with me now, anyway."

Alex stood and began pacing the room. "Oh, come off it. You can have him jumping through all kinds of hoops if you wanted to. That's just not your style. I think a few well-placed kisses and come-hither smiles will do the trick. He'll sleep with you, especially if he knows that you're trying to help him." He sat on the corner of his desk.

Michelle was just about to tell him where to go when his phone rang. She watched his smile slowly fade.

"Hey, Brad. No, I'm not busy. Can I put you on hold for a minute?" He looked at Michelle for guidance. "What do you want me to tell him?"

"Nothing. How did he know your number?"

Alex said he didn't know. "Maybe I gave him a card last night, I don't think so. He does know this is where he worked. It wouldn't be that hard to ask the operator for Alex Cole, especially if he identified himself."

She rose and picked up her purse. "I suppose that could be true, but I know you. You're up to something. But it will all come to the surface in its own good time," she warned. "Thanks for all your help. See you later." She kissed him on the cheek and went to collect her kids from Mary.

As she pulled out of Herrington Global's parking lot, on impulse she decided to retrace the most likely route to Kennedy Memorial Hospital. Herrington was one of the largest businesses in the Dallas-Fort Worth area, yet the company headquarters was in Arlington, a mid-sized city. The large building dwarfed every other structure down-town. It was the only 25-story building in Arlington.

But there was no direct route from Herrington to Arlington Memorial. Brad would have had to walk to an always busy Cooper

Street and then walk about five miles, passing a busy mall, to the inter-state to get to the hospital. Why didn't he just have walked down the street to Arlington General? It was probably only a ten-minute walk from Herrington.

Someone had to have seen him and picked him up. Perhaps a person who didn't want to get involved. Perhaps, a person who didn't want any questions asked. She should go and touch base with Dryson Jones.

But Michelle feared the day's nonstop outings were taking their toll on the kids. She couldn't take her two small children to a police station, no matter how important this was. She decided to call Sergeant Jones later instead.

CHAPTER 21

By the time Michelle and the kids arrived home, Brad was fit to be tied. She had been gone all day and didn't offer any explanation as to why she hadn't called and checked in with him.

But he didn't explode at her in front of the children. He waited patiently until after she had fed the kids and then had put them to bed. They were exhausted and went to sleep right after dinner.

He sat on the couch looking at the papers Alex had given him the day before. The words and symbols on the paper made no sense. He sensed that if he could just break the code, he would have the answers to putting his life back together.

"You're not forcing memories, are you?" Michelle came into the room and took a seat near him on the couch. "How are you feeling?"

"Pretty good for a man who's been worried about his family all day. You know, you could have called and talked to me. Where were you?" His lowered his voice, knowing that if he yelled at her, Jeremy would probably fly downstairs to protect his sister.

She turned to face him. "I was following a hunch. Do you remember anything about that night you were attacked?"

"How many times are you going to ask me? If I knew I would tell you."

"You don't have to bite my head off," Michelle snapped. "I just thought maybe today something might have come back to you."

"Why didn't you call me? I was worried someone had attacked you or something."

"I didn't call you because I was checking a few things out. If there had been a problem, I would have called you."

She was patronizing him, of course. They both knew she had his car keys and had made it clear that Jeremy had strict orders not to let him drive. Even if she had called him today, there was little he could have done if she had run into trouble.

Realizing that, he calmed way down. "I'm sorry. You're right, as usual."

"What does that mean?" Now her tone was accusatory.

But Brad retreated. He spoke in a calming voice. "I meant that I'm not thinking clearly. I'm thinking like a husband. I want to protect my family, but my family is protecting me. So you're right. I couldn't have done much."

She moved closer. "Brad, I didn't mean to make you feel less in your role in the family. I had to take care of some things."

"I had a visitor today." He couldn't contain his news any longer.

"Was Jeremy here? Who was it?"

"Yes, he was here. It was my boss, or rather, my late boss's boss."

Michelle held her breath as if bracing herself for the bad news. "What did he want? Did you tell him that the doctor hadn't released you yet?"

Brad placed his hand on hers. "Will you slow down?" He laughed at her worried expression. "I'm not exactly handicapped, you know."

"I know, Brad. It's just that…well, I should have been here with you."

He liked the way she put it. Being there with him, yeah, that sounded like she was ready to forgive whatever terrible thing he had done to her. Her next words put an end to his basking.

"You shouldn't sign or agree to anything without me or your sister present, since your memory hasn't completely returned."

How could she give him hope one moment, and then snatch it away the next? He felt a creeping sense of dejection. "I didn't sign anything. He offered me Frank's job as president."

She was stunned. "Wow, Brad. That would be quite an accomplishment, and you're ahead of your career goal."

"Yes, it is. You know how hard it is for blacks in the corporate world, especially at a global company like Herrington. I knew that job in London would be a big stepping stone. But I told him that I would need to talk to you. It also means more money for the kids' college funds, more money for us, and I get more vacation time. So what do you think?"

"I think it is a good career move for you. And you wanted to start a mentoring program at Herrington for minorities. Maybe now you'll get your chance."

He remembered that idea now. He'd mentioned it to Michelle one night, several years ago. He didn't think she was listening, another thing he was totally wrong about. "Thanks, Shell."

She looked up at him, shock evident on her face. "What did you call me?"

He'd blown it again. "Shell."

"You used to call me that when we were dating before."

He was going to have to stay on his toes if he wanted to find out what happened in their marriage and not reveal his memory was coming back.

"You mind if I call you that now?"

"No, of course not. So are you going to take the job? You know you haven't been released by the doctor yet?"

"He said they'd wait until I was able to come back to work. Now I have a question for you that has nothing to do with work."

"Okay."

"What was our first date like?"

Michelle's face split into a grin. "It was spontaneous. You came to my office looking for a house. I took you all over Arlington, and you decided on a condo in South Arlington."

"That was our date?"

"No," she said wistfully. "It was getting late, and you wanted to eat at this steak restaurant to celebrate finding something so fast."

"And?" Brad prodded, remembering the events of the evening as if they were yesterday.

"We had dinner. After dinner, you wanted to see more of Arlington so we drove around town. It was getting late, so I took you back to your rental car and that's when you kissed me. You apologized instantly for being so forward."

"Did you slap me?"

She actually giggled. "No, there wasn't time. I kissed you back."

"Well," Brad said.

"I know, I'd never done anything so spontaneous in my life. And then I asked you back to my place."

"Sounds like someone is an incurable romantic."

"Yes, I am. That's why I know we belong together, Bradley. I knew it then, I know it now.. We just have to work out the edges. I fell in love with the man you were then. You worked hard, and I have nothing against that. I just know there's a balance between work and family."

Brad knew they belonged together, too. Maybe the rough edges would be a thing of the past very soon. "I love you, Shell, and I know we will be able to strike a balance that works for everyone."

"I know, Brad. We can make a chart of what we think went wrong and go from there."

Brad didn't want to take a practical approach to something this important. They were on the same page on most things, but affairs of the heart were definitely Michelle's area of expertise. "Tell me how I proposed," Brad said.

Michelle laughed. "You sent me an e-mail."

"Oh, that sounds awful. You said yes to an e-mail?"

"No, you didn't mean to send it. You were sending it to Alex to ask him how it sounded, but somehow it was sent to me."

"What happened?"

"Well, I called you, but you were in a meeting. So I replied to the e-mail."

Brad laughed, remembering how embarrassing the whole thing had become. "Alex got that e-mail. There was some kind of glitch in the system."

"Yes. Alex didn't know if I was proposing to him or if I was asking him to propose to you."

He laughed harder. "Yeah, before it was over, everyone at Herrington had gotten that same e-mail. I was so embarrassed."

"You didn't ever answer me back, so I went to your office and Mary, your secretary, asked me if you had proposed to me yet. I told her no. Then she told me that you would."

"I proposed to you at my meeting. You had the nerve to say no, and you accused me of doing all that on purpose. You walked out."

"Then what happened?"

Brad moved toward her. "I left the meeting and followed you. You wouldn't answer your cellphone; I chased you all the way to your house. Finally, you let me inside and I proposed properly. We married a month later."

"Yes," Michelle whispered. "It was the best proposal."

Brad put his arm around her. "That's what I want. I want us back like that. No matter what happened in our past, we can get through it."

Brad kissed her. "I want the smile you had on your face when you were talking about my proposal. I want you to always look that happy."

"Brad, that wasn't entirely your fault. I lost part of myself when I sold my business to become your wife. True, I had been thinking about getting out of the real estate business before I met you. I know there's more out there for me. I want to explore my artistic side of my talent."

"I would never hold you back."

"I know that now. Before I guess I was afraid to just do it. I can take some classes while Peri is in preschool this fall, and Preston could go to daycare for a few hours. I've always loved art."

This was his chance. Life was given him a golden opportunity to show his support for her dreams just as she had his. "I think you should do it, baby. Since I've been out of it, I have realized life is what you do with it. I know I keep going on about college funds, and trips, but all that doesn't mean crap if you're not doing something you love."

Michelle looked at him with moist eyes. "Really, Brad? You mean it?"

"Yes, baby. I think you should go for it."

CHAPTER 22

As soon as Michelle heard Brad's even breathing, she got up. She went into the bathroom, perplexed. What had just happened? Yes, she and Brad had made love, but it was so different from the last time.

Brad Killarney knew how to have sex one way: missionary. He hated not being in control. Tonight, he was as gentle as the last time, but he let her take control.

She took a quick shower and put on her nightshirt. Planning ahead, she figured if she had to call for Jeremy to help her, it would be nice to have on some proper nightclothes. She then slipped back into bed. Brad's arms encircled her, his naked body snuggling against her. She really wished she could keep this Brad. He was all the things missing in their marriage: caring, sharing, and romantic. She fell asleep, with visions of Brad making love to her filling her head.

When Michelle woke both Peri and Preston were standing by her side of the bed. Peri was tapping her mother not too gently on the arm. Michelle looked over at Brad's side, but he was gone.

"How did you guys get in here?"

Peri gave her a "you're stupid" look before answering. "Daddy let us in. He is fixing breakfast for us, but we want to know if you want pancakes or not."

Her daughter wasn't getting through to her mother. "What do you mean Daddy let you in?"

Peri sighed impatiently. "We knocked and he opened the door."

That was simple. "Oh. No, honey, Mommy wants to sleep a little longer."

Peri nodded, leading her brother from the room. Michelle knew she should probably get up, but her body just wouldn't cooperate. She went back to sleep instantly.

Later, when she woke, her body was a little more agreeable, allowing her to sit up. Brad walked in without knocking.

"Brad, you're supposed to knock. The kids might see you come in like that."

He rolled his eyes upward. "The children are asleep. Jeremy is seeing a client downstairs. And I'm here to check on you. How are you feeling?"

She couldn't deny it. She felt pretty woozy. Almost as if she had the flu or something flu-like, but it was summer and they lived in north Texas, popular for hot weather. "Just tired, I guess. I just need some time to get my strength back. I was just going to get dressed." She threw the covers back and saw that she was nude. "I know I put clothes on this morning," she said, looking sideways at Brad. "Okay, what happened to my nightshirt?"

Brad had the nerve to look innocent. "It's your fault," was all he would say.

"What is my fault?"

He moved closer to the bed. "You felt too good in my arms. I couldn't sleep."

Michelle could feel her skin heating up, slowly the memories flooded back to her. Sometime over in the night, Brad reached for her and they made wonderful love. He was tender and thoughtful and turned her world inside out.

"Well then, that's your fault," Michelle pointed out.

"Yeah, right." Brad laughed and sat down on the bed. "Hey, since we got a little time, how about an instant replay?"

She knew her mouth was hanging open in astonishment. "I can't believe you!" She started laughing. "How about you fix me some lunch?"

He rose and saluted her. "Yes, ma'am." He kissed her on the fore-head. "Why don't you take the day off? You know, recharge your batteries."

"I can't. I have to start planning for Mom and Dad's welcome home party. They'll be home in a few days."

"I think you can plan from the bed. Why haven't your parents called? I've been here almost two weeks. Even my sister calls you. My mom has even called."

"My parents don't call unless there's a problem. Plus, they know Jeremy is here."

"I can just see your mom's face when she returns and finds me under her roof."

"Me, too. I sure hope your insurance is paid up," she teased.

"Me, too." He blew her a kiss and walked out of the room.

She really wished she could keep this Brad.

"Brad, is Michelle coming downstairs today?" Jeremy walked from the living room and met him on his way downstairs.

"Where's your client?"

"Gone."

"She's not feeling well, so she's going to stay in bed."

"Oh, my God. The last thing we need is her getting sick. What's wrong with her? Do I need to take her to the hospital?" He walked in the direction of the stairs.

"Whoa, Jerry. She's just a little tired."

"What's wrong with my sister? What did you do to her?"

Brad was trying to contain his temper. "Cool down, Jeremy. She's just feeling a little tired. I'm going to fix her some lunch."

Jeremy nodded. "She probably hasn't had much sleep in the last two months. With all the stuff you guys have been through, I could see her being run down."

"She wasn't too run down to demand I fix her something." Brad walked to the kitchen. "Let me know if you hear the kids stirring."

He pondered what to fix his wife. He knew it had to be something at least partly healthy. He decided on a turkey breast sandwich on wheat bread accompanied by fat-free chips. He placed the sandwich, a glass of iced-tea on a tray.

Jeremy stopped him as he neared the stairs. He had a handful of letters in his hand. "Brad, can you take Michelle her mail?"

Brad took the letter and placed it on the tray and headed up the stairs.

Michelle sat up in bed at the sound of Brad's footsteps. He walked into the room with a tray and the mail.

"I thought you might want to look at this." He held up the letter. "It's addressed to Mrs. Brad Killarney. You've never gotten mail like this before, and it doesn't have a return address."

"What's the postmark? I don't open anything without a return address." Recent mail threats in the UK and the States had taught her better to be safe than sorry.

He turned the letter over with his thumb and forefinger. "There's not one. I'm calling the police." He put the letter on the night table and dialed the sergeant.

"Call Dryson," Michelle said.

Listening to Brad's side of the conversation, Michelle relaxed a little. "He'll be here in thirty minutes. He said not to touch the letter."

"Duh!" Michelle said. "Did that touch my food?"

Brad looked down at the tray. "I'd better go fix something else. Just in case."

After Brad brought her some lunch, she decided she was just going to rest her eyes for a few minutes until Dryson arrived. But it was over an hour later when Brad shook her awake.

"Dryson is here, baby."

"Okay, I'll be down as soon as I dress."

"I'll wait for you." He sat on edge of the bed.

Michelle knew he wasn't moving, so she would have to. She got out of bed and dressed. They went downstairs hand in hand and met Dryson in the living room. Brad carried the letter in a box in his free hand.

"Jeremy said you weren't feeling well. But I wanted to see that envelope," Dryson said, rising to greet them.

He took a pair of disposable gloves out as his pocket and took the box from Brad. Handling the letter carefully, he listened to it, felt it, and finally he sniffed it. Dryson took a knife out of his pocket and slit the envelope open.

"I think you might want to see this," he said, handing the note to her.

Michelle read the letter. "Why would someone send this to me? I'm just trying to clear my husband, nothing else."

Dryson spoke to her in a soothing tone. "Someone wants you to stop poking into Herrington's records, which tells me that you must be on to something."

"But I don't want to get killed for it! But I think this has something to do with Brad's attack and Frank's murder. I think they're connected."

"Yeah, I think so too. I looked into Frank's insurance policy, and what I found was kind of puzzling."

"Why?" Michelle didn't think it could get any stranger than it was.

"Well, he named Harry Phillips as the beneficiary."

"Who's that?" Michelle had hoped it would have been his current wife, ex-wife, or a son or daughter.

"Here's where it really gets strange. It's his former employer." Dryson took a notepad out of his pocket. "I talked to him, earlier. At first, he wasn't willing to cooperate. But I pressed him, and finally he gave in."

"What did he say?"

"I really shouldn't be telling you this, but you gave me the idea. He told me he was beneficiary to the policy because he had adopted Frank's son."

"You're kidding."

"No. As the story goes, Frank was dating a woman named Mary for a brief time. A child was conceived and was adopted by Mr. and Mrs. Philips about six months ago. Frank wanted to leave the kid something, and since he wasn't allowed any contact with him the agreement was drawn up."

Michelle thought out loud. "So he didn't know what sex the child was, or its name, when he came to Herrington, so he left the money to the adoptive father. So that ruins my idea about why a family member has not claimed the body. Unless Mr. Phillips is in financial ruin."

Dryson shook his head. "Already checked. He didn't need the half-million-dollar policy; he's worth several million himself, as are the other partners. I checked them all out. They are all worth at least five million each, so money wasn't the issue."

Michelle sighed in despair. "Has anyone claimed his body yet?"

"No, and we even went to his wife to claim the body so he could be buried, and she flatly refused, especially when she found out she wasn't the beneficiary. The kids did the same."

Michelle nodded. It seemed a shame. Everyone deserved a decent Christian burial. "Is there any way I could look at the murder scene photos?"

Dryson was about to object.

"I know I'm asking a lot," Michelle pleaded. "But I just want to see for myself, and since someone is sending me notes, maybe something will jump out at me."

"Okay, I'll see what I can do." He eased out of the chair and rose. "I'd be careful, Michelle. Someone knows what you've been doing and they're scared. Who knows what could happen? If you see anything strange just remember to call the police, okay?" He held her hand. "You're very special and I wouldn't want to see anything happen to you."

"I will be careful. But I have got to know what happened."

CHAPTER 23

"Brad, why don't you look at those papers again?" Michelle sat next to him on the sofa after she had put the kids to bed. His long legs were stretched out under the coffee table and he looked quite comfortable, enjoying the quiet.

He straightened up and reached for them. "I don't know, Shell. It seems like a waste of time to me. I tried earlier today and couldn't break it."

"Maybe if you could remember the last time you used the codes, it would bring something back. Alex said that even before you became vice president, you always coded the reports until you could verify funds. Maybe you did it with this one, too."

"When did you talk to Alex about this?"

"A while ago. When you first came home from the hospital."

"What kind of report was it? I have a hazy memory of some kind of report that Frank was asking me about."

She tried to keep calm. A breakthrough to the past? "It was a financial report for the stockholders and the board of directors. To my understanding, no one person had access to the entire report until you finished your part. Do you remember anything about that report? Anything at all about the three million dollars?"

He closed his eyes and leaned back. She could see he was trying to force a memory. A headache would soon follow. "I see the file on my desk, in my apartment. The phone rings, I grab the file and head for the truck."

"Do you remember what happened to the file?" She felt awful for pressing him, but she was sure they were on to something. The end result may well be worth her pushing.

"I put it away," he told her.

"What?" Michelle grabbed him by the shoulders, shaking him. "What do you mean?"

Brad looked at her quizzically. She released him immediately. Taking a deep breath, he said, "I put it away. On my way to the office, I got a call from Frank wanting to know how long it would be before I would be there. Something in his voice didn't sound right. I knew they were going to make me sign the report, whether it was right or not, so I put it away."

"Who's they?"

He shook his head. "I don't know. I could have sworn I heard voices in the background."

Michelle had pushed him too far, but didn't know how to stop now. There were too many unanswered questions, too many possibilities, too many dangers waiting for them.

He rubbed his forehead. "I'm sorry, I need to rest a minute."

She felt guilty for pushing him. "I'll be right here by your side." She held his hand as he leaned against her.

He was soon asleep, and Michelle's mind began to dart about. Were they in any danger? How would they know? His puzzling answers were still ringing in her ear. She and Dryson had combed the truck and had come up empty. But where else would he have put it away?

He was a stickler for details. Maybe the report was on a disk somewhere. But they hadn't found a disk in the truck. All they found were his PDA and his cellphone. His wallet contained only cash, credit cards, and scraps of paper. But Dryson searched and found nothing out of the ordinary. Otherwise, the police would have kept it.

Worn out from knocking her head against the wall, Michelle soon fell asleep as well.

The next time she opened her eyes she was in bed, in her nightclothes, and Brad was asleep next to her. He had carried her upstairs, dressed her for bed, and crawled in beside her, instead of going to his room. But she didn't care. She was glad to have the security of his arms around her.

Brad woke up alone in the bed the next morning. Michelle was probably downstairs making breakfast. He hadn't meant to sleep in her bed last night. He had only intended to lay beside her to insure that she was sound asleep. But her quiet breathing and her snuggling had lulled him to sleep.

He got up from the bed and went to his room. He showered, dressed, and went downstairs. The picture he saw warmed his heart. Peri and Preston were eating a breakfast of eggs, bacon, toast and jelly. Michelle was sitting between them, as she had done for the last few years of their marriage. She smiled as Preston gave her a sticky jelly kiss. Delighted, she returned her son's kiss.

He wanted to get them back to this place.

"Good morning, Brad," Michelle said, rising from her chair. "I'll get your breakfast."

"No, I can get it." He noticed she wasn't eating. "How about I get yours?"

Yet another surprised, she marveled. "Okay. But only one piece of bacon."

He paused ever so briefly and then said, "I remember that you loved bacon."

Her jaw dropped, and he nearly dropped the plate he was holding. "Wow, I can't believe it."

He shook off the feeling that he had been absent in his own marriage. Quickly, he prepared the plate for his wife and passed it to her.

"Do you remember how I take my coffee?"

"Three sugars, two creams; hazelnut, of course," Brad said, certain he was right.

Michelle was impressed. "You never remembered that before," she said softly, a hint of awe in her voice.

"Maybe I did but really didn't." He remembered a fight about his inability to remember this sort of thing.

He prepared her coffee to her liking and gave it to her. They were all eating together—just like a regular family.

The kids gobbled their food and asked for seconds; before Michelle could rise, he beat her to it. "You rest. I'll get it for these endless pits." He took their plates and went to the stove.

He was about to sit back down when Preston said, "Juice, Daddy."

He vowed to share more of this kind of domestic togetherness. He poured his son's juice; Peri didn't want juice. She waited until he sat down to ask for milk, instead. Michelle was laughing.

"Remember, you wanted to see what it was like."

"Yes, I did. Remind me of this the next time I volunteer."

Still laughing, Michelle finished her meal. Finally, the kids stopped eating. Preston signified he was finished by throwing his bacon on the floor. Michelle lifted Preston out of his high chair and wiped his face. "Peri, you and Preston go watch TV and we'll get dressed in a minute."

After the kids left, Brad and Michelle were alone. They faced each other with a tenderness he hadn't thought possible. Maybe her resolve was weakening. Maybe she was ready to be a family again. Maybe.

If only he knew what he had done in the past to make her doubt now.

"Brad?"

He snapped out of his daydreaming. "Oh, sorry. Zoned out for a minute." His untouched eggs were now cold.

She reached across the table and picked up his plate. She walked to the microwave, reheated his food, and returned the steaming plate to him.

"Thanks. I was thinking of getting Jeremy to take me to Herrington today. What do you think?"

"Are you ready for it?"

"Yes." He wanted her to go with him, but he wanted her to suggest it. "I think so. I was going to call Alex. I want to get into my office."

As he had hoped, Michelle suggested she should accompany him. "I was thinking I could take you instead of Jeremy. That way if something came to you, I'll be there. I'll ask him to babysit for a little while today."

"Great." He could feel the bond between them tightening. "I'll call Alex and let him know we're coming."

Michelle rose from table and started scraping the plates to put in the dishwasher. But Brad stopped her. "Why don't I clean up the kitchen and you get dressed?"

"Man, when you change you really change, big time."

As they later drove to Herrington, Brad studied the landscape along the way. "Any of this looking familiar?" Michelle asked.

"No, nothing," he answered. "Can you park where they found my truck?"

"I think your parking placard might be in the glove compartment. Can you look in there?"

As soon as he popped open the glove box, a jumble of images came rushing at him. A flash of light, noise, somebody calling his name. Then he was in the hospital and Michelle was at his bedside holding his hand. He shrugged the images off and looked for the familiar Herrington logo. The blue plastic plaque seemed to wink at him. Or was his imagination in overdrive? "Found it."

"Great." She took it and hung it on the rearview mirror. She turned to him, empathy written all over her flawless brown face. "If it's too much for you, just let me know and we'll leave."

He loved her. No doubt in his mind. He loved her mostly because of the way she was looking at him at that very moment.

"I have to face my demons sooner or later. If I do it now, maybe I'll find the key to my past."

His heartbeat accelerated as she steered the SUV drove into the parking garage. His palms became sweaty, and his head began to throb. Something was going to happen. He braced himself for whatever it was.

She parked in his spot. "Do you remember anything?"

Brad squeezed his eyes shut. The memories were coming back. Maybe too fast. "That night I can remember being in the back of a car. I hear muffled voices, but no one is talking to me. The car stops and someone forces me out and leaves me in front of a building."

"Was it the hospital?"

"Yeah, I guess so."

"That could explain how you got from here to the hospital without anyone seeing you. Someone found you and took you there. But who?"

"I don't know. All I can see is the inside of the car."

She patted his leg lovingly. "It will probably come to you later, when you least expect it. Let's go inside." She slid out of the SUV and came around to his side to help him out.

"Michelle, I'm not helpless. I can get around just fine on my own." She was back to treating him like an invalid. Maybe it was because they were at Herrington Global and neither knew what was around the next corner.

"Of course, Brad," Michelle said, sounding patronizing. She took his hand anyway and led him to the elevator.

She pushed the button for the tenth floor. Soon they would be in his office. "What happens when I don't remember anything?"

"Then we'll go home and try something else." She stroked his arm, trying to calm him down. "Whatever the outcome, we need to do this."

Exiting the elevator doors, he held his breath and then slowly let it out. He relaxed a bit and allowed Michelle to lead him down the hallway. As they rounded a corner, a mature black woman, sitting behind a large desk, was looking at him intently. Clearly she knew him, but he couldn't think of her name.

In the last two weeks, Michelle had become hypersensitive to the slightest change in him and knew when he hit a blank wall. She spoke up when the woman kept staring at Brad, but said nothing.

"Brad, you remember your secretary, Mary."

He nodded yes, mainly because this Mary seemed like she was on the verge of tears. "Hello, Mary."

She sprang out of her chair and ran to him, hugging him, and almost knocking him over. "Oh, Mr. Killarney, I was so worried. I thought you were dead."

I'm almost as good as new," he said, glancing at Michelle. "A few things are still sketchy."

She looked from him to Michelle. "I know Michelle is taking good care of you; she always has. I told her all you needed was the love of your family and you would be just fine."

Mary finally loosened her iron grip and sat down. "It's just so good to see you. My husband will be happy to know that you're doing much better. We didn't think you would walk again."

"Brad!" Alex came up and led them away from Mary and down to his office.

Some of the things Mary said nagged at him, but for now Alex was claiming all his attention.

"Hey, are you sure you're ready?" He opened a desk drawer and retrieved a set of keys. "We can do this later."

Brad was not going to back off now. "No, I'm ready. Besides, Michelle's here with me. I'll be fine." He kissed her on the cheek.

Alex laughed. "Man, you've really changed. When did the public smooching start?"

Brad chose to ignore his friend's remark. "Let's go look at my office."

The three walked across the hall to Brad's office. Brad felt a hot sensation as soon as they entered the room, and went straight to his computer.

Slowly, his user codes and his passwords all came back to him. He checked to see how many times his codes had been accessed in the last two weeks. "I knew it."

"What?" Michelle and Alex both asked in unison.

Brad smiled. "I wanted to see how many times my codes had been used since I have been out of commission. They haven't been used since the night Frank was killed and I was attacked."

Alex looked doubtful. "I've used your computer, so that can't be right."

"No, I have a special code for the reports. I must have somehow sensed someone was going through my computer when I wasn't here."

"How can you remember that code, but not something you created?"

Brad wished he knew the answer to that one, too. "I just can. It says it was accessed at about eleven p.m. and logged out about two in the morning. Did my office look as if someone had gone through it?"

"I don't know," Alex said. "Cleaning had already cleaned it once, before we decided to seal it off."

"Who decided?" Something didn't feel right. "Why seal off my office when I was already at the hospital when he was killed?"

Alex whispered, "The missing money."

Michelle listened as the two men revisited that night. But something Mary had said earlier had convinced her that the secretary knew something she wasn't telling.

"Hey, guys, I'm going to chat with Mary. Just call me if there's a problem."

She stepped outside Brad's office and noticed Mary was wiping her eyes. "Mary?"

Mary looked up, startled. "Michelle, I didn't hear you. Is everything all right?"

Michelle knew she would have to tread carefully with Mary. "Is there something you would like to tell me?" She sat next to her and took her hand. "I know you love Brad like a son, but if you know something about that night he got attacked, please tell me. It could help answer some questions as to who his attacker was."

Mary nodded, tears streaming down her face. "I don't want them coming after me!"

Michelle took a tissue from the Kleenex box on the desk and handed it to Mary. "If you don't say something, they will get away with a very violent crime. Don't you think Brad has been through enough already?"

She was about to cave. "Yes, I wanted to tell you, or Mr. Cole, or somebody, but Charlie, my husband, thought it best we didn't get involved."

"Did you see him get attacked?"

"Not exactly." Mary made a big production of blowing her nose.

Michelle was trying to be patient. "Then what, exactly?"

"Let's go have some coffee," Mary suggested. The two then walked to the break room.

Michelle knew that whatever Mary was about to tell her was going to change all of their lives.

Calmer now, Mary began her story. "Charlie and I had gone out for dinner. I remembered that Mr. Killarney wanted me to mail some papers out for him, since he had taken the afternoon off. But when Mr. Sims came back to work looking like someone had beat the crap out of him, I left without those letters. So, after dinner, I told Charlie to drive by the office so I could pick them up and mail them. When we pulled up in the parking lot, we saw three men beating Mr. Killarney."

"Three?"

"Yes. One guy had a baseball bat, another guy was kicking him and the third guy had a gun. He was aiming at Mr. Killarney's head when we drove up. Charlie flashed his bright lights on them and they scattered like mice. They drove off, leaving poor Mr. Killarney unconscious and covered in blood."

"Oh, no," Michelle groaned. "Poor Brad. Imagine the pain he must have been in."

Mary nodded. "Yes, it took Charlie almost five minutes to get him in the back seat of our car. He's so much larger than my Charlie."

Michelle managed to smile through her tears. Charlie was about five eight, and Brad easily stood six two. "I'm sorry, Mary, but why didn't you all just take him to the nearest hospital instead of that one?"

"I knew that hospital is on his insurance. I figured if we could just get him there, they would take care of him."

"But why didn't you take him in? The hospital said he stumbled in and passed out."

Mary bowed her head in shame. "Yes, I am sorry about that. I was listening to my idiot husband. We've been married forty years, and that's the first time he's given me really bad advice. He thought the police would have suspected us. Charlie had a bit of a checkered past, way back when, and he didn't want to get into trouble."

Michelle was trying to understand. She really was. "But Mary, who would have suspected you guys of doing something so violent?"

"Well, in our struggle to get Mr. Killarney into the car, we got his blood all over our clothes. Then when he started throwing up blood, we didn't know what to do. We probably shouldn't have moved him and called an ambulance, but he looked lifeless."

"And if you both had blood on your clothes, they would have thought it was a robbery, since he didn't have his wallet."

"Yes, but I didn't know that until the next week. It has been a burden carrying all that around. Mr. Cole said he had amnesia, and I wanted to tell you then."

"But how did you get him upright to walk into the hospital?"

"I guess the Lord was with us. For one brief moment, he came to. He called your name and said he was sorry. We parked as close to the entrance as we could without being noticed and kind of walked him to the door and left. I felt so awful for that."

Michelle finally understood. Though Mary's logic was strange, she could understand. "Could you identify the people?"

"Yes, I could." Her voice trembled slightly.

"But you would rather not. You think they are going to come after you?"

"Yes, I do. I know they are. They already said they would."

"When?"

"There's a note in my mailbox every day warning me not to go to the police."

"Do you have one with you? Could I see it?"

Mary nodded. "There's one in my desk. It's really strange because they're always in the mailbox at home, but there's never a postmark. I think they're putting them in my mailbox, because it's always on top."

They walked back to Mary's desk and she got one of those notes for her. Michelle inspected it closely. It had the same verbiage as the letter she had received. "Oh my gosh. This is just like the one I got. It has to be the same person."

"What should I do?" Mary asked.

"Don't tell anyone else about picking up Brad. I think they're more interested in getting at Brad than at you. They probably think you're too frightened to tell anyone. But as soon as I find out anything I'll let you know." Michelle hugged Mary. "Thank you for telling me. I can't thank you enough for getting Brad to the hospital."

"I'm glad he's okay. I wish I would have gone in with him."

"They probably would have kicked you out, since you're not a blood relative. They barely let me see him, and I'm his wife."

"Does that mean you guys are back together? Although I was happy to be his secretary again, I was sorry to hear that you had separated. I know you are his soul mate, so I know you will work things out. Look how you are now, holding hands, like young lovers."

Michelle only smiled, not wanting to destroy Mary's rosy vision of them getting back together. Michelle wanted that, too, but didn't want Mary disappointed if they did proceed with the divorce.

But Brad had changed. He was more loving, patient, and gentle. There had been no more talk of the promotion, but it was never far from her mind.

"If you need a babysitter so you and Brad can have a night alone, just let me know," Mary offered, winking at Michelle. "I know you've probably been running yourself ragged between Mr. Killarney and the kids. Every woman needs a night off."

"Thank you, Mary. I'll keep that in mind. I'm sure Brad will want to take you up on that really soon. But my parents are due back next week."

Mary laughed. "I can't imagine Mr. Killarney and your mother under the same roof. But she did talk to him a few times before they left for the cruise. Why, that day she came up here, I was ready to call security, but it went well."

Again, Michelle's mother surprised her. She had been to see Brad, probably to suggest he take the art class. Was her mother pushing her and Brad back together from both sides, with her caught in the middle?

CHAPTER 24

Brad rummaged through the file cabinets in his office, hoping to find something that would jump-start his memory. But he needed some insight into Michelle's thinking. He paused in his searching and turned to Alex. "Hey, can I ask you something?"

Alex was leery. "You know, whenever you ask me that, you have usually pissed Shell off or something. That's not the case, is it?"

Brad ignored his best friend's barb. "I was a bad husband, wasn't I?" Alex's silence was his answer. "Okay, I must have been awful. I've asked Michelle, but she won't talk about the past. Neither will Jeremy. You're my last hope."

"You're putting me in an awful spot. I think this is something that you need to find out on your own."

"So I was pretty bad. I wasn't cheating on her, was I?"

"No, nothing like that. You believed in your marriage vows. You just kind of took her for granted. Like you knew she would always be there."

"How did I do that?"

Alex wasn't enjoying this. "Well, you started working a lot more. When I came to see you guys in London after Preston was born, I could see the strain on her face. It was like after Preston, you kind of shut down. Work became your focus and Michelle did what she could, but it takes two in a marriage. She looked unhappy. She loves art and she couldn't go to any of the museums in London because you hated them and you didn't want to watch the kids. And you know she didn't like leaving the kids with babysitters, especially with Preston being so young. When I came to London was the only time she was able to go." Alex stared at him from across the desk with sad eyes, remembering the past.

Alex continued his walk down memory lane. "Yes, she said she'd had enough and didn't want the kids growing up in an environment like that. I convinced her to give you one more chance to straighten up."

"I guess it didn't work, huh?"

"No, not really. In all honesty, lately she's been looking like the old Michelle. You know, happy and enjoying life."

To Brad she did seem more at ease, but he had no real frame of reference. "I keep having flashbacks to things that happened in London. I just know I have to be with her for the rest of my life."

"What does she think of the president of investments promotion?"

"You know, I thought she would have been happy, but she keeps saying it's up to me. I think it's a good move, but I like the way things are right now."

"Well, that's something."

Alex shook his head. "Is she still going to that class?"

"Yeah. Since my attack, I think she's using that as her escape from being with me 24-7. She even went out with some woman one night, for girl's night. I must admit I had been trying to wear down her defenses." Brad didn't mention he had called that night and had waited up for her, angry and agitated.

"She's changed a lot since you guys separated. I don't know if it was her living at home with her parents or what, but she's a lot stronger than she was."

"So what are you trying to tell me?"

"To get her back, you're going to have to up the bar. The things you're doing now, she likes. You know, spending time with her and the kids, cooking meals without being asked. You will definitely have to keep them up to keep her."

Brad looked pained. Having to make up for years of bad habits would be hard, but he could do it. "I was so awful, I don't know where to begin making up for all of the past," he said.

Alex agreed. "But wait until you have your memory back before you start falling at her feet. You can't make up for the past; you can only change the future."

Alex's statement puzzled Brad. But his friend didn't elaborate. Was the separation just as much her fault as his? Still wondering, he returned to his search. "Hey, is Frank's office open?"

"No, but I have the key. I still can't believe that no one in his family wants to claim any of his things. I'll have to box them up soon and throw them away."

Brad looked up from the papers he had been sorting. "You mean all his papers are still here? Pictures and everything? What about his car?" Brad had a brainstorm.

"His car is probably back at the dealership since he had just gotten it a few months back. It was a lease. You know what's a mystery? As president of investments, Frank had to be pulling down some good change, but he lived in a rented house, had a leased car and didn't own anything. Where was his money going?"

Brad was just as baffled as Alex. "I don't know. He just remarried last year. Maybe his young socialite wife was spending all his money or he was paying child support."

Alex shook his head. "No, he prided himself on telling us how he gives her an allowance. He claimed the first wife took him to the cleaners in the divorce and he wasn't going to let that happen again. "

Brad didn't know what to think. "Man, this is the weirdest thing. Can we check out his office? He was my boss, so I had to have given him some notes and such."

Despite his misgivings about going into the dead man's office, Alex agreed and got the keys from his desk.

Brad stepped into Frank's office and felt an intense feeling of betrayal. He went directly to the computer and turned it on. Something told him to lift the keyboard. When he did, he discovered a scrap of paper. It looked like a card sample.

Brad set the keyboard down and glanced inside the desk drawer. "God, he was such a pig."

Alex laughed. "Tell me about it. Between you and me, he won't really be missed."

Brad shivered slightly. The room felt strangely cold. "That's pretty rough. Was there anyone at his funeral?"

"Well, that's hard to say, since it hasn't happened yet."

Brad was confused. "I'm not following you. Are you saying his body is still at the funeral home?"

"No, I'm saying his body is still at the county morgue. No one claimed it. The county is burying it tomorrow."

Brad slumped in the chair. "You have got to be kidding. I thought his next of kin had to claim his body as soon as the coroner released it."

"Not in the state of Texas. You aren't legally required to claim the body. Claire, who is Frank's next of kin, refuses to do so."

"That's why this room is so cold. His soul is restless."

"You've been listening to Michelle again."

"Yeah, I think she might have mentioned something about the stars and karma about twenty times in the last two weeks."

"And you're cool with it now? You used to hate it."

Brad was very cool with it now. He realized it was part of her. He hoped to hear about the stars, moons, and destiny every day until he could not take another breath. "I do seem to remember her spouting that spirituality stuff early in our marriage."

Alex opened Frank's file cabinet and started searching it. "Yeah, you used to called it 'stars and crap.' I think you've changed, Brad. Since most of your memory has returned, you can't blame it on your amnesia. I actually think you might be ready to resume your marriage."

Brad felt as if he had passed some kind of test. "Yeah, I think so, too. Now if I could just convince Michelle of it."

Alex's blue eyes sparkled with challenge. Brad knew that meant that he was having a brainstorm. Alex snapped his fingers, heading for the computer. "I know what would endear you to Michelle."

"What?" Brad feared the worst.

Alex motioned for Brad to get out of the chair so he could operate the computer. After Alex plopped down in the leather chair, his fingers were flying over the keyboard. "Ma and Pa Kettle are coming back Monday, right?" he asked, referring to Michelle's parents.

"Yes." Brad was dreading when the spirited Emily Shaw returned and found him living under her roof.

"Why don't you plan the party for Michelle? It would show how much you're willing to do to make her life easier. And if you and Emily could actually get along, that would be icing on the cake. I still can't believe she came up here and there was no bloodshed."

"Hey, I think I was more shocked than anyone. Especially with the way she was treating me every time I went to the house to pick up the kids. I thought she came up here to kill me."

The men laughed. Alex continued his brainstorming. "You could have a surprise party for them at a hotel."

Brad shook his head. "No, Shell wants something intimate and at home."

Alex stopped his work, just long enough to smirk at Brad. "If I didn't know better, I'd say you were whipped."

"I am." Brad walked around the office, trying not to face Alex. He knew he was wearing a stupid expression on his face and didn't want Alex making fun of him.

He noticed the one and only picture in the office. He picked it up and studied it. It was Frank and his boss. But something about Frank began to gnaw at him. He studied the picture and closed his eyes against the pain.

It was like a flash. A bright flash. Frank's sinister smile as he met Michelle for the first time. Michelle's uneasiness about him. Then there it was. Michelle on top of Frank on the sofa. It all came crashing back. He walked into his house and saw his wife on top of his boss. Her hands were out of view, but now he could see that Frank had a grasp of them. She couldn't get away.

He dropped the picture on the floor, attracting Alex's attention.

"Brad, what is it?"

"I know why. It was my fault." He sat on the floor holding his head in his hands. "It's all my fault. She tried to tell me, but I wouldn't listen. I didn't want anything interfering with my project. Michelle told me how uneasy Frank made her feel, but I didn't listen. I deserved to be alone." He sobbed, not caring if Alex saw him or not.

Alex comforted him as best he could. He gently patted Brad's shoulder, almost giving him a manly hug. "Brad, you were different then. I'm sure once you tell Shell you remember and you talk about it, it will all work out."

He shook his head. "No, I don't want her to know that I know. I've got to make her love me unconditionally, so she'll forgive me."

"Brad, one thing I know about this marriage thing is that you can't make her love you. You'll just have to bust your chops showing her how much you love her." He helped Brad to a chair. "Tell me what exactly do you remember?"

"I remember her telling me how Frank hanging around was annoying her. My replacement had arrived from Scotland, and Frank arrived to oversee the transition. But he didn't spend much time at the office. When he was there, he was on the phone with his wife most of the time." Brad thought back to one of those conversations he had overheard, due mostly to Frank pressing the intercom button.

"What did you hear?"

"It didn't make sense then, but now it does. Especially with all the information we're uncovering about the real Frank Sims. She was complaining about their financial status. She sounded like a shrew, and all Frank said was that he was taking care of it. I looked up to that guy."

"I tried to tell you something was fishy about him. Not that you didn't deserve that promotion, but I thought it was strange Frank recommended you without actually working with you."

Brad thought it was strange, too, but didn't want to dwell on it at the time. Now, however, he wished he had taken Michelle's concerns more seriously. A horrible feeling settled over Brad. "You think she really wants the divorce?"

Alex shook his head. "Man, I don't understand you. She took you in when you didn't have a memory."

"She had to do that."

"Maybe. But she didn't have to make love with you. She didn't have to investigate those hours you were missing. She didn't have to do any of the things she's doing for you. I know she loves you."

Brad realized his best friend was right. Maybe she loved him. Was it enough to forget the past and look toward the future?

"What are you guys doing in here?" Michelle stood in the doorway. "Brad, are you all right?" She walked to him, putting her hands on either side of his face, looking directly into his eyes.

"Yeah." He took a deep breath. Concern for him written all over her face. "I'm fine. I guess this was just a little much today." He kissed her gently on the lips, slowing drawing her closer to his body in a hug.

"Whoa, fella." She laughed as she backed away. "Alex is going to think we're some horny teenagers."

Brad didn't really care what Alex thought at the moment, pulled her back to him and kissed her again. "Alex doesn't mind, do you?"

Alex smiled at them. "No, I love the picture I'm looking at right now."

Michelle nodded, grabbing Brad's hand. "We'd better get going. Why don't you come over for dinner? We can compare notes."

"Sure, Shell. See you about seven."

Brad laughed, letting Michelle lead him out of the office. As they rode the elevator in silence, Brad had time to ponder the information he discovered earlier. She leaned against him, igniting a fire in him.

"Brad, when we get home, you should take a nap," Michelle suggested. "Hopefully the kids are asleep and the house might actually be quiet."

His arms inched around her, bringing her closer to him. "I'll only take a nap, if you do. Provided the kids are asleep."

"I have to get dinner started."

"I'll help you. So you still have time for a nap."

"Why Brad, I think I'm really liking the new you." She turned in his arms and kissed him, just as the elevator doors opened, putting a dash of hope in Brad's heart.

After some heavy debating, Michelle gave in and agreed to take a nap with him. Slowly, he was wearing her defenses down.

He thought she would have problems sleeping next to him, but she was asleep instantly. Even with all their clothes on, he felt closer to her each time they were together.

A knock on the door interrupted his musing. He eased out of bed and answered it. Jeremy stood there smiling.

"I was just wondering if you guys were coming up for air. But it looks like you're just sleeping."

Brad smiled. If Jeremy only knew what he felt just by holding her in his arms was almost better than sex, he would probably laugh in Brad's face for being mushy. "Yeah, just taking a nap before dinner."

Jeremy nodded. "Well, I was going to run to the library. The kids are still asleep. I just wanted to let you guys know."

Brad nodded, walking down the hall with Jeremy. "It's okay. She's pretty tired. I don't think she's fully recovered from the other day." He opened the door to Peri's room and noticed she was still asleep.

After saying goodbye to Jeremy, he checked on Preston. Seeing that his son was still asleep, Brad closed the door, and headed to the kitchen.

Michelle woke up alone. The spot where Brad should have been was cold and the evening sun lit the room. She sat up and collected her thoughts. Glancing at her bedside clock, she noticed it was six-thirty. Dinner! Why didn't Brad wake her? Alex would be there in thirty minutes. She rushed out of the room, checking for the kids in the process. They weren't in their rooms.

She marched into the kitchen and stopped cold. Brad was cooking dinner. The kids were helping him. Helping Brad make dinner, this was very surreal. He hated having the kids underfoot when he was working.

Peri was folding the table napkins and Preston was watching his sister. "Hi, Mummy. Daddy is making dinner."

"I see, honey. I'm very impressed."

Brad looked away from his cooking chores and smiled at her. "I wanted to surprise you. But everything is not quite ready. The chicken has about twenty more minutes."

Michelle sat in a chair next to Peri. "That's fine. Don't forget Alex is coming for dinner."

"I know," he said. He turned back to the stove. "I wasn't sure if you wanted a salad or not. Personally, I don't think you need to eat that rabbit food, but it's your decision."

When was the last time he said that? Nothing was ever left up to her. "I don't want salad tonight." She walked over to Brad. She hugged him from behind. "Thanks for asking."

She felt him tremble. "Hey, you'd better watch yourself." He turned and kissed her.

"I'll set the table and let you finish your masterpiece." Michelle also needed to get out of the there before they erupted in the hottest passion session ever. She herded the children into the dining room.

The doorbell rang. "Probably Uncle Alex," she told the children. She answered the door and ushered Alex inside.

"You look great, Al. Brad is making dinner."

"Brad is making dinner? Brad Killarney? I am shocked, to say the least. You're making a husband out of him, aren't you?" He smiled at her.

"No, I'm not. That's all his doing. I didn't tell him to cook, he did it all by himself," Michelle said proudly.

Alex laughed. "Okay, I'm not going there with you. I understand what it is to be truly in love. I hear it's a wonderful experience, according to Mary."

Michelle grabbed his hand, leading him into the dining room. "Hey kids, it's Uncle Alex."

Alex sat at the table and the kids squealed in delight. Running to him and not giving him a minute to breathe, Peri jumped in his lap, and began telling him about everything she'd done since she'd seen him last.

Michelle smiled as Brad brought in the food. She offered, but he refused her help. She sat in her chair like a queen and waited to be served.

CHAPTER 25

After dinner, Michelle herded the kids into the den to watch a little TV before bedtime. The adults went to the living room to discuss what they had discovered at Herrington. She and Brad sat side by side on the couch. Alex sat across from them on the loveseat.

"I had an interesting talk with Mary." She announced as she finished her glass of tea. "Do you remember anything about how you got to the hospital?"

Brad shrugged. "The clearest memory is of being in the back of a car and hearing mumbled voices."

"Mary and her husband took you to the hospital. She forgot to mail some letters for you and she was returning to get them when they interrupted your attackers."

Alex gasped. "Well, it makes a little more sense."

"What?" Michelle couldn't help asking.

Alex cut his eyes at Brad. "The next morning she was a nervous wreck. She also knew that Brad was in the hospital and Frank was killed the night before. I mean, yeah, they found his body that morning, but they had moved it out of the building by the time she had gotten there."

"Okay, that's weird." Michelle drained the last of her tea. "How could she know Frank was dead when he was killed after Brad was attacked? I think she saw more than she wants to admit."

Alex nodded. "She's already a nervous wreck. I walked up behind her one day last week and she almost jumped out of her skin."

"She's been getting threats in the mail. But she doesn't want to get involved," Michelle added.

Brad shook his head. "Poor Mary. She never could take much before she freaked out."

Michelle didn't say anything. She tried to still her movements, so Brad couldn't tell he'd had another breakthrough. "I'll get the kids ready for bed." She jumped up from the table and headed for the den.

Brad watched her leave and shook his head. "What's with her?"

Alex threw his napkin at him. "You had a recollection, you idiot. She thinks you'll freak out, so she's pretending that you didn't." He whispered. "If you're pretending that you're not all the way well, you'd better cool it on the recollections."

"But I wasn't faking. It just came to me. Mary is always freaking out over something or other. But I do believe that someone is threatening her, and I think that someone is in the company."

"Who?"

Brad shook his head. "I wish I knew. Then I'd know who sent Michelle that letter."

Alex's look of confusion was priceless. Alex was always on top of everything. Brad knew he had to clarify.

"Someone sent Shell a letter, and it was on Herrington executive stationary. I didn't notice it until Dryson held it up to the light. But that letterhead is out in the open and anyone can get it."

"Man, this is just getting crazy. Do you remember anything about that report?"

"No, but I'm going to study it tomorrow and hopefully something will get through my brain and I can recognize the code." Brad heard the bath upstairs. Michelle was giving the kids a bath.

"Hey, why don't you come by tomorrow? She's getting the kids ready for bed and I feel I should be helping. I know she wants to go to the gym, I heard her asking Jerry to keep an eye on us. Should be about eleven."

Alex grinned. "Look at you. Are you still sleeping apart?"

Brad smiled. "That's the next thing on my agenda. One thing at a time. Now it's bath time."

Alex nodded and walked to the front door. "Man, the guys aren't going to believe this. Have you decided about the promo?"

"Not yet. But I have to make a decision soon. I know everyone's waiting for my answer." Brad opened the door for his friend.

"See you tomorrow. Maybe we could have lunch or something?"

"Maybe." He patted Alex on the back as he left the house. As soon he heard Alex's BMW drive off, Brad ran up the stairs.

He opened the bathroom door, laughing. Preston was playing in the water and Michelle was soaked. He knew Peri was probably in her room, waiting her turn. Michelle didn't believe in letting them bathe together. Besides the fact that Preston loved to splash in the water.

"Why don't you let me take over here?"

"Oh, no Brad. You've had such a busy day. You need your rest." She dried her face, just as Preston started another splashing session.

"You need your rest, too." He walked further inside the bathroom. "Why don't you let me take over with the Olympic swimmer and you can take care of Peri."

She nodded, drying off the best she could. "I can't believe such a little boy would like so much water."

Brad nodded, watching her. He felt like he was at a peep show. Her shirt was soaked, and the outline of her lacy bra was clear. She had to know what she was doing to him, because she asked innocently, "Could you dry my back?"

"You know that's not fair, unless you want company tonight." He took the towel from her hand and turned her around slowly stroking her back more than actually drying the moisture.

"I think I hear Peri calling me." She darted out of the bathroom before anything else happened.

Brad laughed as he endured Preston's waterfall. Yeah, his plan was working nicely. Soon he would confess his memory had returned and they would be a family again. This time nothing would break them up.

After he finally got his son out of the bathtub and ready for bed, Brad felt like he had missed his own surprise party. How could he have let Michelle alone carry on all duties that should be shared?

Bath time with Preston was an event he didn't want to miss again. Although he was soaked, it was worth every drop of water he endured.

Michelle knocked on Preston's door. "Brad, are you going to read to him?" She walked into the room. It was her turn to laugh at his soaked shirt.

He looked around the room, and sure enough there was a small bookcase with at least thirty books. "Sure, I'll read to him. What's his favorite?"

"Just about any of them. I can read to him, I don't mind."

He shook his head. "No, I need to get to know my son. You've been having all the fun, I want to have some, too."

"Okay. Remember, you asked for it." She walked to the bed and kissed her son goodnight. "I'll leave you men to it." She laughed, closing the door.

After Brad read the same story five times, he understood why she was laughing now. Finally, Preston was asleep.

It was a sense of accomplishment he hadn't felt in quite some time. More exhilarated than when he landed a multi-million dollar contract, he put his son to sleep. Even when they spent the weekends with him, Brad would let the TV do his part. He let them run wild, he knew that, but always knew that Michelle would get them back on track.

It felt good knowing that he could be a part of the family. He wanted that more than life itself.

He walked past Michelle's room and heard her talking on the phone. If he strained he could hear the conversation. But after Michelle screamed in laughter, he knew it was his sister. They were as thick as thieves. He shook his head and headed for his room.

"Mel, when are you coming home?" Michelle propped herself against her stack of pillows.

"I'm wrapping up a few loose ends. I should be there in about a week, give or take a day or two. There's a reason for my call."

"What is it?"

"Would you believe the death of Brad's boss has made the news over here?"

"That's weird," Michelle said. "Maybe it's because he was in London for a while?"

"Well, not exactly."

"Then what, exactly?" Michelle asked.

"At a meeting yesterday, Frank Sims' name came up, but not in a good way. So you know curious I can get. I enlisted the help of a friend."

"I just bet. Was he Scottish or Irish?" Michelle asked, knowing her sister-in-law's preference for European men.

"A Scot this time. Ian is a great computer hacker. Over drinks we were talking about computer searches, and he agreed to retrieve the information for me."

"Yeah, and I bet you were batting your eyelashes at him while you were plying him with drinks. Well, what did you come up with?"

Mel laughed. "I'll be so glad to leave the United Kingdom. I can't wait to get home. I think I'm going to curtail my plane hopping; this merger has zapped me."

"You always loved the challenge."

"I still do. It's this hopping from England to Scotland to Australia, all in the course of a few days, that's starting to get to me. Yeah, I have enough frequent flyer miles that I could go around the world several times, but I'm tired now."

Michelle knew what it was. "It's because you getting ready to turn fifty soon isn't it?"

"No, it's because I was hit on by almost every single man in the UK. It was nice at first, but it got old. Once they discovered I was single with no kids, oh, my gosh."

Michelle laughed. "You know you love it."

"Yeah. I guess you're right. I'm feeling the big five-oh approaching. But to talk about Mr. Sims. Girl, why did Herrington hire him? His credentials are horrible. He had no business being Brad's boss."

"What are you talking about?"

"Well, he was asked to leave his former job. I know a guy at Phillips, Castle, DiBacca and Carlson Investments, and he told me it was some stuff about some woman got pregnant. They were tired of all the scandals surrounding him. Plus, he couldn't keep any clients. In his divorce, the wife got everything. He didn't have any investments of his own. How on earth could he convince someone to invest their money, when he didn't invest any of his own. Now I know he should have been pulling down some pretty good money, yet he didn't own anything, not even the furniture in his rented house."

Michelle knew he didn't spend any money on clothes. Frank Sims bought all his suits off the rack, preferably at a secondhand store. She knew that from the time he spent with her in London. "Where was his money going?"

"I really couldn't tell. His checks weren't direct deposit. He did have three different checking accounts, but none of them had over a few thousand in it."

"Well, I think if we could find those missing securities we could answer all the other questions about this mess. You know his body is still at the morgue?"

Mel muttered something under her breath. "Shell, don't you start feeling sorry for him. He caused you nothing but pain. Remember that."

"I know, but everyone deserves a funeral." She took a deep breath, hoping when her time came it wouldn't end up like that. "Brad is doing much better."

"I'll bet. I bet he wasn't complaining the other day." Mel laughed. "I know he was happy."

"I still can't believe I acted like that. You know as much as we did it, you'd think that would be the furthest thing from my mind, but it's not. He's been flirting with me."

"My brother. The king of anal? Brad's never flirted a day in his life."

"Yes. He's been all flirty and touchy-feely lately, and in public, too."

Mel's voice erupted in laughter. "I can't believe it. I've been telling him for five years to start showing some kind of affection and now he's finally doing it."

"The only thing is that he's not himself." Michelle reminded her sister-in-law. "What happens when all this is over and he returns to his usual brick-wall self? I'm afraid I might not love that Brad now."

Mel sighed. "I know, it's like you've been eating hamburger all your life, then someone gives you steak, it's hard for you to go back to hamburger."

"I just don't know what to do, but I know it's already too late. I love the new and improved Brad. You know he gave Preston his bath tonight and read to him."

Mel laughed. "You know when you guys separated, I told him he was an idiot. Not just because we're friends, but because he was just trying to hide his own shortcomings. He was trying to hide his feelings. I think this amnesia thing was good for both of you. You see how life should be with him, and now you can tell him exactly what you want."

Michelle realized her globe-trotting sister-in-law was right. "Thanks, Mel. I can always count on you and Mom to set me straight." She glanced at her clock. "Hey, I just realized that it was about three in the morning there. What are you still doing up?"

"Well, Ian, that's the computer hacker, just left my room. After fending off his very Scottish accent and advances, I was too wired to sleep."

"Did you want to talk to Brad?"

"No, I wanted girl talk. Since he hasn't seen me since I left, I thought he might not remember me. Anyway, I'll see him in a few days."

Michelle knew that Mel and Brad were extremely close, and for her not to talk to him was killing her. "I understand, Mel, and I'll give him your love. Good night."

"Night, Shell." She ended the call.

Michelle placed the cordless phone on the table, just as Brad knocked on her door. No, she reminded herself. *I'm not sleeping with him again.* "Come in."

He walked inside her room. "I just wanted to say good night. I'm going to take a shower."

"Looks like Preston already gave you one. I don't know where he gets the thing about water from."

He walked dangerously close to her bed. "I don't know. But I'm really drained, so I'll probably be out like a light."

Why was he walking closer to the bed? She immediately jumped up to meet him. "Me, too." She faked a yawn. "I'm exhausted."

Brad smiled at her, leaning to kiss her. "I know what you're doing," he said against her lips. "I'll give you a reprieve for tonight." He kissed her softly on her lips and left the room.

Michelle sighed and prepared for bed. Her body was humming with sexual awareness. She was waiting for him to make his move, but he didn't. He didn't press for anything other than a gentle kiss.

She sat on the bed, waiting for Brad to knock on the door again. But after an hour she realized that he really went to bed. Wanting to get her mind off of sex, she reached for the note pad and compiled her notes.

Now that the mystery of how he arrived at the hospital was solved, Michelle wanted to know who attacked him. Who would have a reason to hurt him? What is on that blasted report? Maybe if she could find out what was on the previous report, she would know what to look for.

But even thinking logically about the case, part of her brain was still thinking about going to Brad's room. She threw back the covers, grabbing her robe. In five years of marriage, sex wasn't ever like it had been the last two weeks. If she had to make a choice about which sex had been better, she would have to choose the sex she was having now.

But she didn't go to Brad's room. It took every fiber in her being not to barge in and demand sex. She didn't, thank goodness. She decided to search his Range Rover one last time. If she could just channel some of that frustration into doing some good, maybe she could solve the puzzle.

As she opened the door leading to the garage, she got the surprise of her life. One, the garage door was up, and two, someone was going through Brad's truck, and it wasn't Brad. She tried to scream, but the sound was rooted in her throat. How did he get in the garage? She turned to run but knocked over the trashcan by the door, startling the intruder.

He looked up and dropped the tire iron he held in his hand. "Okay, Mrs. Killarney, I don't want to hurt you. I just want to get out of here." He took a step toward her. "Just let me get what I need and you'll get to live another day."

She was rooted in that spot. She didn't want him going inside the house and hurting the children. "What do you want?"

"The Palm Pilot."

But it was in the truck. "I don't have it. I mean, it's in the truck. Or it was."

"I think you have it. I'd hate for something to happen to your children like what happened to your husband."

"So would I," a masculine voice answered.

Michelle gasped as she noticed Dryson behind the intruder. He quickly handcuffed him, and his partner escorted him to the patrol car.

"How on earth?" Michelle asked, when she got her voice back.

Dryson re-holstered his gun. "Well, with all the things happening at this house and with you guys, I convinced my superiors that someone should watch the house around the clock. We saw him breaking in to the garage. I wanted to see what he was going to do."

"He was asking about Brad's Palm Pilot. But he didn't find it. I knew we left it in the truck."

Dryson nodded. "You think it's in the house?"

Michelle shook her head. "I don't think so, unless Brad took it. I'll ask him in the morning. How did he get in the garage?"

"Well, there's a new item in the criminal world. It can access a locked garage, unless it's attached to an alarm system. I suggest you get an alarm on it as soon as possible."

"If that crook knows about the Palm Pilot, do you think others will try to break in as well?"

Dryson studied her carefully, before he answered. "I'm afraid so. Apparently there's something on there that will incriminate someone and they are willing to kill to get it. We will place a police car out front."

"No. I don't want the kids thinking something is wrong. Unless it's an unmarked car, otherwise it would hurt the case having an official police car outside. The criminals won't try again. I want this mess cleared up. I'm tired of trying to figure out what happened to Brad and Frank. Any luck on those photos?"

"Yes, I should have them by Sunday. I'll meet you in the park, so Brad won't think I'm trying to steal you away."

"He does not."

"Michelle, that man looks at me like he could kill me. Especially that day, you were in bed, I thought he was going to kill me with his bare hands. He's a pretty big guy."

Michelle knew Brad wouldn't hurt a fly. He wouldn't mind another man in the house. He certainly didn't when Frank burst into their lives. "He won't mind. I know Brad. Thanks for coming to my rescue, again. Why don't you come by for breakfast?"

"You know I can't resist home-cooking. I'll see you in the morning." He left the garage, heading for the unmarked police car.

Michelle closed the garage door, checking to make sure it was secure. Making a mental note to call the alarm people first thing in the morning, she went upstairs.

CHAPTER 26

Brad woke early Friday morning. As he faced himself in the bathroom mirror, he smiled. His plan was taking shape, if he could only figure out what happened to him the night he was attacked, and everything would be just fine. He would soon be able to confess that most of his memory had returned, Michelle would take him back and they would once be a family again.

The night before, he knew that she expected him to sleep with her and he had exerted willpower he hadn't known he was capable of, but he slept in his room alone. That should have impressed Michelle. It impressed him.

He dressed in a jeans and T-shirt and headed downstairs. As he neared the kitchen he heard voices. Two male voices. One was Jeremy's, but the other sounded familiar.

He stalked into the kitchen and his blood immediately boiled over. Dryson, the police officer, was sitting at the table, like he had been doing that for years. He was still dressed in his uniform. Preston was sitting in his lap, playing with his badge.

Brad felt like someone had taken his favorite toy away and was about voice his opinion when Michelle caught him by the arm and dragged him out the kitchen and into the hall way.

"Don't you even think about making a scene, Brad Killarney," she warned. "I invited Dryson, so you be nice. He's been very helpful in letting me have access to information I shouldn't have."

The old Michelle would never have done this. She would have just hoped for the best. He liked the new, take-charge Michelle. "What do I get for not kicking his ass, for trying to take you away?"

"Nobody is taking me anywhere. Including you. Just remember that. Dryson is a friend of the family and has saved me more times than I want to count. He's divorced and doesn't get home-cooked meals often, so you just better be nice." She softened her words with a tender kiss. "Just a little incentive." She walked back into the kitchen.

With a lick of his lips, he followed her in the room and took a seat at the table. "Good morning, Dryson. What brings you by this early in the morning?"

Michelle breathed audibly. She was not pleased with this line of questioning. "What Brad means, Dryson, is that he's glad to see you."

Brad watched Michelle finish fixing breakfast. She was smiling. Soon she placed a plate in front of each of the children and then placed a platter in front of the adults. "Hope you guys are hungry. I made plenty."

Brad wanted to comment, but the pancakes and bacon looked too good, and he was starving.

Michelle watched with pleasure as the men ate with gusto. "This just does my heart good that you guys are hungry, but do you think you could save me some?"

Brad laughed. "Baby, it's sooo good."

Jeremy gasped. "Brad, I don't think I've ever heard you call her anything but Shell. Wow, you've grown."

Michelle sighed as she waved good-bye to Dryson. Brad was still on his best behavior, volunteering to take the children upstairs to help them dress for the day. She started collecting the dirty dishes and put them in the dishwasher.

Brad walked up behind her, hugging her. "What are you doing today?"

She shuddered as his body rubbed against hers. Something as mundane as answering him became a game of foreplay. She exhaled as he nibbled her neck in rhythm of his hips. "I'm taking the kids with me to the park, then we're going to the mall and grocery shopping. Did you want to go with us?"

"No, Alex is coming by at later, so we can have lunch. I was hoping you could join us."

"I wish I could, too, but I've got a million things to do, if I want to have a surprise party for Mom and Dad on Monday night."

He nodded, turning her around to face him. "I'll miss you today." He kissed her. "Maybe we can make up for it tonight?" He kissed her again, this time letting his tongue work its magic.

Michelle felt her knees buckle with passion as his kiss deepened. She was ready to take his hand and run upstairs but the kids ran into the room.

"Mummy, are we ready to go?" Peri was dragging the bag Michelle usually took to the park with them. In that bag were a book, snacks, drinks, antibacterial soap and towelettes.

Brad laughed as he looked through the bag. "Man, you're ready for anything, aren't you?"

She grabbed the bag, checking to make sure everything was in its proper place. "Yes, I try to be. Don't forget if you need me to call my cell."

"I think it's ingrained in my brain. Call you if there's a problem." Brad kissed her.

Michelle nodded, not wanting to start a debate about his memory loss. "Okay. Come on, guys, kiss Daddy and we'll be on our way."

And then they were gone.

Brad sat in the den, studying the gibberish on the paper Alex gave him days earlier. Nothing was making sense. He hadn't been able to break his own code. If only he could figure out one of the symbols, the rest would fall into place.

The doorbell disturbed his thought process. He knew Jeremy would answer it. He tried to keep his concentration on the paper.

"Brad, your boss is back." Jeremy announced standing in the doorway. "He's in the living room. Shell doesn't like strangers all over the house." Jeremy reminded him, explaining why he didn't show him to the den.

Brad nodded, rising to meet the man. He didn't have an answer for him yet. He walked to the living room. Conrad Jameson sat on the couch talking on his cellphone. Brad strained to hear the conversation.

"I told you I will take care of it. Just keep your mouth shut. What about the woman?"

Brad was concentrating so hard on listening; he didn't see Preston's toy truck in his way. But Jameson heard him.

"I'll call you back." He snapped his phone shut, stood and faced Brad. "Brad, I didn't hear you."

Brad motioned for him to sit down. "You wanted to talk to me?" He sat down and faced him.

"Yes, I did. I wondered if you had come to a decision yet. The board of directors is anxiously awaiting your answer. Have you discussed this with your wife yet?"

"It's been tabled for the moment. But I will have an answer for you soon."

"Are we waiting for your wife to give her approval? I didn't know she would have this big an influence on it. How does she like being back in the States?"

"Fine. This is her hometown."

Jameson nodded. "Do you know when you will be released from the doctor?"

"No, I have an appointment next week. So that would be the earliest I could give you an answer. Have you always been here?"

"No, I was in Glasgow, Scotland, until about a month ago. There was a reorganization in our department and my job landed me here. How do you stand this heat?"

Brad chuckled. "Texas heat takes some getting used to. When I transferred down from Boston, it was this time of year and I thought I was going to die of a heat stroke."

"Well, I hope I'm not here long enough to get used to it. As soon as this mess is cleared up, I'll be on my way to Seattle."

Brad nodded. The Seattle division was new, and rumor was the company was going to split into four divisions, with each one acting independently of the others. So how did Jameson figure into all that?

Jameson glanced at his gold Rolex and rose. "Well, I'll be going. Give me a call when you know more about when you're coming back. And if you want the job." He handed Brad another business card.

"I'll let you know something as soon as I do." Brad extended his hand, taking the card.

"Thank you, Brad." He left the house. Brad studied the card. The plaid symbol in the left hand corner of the card was unmistakable. Where had he seen it?

As soon as he was out of sight, Alex drove up. Brad laughed as Alex approached him. "You just missed Jameson by thirty seconds," he said, waving Alex inside the house.

"Jameson?" Alex headed for the couch. He looked around the house as if he thought the kids would come running around a corner and attack him.

"The president of operations. The kids are gone with Shell."

"Oh. No one has seen that guy in the last few weeks. Not that you're not important or anything, but why is he coming to see you?"

"I told you he offered me Frank's job."

Alex nodded. "Oh. I didn't know he was the one offering it to you. I thought he would just have a director do it, or just call you."

"How did he know I was staying at Michelle's parents? It's not like this address is any of my legal documents at work. My mail from the company is still coming to the apartment. Jeremy checks it for me."

"Maybe he asked Mary?"

"He didn't mention how he got the address, or even how he knew the fact that I'm living here at my in-laws."

Alex scratched his head. "You think he had something to do with Frank's death?"

"I don't know. But he knew all about Michelle and that we just returned to the States."

"Maybe there's a leak somewhere. But why would anyone be interested in you and Shell?"

"I don't know. You know the night I was attacked he called my apartment four times."

"Did you talk to him?"

"No, I had already left. But apparently he doesn't think I know about them. I wish I could hatch a plan that would catch him in the act."

"In the act of what?" Alex laughed. "You're starting to sound a lot like me."

"Well, I was just thinking, that if he was responsible for either Frank's death or my attack, maybe he knows about the money."

"And you would get this information how?"

"I have no idea."

They headed to lunch; Brad enjoyed a day out. This was his first outing without either Michelle or the kids in tow. As much as it was relaxing to chat with Alex and drink a beer, Brad missed his family. He missed the children asking a million questions and Michelle doting on all of them.

"Okay, Brad what's wrong?" Alex asked as he studied the menu with intensity.

He set his menu aside. "You're going to think I'm nuts."

"I would never."

Brad sighed. "I'm missing my family. I haven't seen them all day."

Alex shook his head. "Well my friend, you have done it. You have crossed over. You have become new Brad."

"What are you talking about?"

Alex closed his menu and focused on his friend. "You're not the person you were before the accident. The Brad I knew could stay away from his family for longer than this and never miss anyone. I think you talked about your job more than about your family. Now it's like your job comes in second to your family."

Brad mulled over Alex's remark. "I can't understand how me having amnesia could have changed me so much in such a short amount of time."

"Maybe those changes were always in you, but you chose to keep them hidden. When you had lost your memory, your true feelings came out for your wife and your kids. Now you've just got to incorporate that with your new life."

Brad could do that. He knew he could. All he had to do was prove it to Michelle.

CHAPTER 27

Michelle breathed a sigh of relief as she left the Party Shop. Her plan was going nicely. She could decorate the house Monday while the kids were napping and before her parents returned that evening. Grinning, she imagined her mother's surprised face.

She strapped the kids into their car seats and, her purchases secured in the back of the Navigator, headed for home. Grocery shopping would have to wait until tomorrow, she mused. It was almost seven, and they had been gone all day. Brad was probably getting antsy.

As she drove, one part of Michelle's brain was on autopilot, the other on Brad. Total recall was close, but would she like the Brad that finally emerged? Could she love him again? The new Brad was loving, caring, and more of what a husband should be.

But was she being fair to Brad? He'd been through so much in the last two weeks. Thank goodness, his injuries weren't worse. His ribs appeared to be almost healed, and his headaches had either disappeared or he had stopped talking about them.

"Mummy, we're home. Can we get out?" Peri asked from the back seat.

She parked in the driveway and freed the kids, who ran into the house ahead of her. She gathered the bags and headed inside. Glancing around the kitchen, she thought she was in the wrong house. Somebody had been cooking, and the aroma smelled like heaven.

She walked into the living room and almost dropped the bags. The table was set. Everything was already prepared for them. Who cooked? "Jeremy?" She called out, but Brad greeted her from the hallway.

"He had to go out for a minute," he said, walking towards her. "I thought I would fix dinner. You don't mind, do you?"

Michelle shook her head, too confused to speak. "How was lunch?"

He took the bags from her hands and kissed her. "Great. I really missed talking to Alex." He stepped back from her. "You know you look really beat. Would you like to take a nap before dinner? The chicken probably has about thirty minutes before it's done."

She shook her head. "That's not enough time for a decent nap. I imagine the kids will turn in early, since we were shopping so much."

Brad glanced around the room. It was too quiet for two small children to be in the house. He walked to the den where they usually watched TV, and laughed. Peri was lying on the couch, her eyes almost closed, with the large remote in her hand. Preston was on the floor, sprawled out and sleeping. Shaking his head, Brad walked back into the living room. "I hate to tell you this, but the kids are already knocked out."

Michelle yawned. "They can't be. It's only seven. They haven't had dinner." She knew they were tired, but not this tired. "Well, they did have a lot to eat at the mall."

Brad shrugged. "Why don't we put them to bed, and when they wake up, we can feed them?"

She didn't want to be alone with Brad, especially after she'd spent most of the afternoon thinking about him. But now since her children had betrayed her, she didn't have a choice. "All right."

After they put the kids to bed, they came back down and Michelle sat at the dining room table while Brad went to the kitchen.

"I'll bring in dinner," Brad said, returning with the chicken and mixed green salad.

"Brad, you didn't have to. I could have called and ordered something for us. But it smells great."

Finally, some thanks. He wanted to make up for all the bad things he had done in his previous life. He wanted to beg her forgiveness, but couldn't. That would give away his game and he wasn't ready for that.

He sat down. "Good. Dig in."

They ate the low-fat dinner in silence, until Brad reflected on the day. "What did you do today?"

Michelle smiled with pride. "I got stuff for Mom and Dad's surprise party. You know they return Monday. It's going to be a night of explanations."

"What is Emily going to say about me being here? I recall we didn't get on all that well."

"Actually, Mom does like you. It's just that recently you're not her favorite person."

"Is there a reason?"

"Yes, there is." She speared a baked chicken breast and plopped it on her plate.

"Are you going to tell me?" He placed a hefty amount of salad on his plate, followed by two chicken breasts.

She shook her head. "No."

Not wanting to start a discussion that he didn't want to have in the first place, he switched topics. "Are you ready for their party?"

Apparently, Michelle didn't want to go there, either. "Yes. Tomorrow, I need to order some meat and cheese trays, but I think that should be everything. What did you and Alex do?"

"We had an frank and honest discussion about you." He reached across the table, grabbing her hand. "I had no idea I hurt you so. I'm sorry."

"Brad, that was so long ago. Let's just forget it." She snatched her hand away. "I know you were only doing what you thought was right at the time."

"Why, Michelle? Was I that horrible a husband, or something worse?"

She rose and walked to the living room. He followed her. She sat on the couch, shaking her head and wiping her eyes. "We just seemed to be going in opposite directions. And it began to gnaw at me."

He sat next to her. "Tell me what you're thinking?" Brad leaned back on the couch and reached for Michelle's hand. She didn't pull away.

"I'm thinking it's just as much my fault we grew apart. When we met, our differences held us together. I worked in the corporate world for fifteen years before I started my own real estate company. I know what it's like to want something and not be able to achieve it."

Brad sat up and stared at her. "What was missing from our relationship?"

"This. Talking, communicating, being a united front. I missed this. When I told you about Frank, you dismissed the idea. He didn't make a play for me, but I somehow felt he was using us."

"Why?"

"Well, now in the cold light of day, I can remember things about our little trips to the park. I think he was meeting someone there. He'd go to the bathroom and be gone for like thirty minutes, and his entire demeanor would be different when he returned. Sometimes he was distant when he returned, sometimes happy."

"You think it was a woman?"

"No, I think it was a man."

This didn't bode well with Brad. "Could you describe him?"

Michelle sighed. "No, that's the problem. The restroom wasn't close. I can remember basic things. You know, tall, white guy, but that's it."

Brad lowered his head. "That could explain a lot. We've just got to keep digging until we get some more facts to make sense of all this."

He pulled Michelle into his arms. "I'm sorry, baby. For all the things I didn't do. I want to make it up to you."

"Brad, you can't make up for the past, we can only work on the future."

The future. At least there was hope. They sat on the couch in silence. Michelle leaned against him. They both were trying to let go of the past and work toward something to make their marriage strong.

He stroked her forearm as she wrapped her arms around him. "Hey, I think the chicken is cold. Why don't we order something?"

Michelle sat up and stared at him. "But what about your meal?"

He glanced toward the dining room. "I'm sure it's cold. I'm in the mood for something ooey and gooey."

"I don't think that's on my diet." She scrutinized him closely. "What are you trying to do, make me gain all the weight I lost?"

He leaned forward, meeting her lips with his. "What's a pound or two gained for some really good food?" He caressed her face gently. "Besides, I could always work it off you later."

"I just bet you could." She smiled, doing something out of character. She sat in his lap.

He kissed her lips with a loud smack.

She laughed and kissed him, enjoying their quiet time together. She rose. "You can call and order the pizza since you're feeling so frisky, and I'll go check on the kids."

He watched her leave. He was so close. They were sharing and being honest about their feelings. It felt good. Sighing, he reached for the phone and ordered the pizza.

As he reclined on the sofa, he realized that Michelle had been gone a long time. Maybe she was slipping into something more comfortable, he hoped.

Those hopes were dashed when his daughter appeared with Michelle. Preston was in her arms. "How long for the pizza? I thought we could watch a movie and eat in here. What do you think?"

He thought that idea was a winner. Better than prime rib, better than steak, and almost better than lobster. Three sets of eyes awaited his answer. "Sounds fine." He reached for Preston. "Where's my wallet?"

Michelle tilted her head at him. "You know, the last time I saw it was when I searched your truck. Maybe it's in your glove compartment. How did you pay for lunch?"

"Alex picked up the check. I reached for my wallet and I didn't have it. The few times we ate out, you took care of the check."

Michelle nodded. "Why don't you look in the truck for it and we'll pick out a movie?"

He nodded, feeling an indescribable emotion. Was it hurt? Anger? Frustration? Or just being a loser? He headed for the garage, but she caught him as he opened the door.

"I never meant to hurt your feelings or make you feel less of a man, Brad. It's just those first few times we went out to eat, you were so disoriented it was easier that I took care of it."

"I know. I appreciate it." He walked into the semi-dark garage. He flipped on the lights, smiling instantly. Next to Michelle and the kids, the Range Rover came next. The car looked regal parked next to Michelle's Navigator. He opened the door and retrieved his wallet.

He remembered the Gucci wallet Michelle had gotten him for his forty-eighth birthday. He had a meeting on her forty-fifth and had forgotten to get her a birthday present. He had so much to make up for, he didn't know where to begin.

He'd start with tonight. As he walked back into the house the doorbell rang. He looked through the peephole, just to make sure it was actually a pizza delivery person. It was. He quickly paid for the pizza and returned to the living room.

Michelle had the kids settled on the floor with paper plates and plastic bottles of juice. He placed the pizza on the coffee table. She put a slice of pepperoni pizza in front of both the kids, and soon they were gobbling down the food. Brad grabbed a slice and a paper plate and Michelle did the same. But she was sitting on the other end of the couch, much too far away.

"Why don't you sit closer to me?" He picked up the remote and started the movie. The children were engrossed in it immediately. Exactly the desired effect.

She shook her head. "Do I have your promise that you'll be on your best behavior?" She nodded at the children.

He patted the space beside him. "Of course. On my honor."

"You weren't in the military."

"Humor me."

He watched as she scooted a little closer.

"Is this better?"

"No. Closer."

She glanced at the children, who weren't paying her any attention. She scooted closer. He motioned for her to come closer still. Finally, she was next to him with not so much as air between them.

"Are you happy now?" She reached for another piece of pizza.

"Yes. I am." He kissed her, moving her legs across his at the same time. "Now, this feels so much better."

"Mummy, are you going to kiss Daddy?" Peri asked from her position on the floor.

"No, honey. We're watching the movie." Michelle tried to untangle herself from Brad, but it was useless. He held her firm.

"I think she should kiss me. What do you think, Peri? After all, I ordered the pizza."

Peri stood and walked to her parents. "I think you should kiss her, Daddy." She giggled at her mother. "Can I have another piece?"

Michelle still tried to wiggle free. "That's your last piece. You'll have bad dreams if you eat too much."

Peri nodded, but didn't leave from her position. "I thought you were going to kiss Mummy."

Brad smiled. "That's right, baby. What kind of kiss? A wet sloppy one, or a little one?" The smile on his daughter's face was priceless.

"A big one, Daddy." Peri reached for her pizza and returned to her seat on the floor.

"Okay, baby." He leaned toward Michelle and felt the heat radiating from her body. Finally, she quit squirming, as if her fate had already been sealed and it had. He whispered against her lips. "This won't hurt one bit." He kissed her gently, then teased her mouth opened with his tongue.

She put her arms around his neck, drawing him closer. When the kiss ended, they were both panting like they had just run a marathon. Desire coursed through their veins like a forest fire through dry woods. The next hour would be excruciating.

After their bodies calmed down, Michelle snuggled next to him and pretended to watch the movie. Her hands began a journey of their own. Gliding over his chest, feeling him up. She looked at him with wide-eyed innocence, as if she didn't know she was turning him on. Brad didn't know how he was going to make it through the next ten minutes without exploding.

CHAPTER 28

Brad snuggled next to Michelle's nude form in her bed. He couldn't believe his luck lately. After they had a family meal of pizza, they put the kids to sleep. He was going to be gallant and sleep alone in his room, but she invited him to sleep with her.

Of course, he couldn't refuse. He slipped into her bed, and into paradise. Before he could get settled and begin his seduction act, Michelle was lying next to him with her head on his chest and her hands roaming. But that was two hours ago; now as he listened to the quiet rhythm of her breathing, he wondered how could have neglected her so in the past.

He had to convince her that he had changed. And he had, to an extent. He would help her decorate the house for her parents' welcome home party. He would try to be nicer to Emily. Although, before the cruise, Emily had been something of an ally in his efforts to win Michelle back. She had told him about the art class and the gym, and had made a point of telling him how long they would be gone on their cruise. Maybe their feuding days were behind them.

"Brad, what are you still doing up?" Michelle raised her head to look at him. "You should be fast asleep after that workout you gave me." She smiled at him.

"Does that mean you're ready for another one?" He hoped so, watching as she climbed on top of him. "I hope that means yes."

She smiled, crushing her body to his. "Where did you get all this energy?"

"I could ask you the same thing. Did you put something on my pizza tonight?"

"Of course not." She giggled as he guided her body to his. Once he was inside her, all conversation and teasing ceased. Michelle moaned loudly.

"Hey, the kids will hear. I know what will shut you up." He raised up, kissing her hard, feeling as exhilarated as being on a roller coaster. He didn't want the ride to stop, so he held onto her for all it was worth.

Later that night, Brad eyes snapped open. A symbol popped in his brain and wouldn't let go. Where had he seen that symbol before?

He slipped out of bed, struggling into his jeans and shirt, heading downstairs to the den. The paper was sitting in front of the computer.

He had seen the symbol; it was on the paper in front of him. But what did it mean? Leaning back in the chair he let out a sigh. All these clues right in front of him, and he was too thick to figure it out. It was getting frustrating.

Then it came to him. That symbol meant something other than the obvious. It was in another language, and it looked like an upside down "v." He would just have to figure out what language and what letter of the alphabet it was. Hopefully, his code wasn't that far off the mark.

He sat in the quiet of the office. Adrenaline surging through his body, a thin sheen of sweat covered his body. He remembered. It was in Greek. Their honeymoon. They went to Greece for their honeymoon, and he was taken with language and how it was written.

He turned on the computer and deciphered most of the note. He would have to get Alex to check some things for him to be sure, but he was almost certain. If he was wrong, his career wouldn't be worth the paper he held in his hand.

With a sigh he turned off the computer and went back to bed. Michelle snuggled next to him, kissing his chest, but never opening her eyes. She rested her head on his chest.

"Are you okay?"

"Yeah." He kissed her hair. "Go to sleep." He caressed her as she settled down and her breathing even out. He hoped she would still want to be his wife when she found out all the nasty truths.

The next morning, Michelle woke up refreshed. She got out of bed, put on her robe and checked on the kids. They were both still sound asleep. She instantly thought of an early morning activity that might do her body good. She hurried back to her bedroom and slipped back into bed with her husband.

She knew he was nude under the covers. It was just take a little nudge to wake him and they might even have time for quickie before the kids woke up. Was that her trying to fit a round of lovemaking in her day? She was acting like a wife, which she wasn't. But her hands glided over his chest, and she decided that she was a wife, at least for that morning.

Brad eyes opened. "Hey, what's this? You trying to take advantage of me?" He pulled her on top of him. "I like it." He kissed her and eased her on her back.

Making love was not like this in their marriage. She felt needed and free at the same time. She just couldn't figure out what she was supposed to feel at this moment. She knew that she felt great.

Finally, Michelle eased out of bed and took a shower. Hopefully, Brad would still be asleep when she left the house. She went to check on the kids. It was too quiet upstairs; she went downstairs and found them in the family room watching cartoons, still dressed in their pajamas. She stood in the doorway watching them, wishing she knew which way their lives were headed.

They were all enjoying the new Brad. He was playful, relaxed, and not concerned with business twenty-four hours a day. But that wasn't Brad. He still hadn't regained his memory, and it had been almost two weeks.

"Mummy, we're hungry." Peri smiled at her mother. "We saw you and Daddy sleeping, so we came down here."

"When did you come in my room?"

Peri shrugged her shoulders. "Earlier."

Well, of course, Michelle thought. Did Peri see anything she wasn't supposed to see? Like her mother acting like a nymphomaniac, for starters. "I'll call you when breakfast is ready. Have you seen Uncle Jeremy?"

"I think he's in the garage." Peri returned to watching TV, dismissing her mother.

"Thanks, honey." Michelle left the room, heading for her brother. She found him searching Brad's truck. "What are you doing?"

"Seeing what anyone could be looking for. Dryson told me about the intruder. Why didn't you say anything?"

"Keep your voice down. I don't want Brad to know. He didn't get anything. He was looking for Brad's PDA."

Jeremy walked toward her. "You mean, he told you what he wanted?"

"Yes. I caught him rifling through Brad's truck." Michelle tried to make it sound normal, knowing Jeremy would blow his top. He had appointed himself protector of all.

"Shell, you should have mentioned this to me. Mom would have my hide if something happen to you and the kids."

"I know. Things just got away from me. I promise if anything else happens I will tell you. I must be onto something, or why would they be watching the house?"

"They're watching the house, too! I can't believe you."

She shook her head. Over the years, she'd forgotten what a worry wart Jeremy could be about some things. "If you don't calm down, I'm not telling you anything else."

He took a deep breath. "I'm sorry, I just freaked out, when Dryson told me about it this morning." He noticed her shocked expression. "I went out to get the paper and I noticed he was parked in front of the house."

"I need a favor." She didn't give him time to refuse her. "Can you watch the kids for about an hour or so? I need to go out for a little bit."

Jeremy helped her. "I will watch them, if you tell me where you're going." He opened the refrigerator and grabbed the milk and orange juice.

"I can't. But after it's over, we'll talk."

Jeremy looked at her as if deciding her fate. Then slowly nodded his head. "All right. I'll watch them. But what are you going to tell Brad? He'll want to know exactly where you're going."

"I know. I'll just have to cross that bridge when I get to it." She started making pancakes, the kids' favorites. "Can you call my babies for breakfast?"

He grunted. "Those babies, as you call them, eat more than some of my dates." He rose to go fetch the children.

She went to the phone and quickly called her friend, Pam. "Hey, I know this is a lot to ask. Can I meet you about eleven?"

Pam was definitely confused. "Sure where?"

"Tarrant County Cemetery."

Pam, bless her heart, didn't ask any questions. "Sure, Michelle." She ended the call.

Michelle exhaled and resumed making breakfast. "Well, that was fairly easy," she whispered to the pancake batter.

The children came in, as noisy as ever, and Peri took her seat while Jeremy helped Preston into his high chair.

She wiped her hands on a towel. "Do you mind watching the pancakes and bacon?" She exited the kitchen and walked upstairs to her bedroom. The shower was going; she headed for the bathroom and opened the stall. Instead of her just informing him that breakfast was ready, she gazed at his form.

"I hope you like what you see?" He smiled as he lathered his body with soap. "Why don't you join me?" He smiled at her.

Michelle blinked, bringing herself back to the present. "No, thank you. Breakfast is ready." She closed the shower door. She shook her head as she headed down the stairs. "I wonder if I'm going through the change? I've never felt this horny in my life," she muttered, heading back to the kitchen.

After they finished breakfast, Michelle told Brad about her lunch plans. To her surprise, Brad agreed with Jeremy watching the kids. Alex was coming over and they were going out as well.

As she cleared the table, Michelle pondered Brad's unexpected consent. That was too easy. She didn't have time to worry about Brad's response to her leaving the house without him; she had to get dressed. After she slipped on slacks and a nice blouse, she left the house. With the help of the computer, she had directions to the cemetery. Brad and Jeremy would both skin her alive if they knew where she was going.

She pulled into the cemetery parking lot, searching for Pam's SUV. She soon spotted the red Lexus and parked next to it.

Pam greeted her with a smile. "Hi, Michelle. You know, my mom thought I was nuts for meeting you here." Pam was dressed in a dark pantsuit. "I have to say, Michelle, I was a little intrigued by all this."

Michelle smiled at her friend. "I do appreciate you meeting me here. I guess I do owe you an explanation."

Pam nodded. "I would like to understand."

She took a deep breath and began the story. "Well, remember when I told you Brad and I were separated? Well, this guy is his boss, and he was killed at the same time Brad was getting attacked."

"Did you know his boss?"

"Yeah, he was actually good to talk to. I think something bigger is going on, and I believe that's why he was killed. We're here because no one would claim his body."

Pam stopped walking and stood directly in front of Michelle. "You mean to tell me you were actually involved with this guy?"

Michelle shook her head. "No, of course not. He was killed two weeks ago, and no one claimed his body. Not his ex-wife, any of his kids, nobody. So the county is burying him today. I just thought someone should be here. He wasn't liked very much."

"No wonder. I understand about you wanting someone at his funeral. But he tried to ruin your marriage, and you still want to be at his funeral."

Michelle nodded.

"Okay, Michelle. I know what's it's like when everyone thinks you have lost your mind. What did Brad and Jeremy say?"

"They don't know. They would have me committed, if they knew. So please don't tell anyone." She guided Pam to the burial plot.

As she suspected, no one was there. The county workers were lowering the pine box into the ground. The two men glanced at her as they began shoveling dirt on top of it. Then they were gone.

Pam whispered, "Man, it even feels cold. I can understand your sentiment now. I hope when it's my time, it's not like this. What a loss of life." Pam wiped her eyes. "How did he die?"

"He was stabbed in his office."

"I wonder if he knew his attacker?"

"I don't know. It could have been a hit man. At first, the police suspected Brad, but when they discovered that Brad had been admitted to the emergency room at the time Frank was killed, he was immediately excluded as a suspect."

"You know Jon is a mystery buff, I bet he would loved to see the evidence."

Michelle remembered from their many conversations, Jon was her husband. "Is he here? I know you said he was coming for a visit."

Pam shook her head. "No, he's coming in another month and he's going to stay for two weeks."

"Hopefully, by then all this will just be a horrible memory." She wiped her eyes. "Well, Frank, I can't say that I'm sorry this happened to you. But you deserved better than this."

The women walked back to their cars in silence. Pam finally spoke. "Why don't we have lunch? That way you won't actually be lying to the guys."

Michelle nodded. It wouldn't do her any good to go back home, with teary eyes. "Thanks, Pam. Are you sure? What about your kids?"

"Mom is watching them. How about Red Lobster?"

"Sounds good. I'll follow you." Michelle walked to her car and hopped inside. Once in the safety of the car, she took a deep breath, glad she followed her instinct and went to the burial. Her heart felt lighter already.

He watched the women leave the cemetery. He couldn't believe that she actually came to the burial. But it figured. She was a forgiving soul. She took her husband in, not knowing how long it would take for him to get well. He had a mind to follow them, but not with that Amazon of a bodyguard with her. He couldn't kill two women. He already had one murder hanging over his head.

Michelle and Pam settled at the table, sipping a glass of wine. Pam was very interested in the case, maybe a little too much for Michelle's peace of mind.

"It seems awful that no one claimed that poor man's body. Who did all his possessions go to?"

"He didn't have any possessions. Everything he had was either a lease or a rental."

"Wow." She sat back in her chair. Tears flowing down her face. "I'm sorry. It's just that he was fifty years old and he had no family members at his funeral. No one claimed his body, and no one cared about him. I'm glad we went."

"Thank you, for not asking any questions this morning." Michelle couldn't quite get over Pam's outburst. "I know it seems awful to us, because we are surrounded by love and that won't happen to us."

Pam emptied her glass of wine in one swallow. "Damn right. When Jon comes to visit next month, I'm not going to let him go back. We're going to make it work. I don't want to end up like Frank."

"I know you won't. Just make sure it's really what you want."

She smiled across the table at Michelle. "What do you want, Michelle. Do you want to reconcile with Brad?"

"Yes. I just don't know what he wants. Or if he's real. I'm so confused right now. I guess I'm going to have to wait it out and see which Brad emerges."

"Would it really matter?"

"No, I guess not."

226

Alex drove to the office in silence. Brad was studying the note carefully. He knew where the money was, or at least he had a good hunch.

"Brad, why do you think the money is still there? Surely whoever did Frank in would have found it by now."

Brad shook his head. "It's just something he said a day or two before he was killed. I think he was supposed to hand it over, but he didn't."

Alex shook his head. "Man, this is so strange, I don't doubt that you're right, but I still think whoever it was would have gotten it by now."

"I'll just have to prove it to you." He held up the sheet of paper. "This tells me that it's still there, but someone is getting ready to transfer it."

Alex pulled into the desolate parking lot. "Okay, let's say that you can figure where the money is and who is getting it. Would it be the same person that killed Frank?"

"I don't know. I still don't know why I was attacked. Especially if Jameson left me a message to bring the report anyway. It was a done deal."

"But the report wasn't on you. It was in my office in code. Only an idiot would hurt the person that could decipher it."

CHAPTER 29

"Mummy, we missed you!" Peri hugged her, almost knocking her mother over.

"I missed you, too." She rubbed her daughter's hair. She really did miss her kids today. With the somberness of Frank's burial, she missed her family.

She picked up Peri and hugged the stuffing out of her. "Mommy loves you." She held her daughter so close the child almost couldn't breathe.

"Mummy hurt." Peri forced the words out of her mouth.

Michelle hugged her again, then let her go. "I'm sorry, honey. Have you eaten? Where's Uncle Jeremy?" She let Peri down.

She shrugged. "He's playing on the computer."

Michelle picked up Preston, hugging him in the same manner. He was her special little man. He hugged her back with the same fierceness. She walked into the den with Peri tagging along behind. Jeremy wasn't playing on the computer, he was studying something on the screen.

"Hey, Jerry. I'm back. I hope the kids weren't too much trouble. Is Brad here? Have you had lunch?"

He leaned back in the leather chair, glancing at her. "How was the funeral?"

Busted. "How did you know? I thought I was being careful."

"Because I can add. I knew that it has been two weeks since Frank's death and no one has claimed his body. Therefore the county was probably burying him today, along with about a hundred other unclaimed people. Plus, I overheard you on the phone. I won't say anything to Brad, but I think you should tell him. But why did you go?"

She shrugged, not wanting to discuss her reasoning. "Have the kids eaten?"

It was his turn to get busted. "I'm sorry, Shell. I started looking at this and I forgot all about them. Usually, Peri reminds me when it's time to eat." He smiled at his niece.

Michelle knew that her brother had a one-track mind. "I need to feed them. Why don't you tell me what you're doing while I fix them some lunch?"

Jeremy nodded. He stood, picked up Peri and tweaked her little nose, making her laugh. "You're supposed to keep me out of trouble." He started down the hall to the kitchen.

After the kids were seated, Michelle looked in the freezer for something quick to fix. "What would you guys like?"

"Hot dogs," Peri answered.

"No hot dogs. How about fish sticks and French fries? Yum. Or how about some baked chicken and mac and cheese?"

Again, Peri answered. "Fish sticks."

"Okay, fish sticks it is." She glanced at her children. Their hands were dirty. "Go wash your hands."

"Okay, Mummy."

While Peri was washing her hands, Michelle put Preston in his high chair. By the time Peri returned, Michelle had placed the meal in the oven.

"Jerry, what were you doing on the computer?"

"I scanned those papers Alex gave Brad a few days ago into the computer. Some of the symbols on it looked familiar. I thought I could decipher it that. So I ran it through a language program, since it seems to be the answer to the murder and Brad's attack."

"Did you find out what language it was?"

"No. I tried Spanish, Arabic, Latin, and Hebrew. Nothing made sense. Does Brad know any other languages fluently?"

"Are you kidding? Brad, Mr. They Should All Speak English, Anyway?" She took the fish sticks and French fires out of the oven. "I've never heard him speak anything else."

"It's definitely a language with lots of symbols. But I'll keep trying after lunch. So how was it?"

He meant the funeral, she knew. "Is Brad back?"

Jeremy shook his head. "Alex got here about twelve. He told Brad about Frank was being buried today, but Brad only nodded. Then they left with those papers in Brad's hand."

"Did he take his Palm Pilot?"

"No. What are you up to, Michelle?"

"Nothing, I just wanted to look through it one more time. Maybe something will pop out."

The fish sticks had cooled enough for the kids to eat. Even though she ate a healthy lunch with Pam earlier, she had to at least eat a few fish sticks with the children. Jeremy also joined them, but he ate a salad. It was the most satisfying meal she had ever had.

Brad and Alex rifled through Frank's desk, looking for the clue that would solve the question of the missing money.

Brad took the folded paper from the pocket of his jeans and studied it again. "Look for something that starts with a four digit number, then a string of letters, then six digits."

Alex grunted. "Isn't that a Herrington account number?"

"Give that man a cigar," Brad added sarcastically. "Of course it's a Herrington account number, but it's a dummy account. Real Herrington accounts end in the alphabet."

"That's right. The initials of the department." Alex licked his finger and drew an invisible number onc in the air. "Like Investments is HI, operations is HO, marketing is HM, and so on."

"Yes, I think that must have alerted me in the first place. Then when I started investigating is when all the trouble started."

Alex nodded. "But, Brian Hall had the job before you and he never said anything. He'd been vp for the last five years, surely he wasn't in on it."

"It's a shame we can't asked him." Brian committed suicide a week before Brad returned to the States.

"He was acting strange a couple of weeks before that happened. I still refuse to believe he'd jump into the Trinity River."

Brad looked Alex straight in the eyes. "I think this is a lot bigger than we think it is. Frank became president last year after Bob Donohoe had a heart attack and died. That was mighty convenient."

"Yes, I was thinking the same thing. Maybe that's why Frank got the job; somebody needed a fall guy. I know he shouldn't have gotten the job in the first place. His reputation is horrible in the financial community. He shouldn't have been hired for any position, let alone president. Who knows how long this has been going on, and how many millions we're talking about?"

Brad shook his head. "I'm almost too afraid to guess. But I would like to catch the bastard who's doing this. That's probably why Brian and Bob were iced."

"Maybe. The day Frank was in the park, he told the mystery guy he wanted out, but he told Frank that it wasn't over. I couldn't get a real good look at him, and could only make out parts of their conversation." Alex coughed. "And the next morning, Frank had a knife in his chest."

"And I landed in the hospital with a concussion and cracked ribs." Brad resumed his search. "You know, when I was decoding this thing I was sure it would be easy. But now I don't know. I know it's here. I can feel it." He opened the top file drawer. "It would be easier if he had a little black book marked 'secrets.' " Brad laughed, opening a file folder.

"You mean like this one?" Alex held up a small spiral tablet. It had the word "private" on the cover.

Brad took two strides to the desk and grabbed the tablet out of Alex's hand. He opened it and started to laugh. "Either Frank was a class-A idiot, or he was really smart."

Alex couldn't hide his puzzled look. "What?"

He showed the pages to Alex, trying not to sound too giddy as he explained the pages. "Look on this page. It has account number

1184GLSCUK767676, dated last year about two months after he took over as president." He flipped the page. "The same account number is on this page, dated about eight months ago, and so on."

Alex nodded, reading Brad's mind. He immediately keyed the account number into the computer. "It requires some kind of special code to access the information," Alex announced.

Brad looked at his best friend. "You're the best computer hacker I know in North America. Get to work. I'll still look in the files. Maybe he left a hard copy somewhere."

Alex started keying different combinations of passwords, but hitting a brick wall on each try. After each failed attempt, he let out a muffled curse.

The picture on the wall, he thought. One day Brad walked into Frank's office and he was fiddling with the picture. It was a reproduction of a Monet. Brad walked to the picture, lifting it from the wall. He was rewarded with a small piece of paper, neatly folded into quarters. He read the paper, and slapped his forehead. "Man, we are so stupid."

"What now?" Alex stopped working on the computer.

"If you were trying to hide something and you were trying to set someone else up, what password would you use?"

Alex scratched his hairless chin. "Well, something that would really incriminate that person. Something that only could be associated with that person." Alex eyes became large as the light in his brain finally came on. "You're not trying to tell me that his password has something to do with you?"

"Yes, it does." Brad smiled. He should be furious as hell, but he smiled. "The password is Shell. I know he heard me call her that when he was hanging out with her in London."

"Then the late Franklin Sims got exactly what he deserved. I can't believe he was trying to set you up."

"I didn't see it until just now. You know, I think he believed I would have just signed the report rather than checking the figures, because he recommended me for the job. Bastard. He thought I would just ignore procedure for the sake of friendship."

"But he didn't know that you were an overachiever and would never have signed something without checking it out thoroughly."

They both watched in amazement as the file opened. Brad studied the chart in front of him. "This shows where the money is, but it doesn't show who told him to put it there. Is there any way we could freeze this so we could know if someone accesses it?"

"You want me to freeze this account?"

"Yes. Can't you put some kind of tracer on it?"

"Yes, but that would take me a while to do that. I don't think they can get to the money," Alex stated.

"Why, just because it hasn't been moved yet? Don't be silly. They're probably just waiting until the heat's off and then they would be long gone. Probably back to their homeland, or to Seattle."

"Okay, what was that?"

"Just a hunch."

"Hey, you said that Frank was in the park with a guy. Could you describe him?"

Brad shook his head. "No, I didn't get a good look at him. Just like the attack. I remember certain things, but it's like my brain blocked out anything descriptive."

"Well, that blows that theory. I was hoping you remembered something other than kicking Frank's ass."

"No, I've had a few nightmares but I can never see their faces." But he could see something else.

"Well, at least we can tell the auditors that we found the money. How did you figure this out?"

"You're going to laugh when I tell you."

"Try me."

"Well, I was staring at this paper last night and some of the symbols looked familiar, but I just couldn't figure where I'd seen them. Then later in bed it came to me. It was the Greek alphabet. I remembered on our honeymoon, I was intrigued by the Grecian language."

"Yeah, you went on forever about Greece when you guys got back. I think I was more excited than you when Michelle announced she was pregnant a few months later. At least you'd quit talking about Greece and the Aegean Islands."

Brad laughed, remembering. "Boy, I had it bad."

"Yeah. So what do you want to do about this?"

Brad shrugged. "We'll put a tracer on it, but I think whoever was in it with Frank will try to do something soon. Especially, since he's finally buried, they'll figure it's all clear." Brad returned the piece of paper to the back of the painting. A piece of fabric fell to the floor. "Hey, what's this? Why would Frank have a fabric swatch on the back of a picture? It's not like he was going to order a suit or anything."

Alex laughed. "Yeah, I know he buys off the rack. I heard Jameson commenting on that one day. He told Frank he needed to invest in a good suit."

Brad shoved the fabric swatch in his pocket. "Hey, is there a picture of Jameson around anywhere?"

"Yeah, I know there's one on the company's intranet. You know, his mugshot."

Brad shook his head. "No, I mean one like when he's all dressed up, like an awards banquet or something."

"That will be in the lobby."

Brad nodded, heading for the elevator. "I've just got a hunch and I've got to see if it right."

Alex huffed, but was right behind him. "What kind of hunch? Man, somebody's going to be stalking us after while."

Brad laughed as they entered the elevator and headed for the ground floor. "Wouldn't you want to be remembered for solving this puzzling crime?"

"No, I don't want to be remembered at all. I would like to still be here."

Soon they were in the spacious lobby of Herrington Global Investments. The glass case was directly in front of them. Brad searched each of the pictures, but didn't find what he was looking for. "Damn. It's not here."

"What?"

He looked at his friend. "If I tell you, then we're both at risk. This way if you don't know, you won't be in danger."

"But I'm already in danger anyway. So what's a little more?"

Brad shook his head. "If something happens to me, I want you to take care of my family."

"What are you, kidding? Nothing's going to happen to you. If they couldn't kill you then, they won't get you now. We're not discussing this. Just tell me what you're looking for."

"No. I've made some mistakes in the past, but I'm not in the future. This is on me, and I'm going to fix this."

Alex sighed. "All right, Brad. Since whatever you're looking for wasn't here anyway, I'll let you keep your secret."

"Thanks, Alex. I think we're done here."

"Thank God." The friends headed for the elevator.

When Brad finally returned home, the house was quiet. It was barely three o'clock in the afternoon, he expected the kids to greet him at the front door, but no one greeted him.

He walked upstairs, checking the kids' rooms first. Peri was sound asleep, as was Preston. Slowly, he turned the knob to Michelle's room and entered. She was sound asleep, as well.

She was burrowed deep under the covers. Would she feel him get into bed with her? Only one way to find out.

He slid into bed beside his wife, smiling as she automatically made room for him, without opening her eyes. She snuggled up next to him, resting her head on his chest. He held his breath until she got comfortable. It felt so right. He would have to confess, and soon.

CHAPTER 30

Sunday morning, Brad awoke with a new sense of direction. He would confess most of his memory had returned, he determined. He had tried several times at dinner the previous night, but the words became tangled around his tongue.

Especially after Jeremy took the kids for the evening. They were actually alone and they both took full advantage of the fact.

After dinner, they took a bubble bath together. This time when he spoke of the future, she didn't stop him with talk of his amnesia, so maybe she was as much in love with him as he was with her.

A man could only hope. He knew today would be full of chores to do. They had to plan her parents" surprise party and he wanted to talk to her about what he found yesterday. But first he was going to fix breakfast for his family. He eased from her bed and went to his room to change. After he dressed in jeans and a button-down shirt, he went downstairs to start breakfast.

Jeremy soon joined him in the kitchen, and he started the coffee as he and Brad talked about the party.

"Will Emily and George be surprised? Or are they expecting it?"

"No, Shell thought this up. She wanted to do something nice for Mom. Where is Shell, anyway?"

"Still knocked out. She didn't move when I got out of bed. She must be tired."

Jeremy nodded, taking cups from the cupboard. "More like emotionally drained. Yesterday was too much for her."

I should have stayed with her, he chided himself. "Were the kids too much or what?"

"She didn't tell you?"

"Tell me what?" Brad stopped searching for the skillet. "What happened yesterday that she didn't tell me about?"

Jeremy cursed himself for bringing up the subject. "Why don't you ask her yourself? I'm not getting in the middle of this. She had a pretty hard day, remember that. Then she came home and had to contend with the kids."

Brad nodded. "I'm not going to pick a fight with her about it, whatever it was."

But Brad wasn't going to focus on that. He chose to focus on the future. Being a family and having their own house. She couldn't be happy living in her parents home.

Although yes, the house could hold them all comfortably, he thought. It had six bedrooms and was considered very large. But he couldn't live under the roof with Emily. That just wasn't possible. Their truce would eventually end and she'd hate him again.

"Yo, Brad," Jeremy called. "Man, you were zoning out. I called your name like four times."

"Yeah, I was out there. I guess I have too much on my mind. Trying to fix all the messes in my mind is hard work."

"Don't I know it." Jeremy poured two cups of coffee, waving one of them at Brad. "It seems when you think you have one thing working out, something else happens."

"What do you mean?"

Jeremy fixed his coffee and sat down at the table. "Before Mom and Dad left on the cruise, they asked me to stay with Michelle to help her with the kids. I figured it would have been awful, but being around them and you guys, it just shows me that I need to get out there and search for my Ms. Right again. So what if it didn't work out this time? I shouldn't give up. I think I'm going to sell my condo so I can be closer to Mom and Dad and Michelle."

"Where do I fit into all this?" Brad asked.

"I figured you'd stay here with Shell."

"You think she'd want to stay here, versus us getting a house nearby?"

"Probably. She's been feeling that home thing. You know our parents are over sixty-five and your kids are the only grandkids. She wants them to be able to enjoy them."

"I'd never thought of that. My parents are pretty much in the same boat. Mel never married, so our kids are all the grandkids they have. I've tried to talk them into moving down here, but no luck. They'd miss all their friends."

Brad started making scrambled eggs as the bacon cooked on the grill. "I know the smell of food will wake them up."

Not ten minutes later, when he was placing the bacon on a platter, Peri, Preston and Michelle walked into the kitchen, dressed in their pajamas.

"This smells wonderful, Brad." Michelle sat down at the table, by the children. "I'm starving."

Brad smiled, placing a platter of eggs on the table, along with bacon and hash browns. "Dig in. I've been slaving over a hot stove all morning."

Everyone started eating and all conversation ceased. Only after the platter was clean, did conversation resume.

Michelle leaned back in her chair and patted her stomach. "Oh, that was wonderful. I don't think I have enough strength to walk back upstairs and get dressed for the day."

Brad cleared the dishes from the table. "Who said you had to get dressed?"

Jeremy choked on his coffee. "I could take the kids off your hands."

"No, Jerry," Michelle laughed. "I'm taking the kids myself. I feel fine." She stood and started down the hall with Peri and Preston right behind her.

Brad laughed as he cleaned the table. Jeremy rose from the table, taking his cup to the sink. "I got some work in the den, if you guys need me for anything."

"We have to plan the party, or rather make a plan of attack on the menu."

Jerry shook his head walking out of the kitchen. "Man, you've changed so much, it's like I barely know you."

Brad didn't recognize himself either.

Later, after planning the menu for the surprise party, Brad watched the kids run around like they were hopped up on chocolate or something. "Who's picking them up?"

"They're taking the airport shuttle service."

"That sounds good. What did you do yesterday?"

"What do you mean?"

"I mean I know you went to Frank's burial. Why did you go?"

Michelle stared at him. "Did Jerry tell you?"

"What? He knew you went there and no one bothered to tell me? No, he didn't have to tell me. I know because I know you. What the hell were you thinking? Somebody is out to get us, and you're out there waving a red flag!" As he said those words, Peri stopped dead in her tracks. "I'm sorry, I know we're not supposed to fight in front of the kids, but this has got me all wound up."

Michelle's gaze burned a hole through him. She just figured it out, and he was going to be in a whole lot of trouble. "Your memory has returned, hasn't it?"

"Shell."

She turned to her children. "Honey, go get your bag, we're going to the park." As soon as Peri scooted out of the room, she lit into him. "Don't you dare try to sit there and patronize me. How long have you had it?"

"A while. I just wanted you to love me."

"For the liar that you are? I can't believe you took advantage of me. Do you know who attacked you?"

"Some things are still fuzzy. I don't have all of it back. I know that I'm a big cause of our split up. I know that you have no business feeling sorry for Frank, especially with all the stuff we have found out about the man in his double life."

"Don't turn this into something about you. Yes, I went to the burial, Brad. Pam and I were the only people there, besides the gravediggers. It just seemed so sad that he had no family at his burial."

"I wanted to tell you, but I don't remember that night, so I'm not completely well. Please understand."

"I understand that you manipulated me. I trusted you and you lied to me." She rose from the table when Peri returned with the bag. "We're going to the park, so I can think. When I return, you can pack your clothes and get out."

His plan didn't work. Big surprise there. "Shell, please just think about what we mean to each other. Just think about it, please. I'm not leaving until you return."

"Whatever." She picked up Preston and grabbed Peri's hand, almost dragging her daughter to the garage.

Helpless to stop her, Brad watched them leave. He was so close to reconciling, and now this giant leap backwards. How to straighten it all out? One thing was certain: he couldn't do anything right now. Michelle was too enraged, and any action on his part would only make divorce all the more inevitable.

After Michelle belted the kids in their car seats, she sat behind the steering wheel, determined not to cry. She had a feeling that his memory had returned but didn't think Brad would be so devious as to hide the fact from her. Did he really think she'd kick him out of the house the minute he was well?

Would she have?

Michelle knew she loved him and was ready to be a family again, but changes would have to be made. He would have to treat her more as an equal and not as a object. Not someone to see to the children and definitely not just an ornament on his arm at company functions. Besides, she still had his keys. He wasn't going anywhere.

"Mummy, are we going to the park?" Peri asked.

Michelle blinked, glancing in the rearview mirror. Peri stared back at her with big brown eyes. "Yes, baby." Finally she started the engine and was about to put the car in gear, when someone knocked on her window. She almost jumped out of her skin.

Dryson motioned for her to let her window down. When she obliged, he couldn't apologize enough. "I'm sorry, Michelle. I was trying to catch you when you weren't with Brad." He handed her an envelope. "Here's a copy of the crime scene photos."

Michelle reached for the envelope. "Do you need them back?"

"No. Just destroy them. Let me know if something stands out to you."

"I will."

"Are you okay?"

Michelle nodded and let her window back up. If she opened her mouth, she would tell him the whole ugly story and probably run back inside to Brad. Slowly she backed out of the driveway and headed for the park. Once there she unbuckled the kids and they followed her to their usual park bench. She took a seat, situating the bag next to her.

"Can we go play?" Peri asked, grabbing her brother's hand, ready to take flight toward the play area.

"Yes, you can. But stay where can I see you."

"Okay, Mummy."

She had so many things to think about. So many things were clouding her views about everything. If she could clear Brad's name and he still took that job of president, what would she do? She would still file for divorce, showing him she meant business.

After making sure the children were where she could see them, Michelle opened the envelope. She studied each picture closely. However, one in particular bugged her.

She had seen that particular pattern of Scottish plaid shown in the troublesome photo on something. Maybe she had remembered from their last trip to Scotland. Or maybe the Scottish festival, the last cultural event she'd attended in London. They were always selling kilts or tartans at those festivals. It was a beautiful pattern. Maybe that's why it stuck out in her mind. She studied the photo of the knife. Where had she seen that knife before?

She closed her eyes, hoping something would pop into her numb brain. Maybe too many things were happening to her at once to completely understand what was going on around her.

Her eyes popped open. Suddenly a scene from the past flashed before her. One of those horrid times Frank accompanied her to the park. In his usual manner, he went to the bathroom across the park, but she noticed a man waiting for Frank. They darted to the side and, like usual, Frank returned to her thirty minutes later, in a bad mood. Her recall of that day was incredible. In hindsight, she should have realized what was going on. Upon leaving the park, Michelle noticed the man getting into a dark sedan and driving past them. The only thing she could see was that crest on the license plate. It signified his family's colors. His clan, as the Scots called it. The same crest was on the knife that killed Frank. It was Herrington Global's operations president, Conrad Jameson. The same man who offered Brad the job as president of investments. No wonder that business card looked familiar. But that man wasn't big enough to have overtaken Brad and beat him up and left him for dead. Plus, Mary said there were at least three assailants.

Immediately, she reached for her cellphone to call Dryson. She didn't feel exactly safe. She quickly dialed his number and told him to meet her at the park.

But now she had to wait for Dryson. She reached for her phone to call Jeremy, when she was interrupted.

"Hello, Michelle. I see you've been studying the photographs."

A cold chill ran through her body. How could he have approached her in broad daylight and she not noticed? She glanced around the park for her children; they were still playing. She tried her best to remain calm. She didn't want the kids running to her, then their lives would be in jeopardy.

"Mr. Jameson, so nice to see you again. I missed you the two times you showed up at my house." She discreetly slid the photos into her bag. "I was just looking at some pictures from vacation."

He smiled at her, chilling her blood. "I think you know what I'm looking for." He sat next to her.

"No."

"I need those pictures. I need Frank's PDA. I know you have it."

Brad paced the living room, deciding his next step. Michelle had been gone almost an hour; surely she would have calmed down by now.

He walked to the den, where Jeremy worked on the computer. "What are you doing?"

Jeremy looked up at him. "I was trying to decipher that paper Alex gave you a few days ago. I ran it through some computer programs, but I can't figure out what language it is."

Brad was moved. Each in their own way, everyone was trying to help him. "It's Greek. I figured that part out already. I found the missing money. Frank was taking it, and they way I figure it, the previous veeps were fall guys. They would merely sign off on the report and he'd dump the money into a dummy account until someone else would take it out."

"Wow, so what now?" Jeremy stared at Brad.

"Now I need to go after your sister. My memory returned a few days ago, and she's pissed cause I didn't tell her sooner. I wanted her to love me again, before I told her. But that only infuriated her more. I just wanted her to see how much she meant to me."

"I know. I figured you were just trying to get her back, but you went about it wrong. Shell isn't the same woman you separated from two months ago."

"You don't have to tell me that. I guess we both changed." Brad took a deep breath. "So are you going to help me find my keys or what?"

"I'll help you look, but who knows where she could have hidden them. I haven't seen them since Dryson handed them to her."

Brad nodded. It was going to be like looking for a needle in a haystack. But he didn't have time. "Why don't you just take me to the park?"

Jeremy nodded. "Okay, she'll be mad at both of us for a while, but not for long. You guys need to work this out." He grabbed his keys and they headed for the garage, but the phone rang. "Hold on." He went to answer it, but by the time he took another step, it stopped. "I guess it wasn't important." He grabbed his cellphone as he reached the garage door.

They hopped in his car and they left. They were barely a block away from the house, when Jeremy's cellphone rang. "Answer that."

Brad picked up the cellphone and to his dismay, it was his least favorite person. Dryson.

"Brad? I thought I called Jerry. Anyway, is Shell with you?"

"No. We're on our way to the park. What's up?"

"I don't know. I gave her some crime scene photos. She called me about twenty minutes ago and told me she figured it out and to meet her at the park."

Brad cursed under his breath. "You think she's in danger?" *Please God, let him say no. Please, please*, he chanted to himself.

"I think she is. I tried to call her back and her phone is off. That's why I'd hoped she was with you. I'll turn on the siren. I'll be there in ten minutes." He ended the call.

Brad turned to Jeremy, who was already speeding. "Punch it, Shell's in trouble." Brad hoped they reached her in time. He didn't want to lose her after all this. "Oh my God, she has the kids with her!"

"I-I don't have it. I never had it," said Michelle. She glanced around the park, spotting the children. They were still playing, safe and sound.

"You don't want me to force you to tell me where it is," Conrad said threateningly. "I have someone watching your children. Every second you don't tell me only means more harm to them. Didn't your husband's brush with death show you that I'm not kidding?"

"Why did you have him beat up?" Michelle asked, desperately trying to buy time.

Jameson smiled. "I really don't like him. He was the first vp that tried to actually do his job and not just sign things. The orders were to kill him, but they got interrupted."

Her heart broke. "Why would you want Brad killed?"

"He's married to you. I thought you would be able to ID me from the time you saw my car in London and somehow tell your husband. My game would be finished."

"But I didn't even remember you until all this started happening."

"I realized that a little too late."

"I got your letter."

"Yes, and you were supposed to get scared like Mary. Now, can I have the PDA?"

"I don't have it," Michelle answered. She glanced around her area, looking for a weapon of any sort. But as usual the park was immaculate. Not a twig or branch nearby.

"How did you know about the money?"

"What money?"

He moved closer to her, grabbing her hands. "Look, I'm tired of playing games." He released her hand and reached inside his pocket, withdrawing a knife.

Michelle couldn't hide the recognition as it crossed her face. He laughed. "I know you noticed the crest. That crest is on every suit I own. Damn my family's Scottish pride."

"Was Frank taking the money for you?"

"He owed me a favor. I needed a pawn. He was easy enough. I recommended him to the board of directors to step in as vice president when Bob died suddenly of a heart attack. Then when the president died, naturally he was promoted again with my recommendation."

"So why offer that job as president to Brad?"

"I had nothing to do with that. The board wanted him. I tried to shoot him down citing his unstable home life, since he was going through a divorce. But rumors were already floating around about Frank breaking up your marriage."

"Is that why you only appeared after I left the house?"

"Yes, I couldn't take the chance you'd recognize me. It would have all fallen into place. And I had to make sure Brad didn't recognize me."

Michelle strained her brain for something, anything, to keep his attention averted from the knife in his hand. But she didn't want to anger him, either. That would mean instant death.

"I've had enough questions. I've searched Frank's house, his office, I know you have his PDA. Just give it to me and I'll be gone. You should know I have no compunction about killing two small children."

Her heart sank. She had to protect her babies at all costs.

"But you know too much and I can't let you tell your husband. Just stand up nice and easy and start walking to the parking lot."

Michelle did as he said. With every step she took, she knew she was closer to her own end, and possibly her children's. When she had a plan formulated in her mind, she slowed down her pace. She spotted a beer bottle near the trash bin.

But he was one step ahead of her. He dragged her along with him. "Don't think you're getting away from me." He strengthened his hold on her. "Come on."

"My children," she cried. "Let me get the children." She fell to the ground, grabbing the beer bottle.

"No. Get up." He attempted to pick her up.

Finally, she had him where she wanted him. She hit him in the head with as much force as she could manage, knocking him off balance. She scurried away as quickly as she could. She screamed for help, but with it being a Sunday morning there wasn't much help to choose from.

The children heard her scream and ran in her direction. She herded them into the car and hoped she could get away before Jameson could get his bearings. She got them into the SUV, not bothering with car seats or seatbelts. "Stay on the floor," she commanded, slamming the door shut. She ran to the driver's side, jumped in, and started the engine. She forced the SUV into reverse and gunned it for all it was worth. She was backing away, free!

But not for long. Her tire was flat. Jameson had shot her tire. She was determined not to get out of the car. The kids had begun to cry. Michelle thought she was losing her mind. She tried to drive away but the car wouldn't move. She saw her life flash before her as she watched the Mercedes ram head first into the side of her car.

After the airbag inflated, the last thing she heard was the monotone voice of the navigation system asking if she needed help.

"Yes," she croaked, then lost consciousness.

Brad's heart was about to pop out of his chest as he and Jeremy entered the park. Police cars were everywhere, as were ambulances and helicopters.

"Do you see Shell's car anywhere?" Brad searched the area for the black Navigator. He didn't see it. "Where in the hell is she?"

Jeremy didn't answer. "Hey, there's Dryson." He brought the car to a stop and jumped out.

Brad jumped out of the car and ran to Dryson. "Where is she? The kids?"

Dryson stared at Brad with tears in his eyes. "I'm sorry, Brad. I didn't get here quick enough."

Brad didn't want to hear that. He grabbed Dryson by the arm. "Where is my wife?"

"She was airlifted to Kennedy Memorial. The kids were a little shaken up, but they're fine. I knew you were on the way, so I told them to let them stay here. But Shell is pretty bad off."

"Where are the kids?"

"This way."

Brad followed Dryson to the ambulance. Peri and Preston sat quietly on the stretcher. "Daddy!"

He reached for his daughter, hugging her for dear life. "Are you okay?"

"Daddy, this man tried to hit Mummy and…"

Brad muffled her cries in his shoulder. "It's okay, honey. She'll be just fine." Jeremy joined him and helped him with Preston.

"You know, Dryson, I'm sure this will make sense later, but right now I need to get to the hospital." He walked back to the car with Jeremy on his heels.

The ride to the hospital was quiet. Even the kids were silent. Brad hoped that Michelle was okay. Not likely, since she was taken by heli-copter to a hospital that was probably only thirty minutes away. He prayed for the best.

Two days later, Michelle was awakened by a beeping noise. She wanted to open her eyes, but it proved quite a struggle. When she did, her room looked fuzzy.

"Hey, you're up." Brad's voice told her. "It's about time."

She turned her head toward his voice. The room came into focus slowly. This wasn't her room. Everything was too clean, too functional, and smelled liked antiseptic. "What happened? Where are the kids?" She tried to sit up.

Brad's strong arms held her in place. "No, you stay here. The kids are with your mother. They went to get something to eat. Jameson rammed his Mercedes into your car. Do you remember the accident? You have some internal injuries." His voice wavered as he continued listing her injuries. "You've been unconscious for two days."

"Two days! The party!"

Brad rubbed her hand gently. "Don't you worry about that. We didn't have the party. We've been up here with you. How do you feel?"

"Strange. Every time I take a breath, my stomach hurts. My vision keeps going funny, and I feel hot."

"I'll call the doctor. He wanted to know the minute you woke up."

She watched him push a button, and a starched uniformed nurse immediately entered the room. She took Michelle's temperature and adjusted the IV. Smiling, she left the room.

"I can't believe all that happened. I can't believe it happened to me. I can't believe that your boss' boss was the murderer. What happened to him?"

"He was arrested along with the thugs that beat me up. Thank God Dryson got to the park when he did. He saved your life." Brad caressed her hand, being mindful of the IV. "The doctor says you'll be in here for at least two weeks."

Michelle ran her hand over her head. Something felt weird. "Where's my hair?"

"You hit your head on the window. They had to cut your hair to make sure they got all the glass out. It will grow back."

Michelle couldn't hold back her tears. "I guess I should be thankful I'm alive. I am, really. I hope the kids weren't too shattered."

"Yes, they were. They were worried about you, so I let them stay up here last night. I hope you don't mind." He coughed and shifted his position. "I know you're not feeling your best, but I want you to think about us being a family again. I'm ready, Shell. When I was sick, you took care of me and I will do the same when you get out of the hospital, if you will allow me to make up for not telling you that my memory had returned."

She stared at her husband. A man who once thought a man crying was a sign of weakness had tears streaming down his face. "Brad, I couldn't have thrown you out. Even if I wanted to, I couldn't bear to be apart from you again. But you should know that I've changed. I still want to be my own person. I mean, when I get well, I want to do something besides be a mom, and a wife."

He nodded, tears in his eyes. "I wouldn't have it any other way. You won't regret this, I promise." He leaned over the bed rail and kissed his wife. "Thanks for giving me a do-over."

ABOUT THE AUTHOR

Celya Bowers was born and raised in a small, central Texas town, just south of Waco. Being the youngest of six children, and having strict parents, she started reading at a very early age. The writing bug bit soon after that, and she began creating stories with characters that looked and talked more like she did.

After attending Sam Houston State University, she relocated to Arlington, Texas, just east of Dallas. She currently works at a mortgage company. Her dream destination is to visit the Emerald Isle, so she can finally get a stamp in her passport. For more information see www.celyabowers.net or email her celyabowers@gmail.com.

DO OVER

2007 Publication Schedule

January

Corporate Seduction
A.C. Arthur
ISBN-13: 978-1-58571-238-0
ISBN-10: 1-58571-238-8
$9.95

A Taste of Temptation
Reneé Alexis
ISBN-13: 978-1-58571-207-6
ISBN-10: 1-58571-207-8
$9.95

February

The Perfect Frame
Beverly Clark
ISBN-13: 978-1-58571-240-3
ISBN-10: 1-58571-240-X
$9.95

Ebony Angel
Deatri King-Bey
ISBN-13: 978-1-58571-239-7
ISBN-10: 1-58571-239-6
$9.95

March

Sweet Sensations
Gwendolyn Bolton
ISBN-13: 978-1-58571-206-9
ISBN-10: 1-58571-206-X
$9.95

Crush
Crystal Hubbard
ISBN-13: 978-1-58571-243-4
ISBN-10: 1-58571-243-4
$9.95

April

Secret Thunder
Annetta P. Lee
ISBN-13: 978-1-58571-204-5
ISBN-10: 1-58571-204-3
$9.95

Blood Seduction
J.M. Jeffries
ISBN-13: 978-1-58571-237-3
ISBN-10: 1-58571-237-X
$9.95

May

Lies Too Long
Pamela Ridley
ISBN-13: 978-1-58571-246-5
ISBN-10: 1-58571-246-9
$13.95

Two Sides to Every Story
Dyanne Davis
ISBN-13: 978-1-58571-248-9
ISBN-10: 1-58571-248-5
$9.95

June

One of These Days
Michele Sudler
ISBN-13: 978-1-58571-249-6
ISBN-10: 1-58571-249-3
$9.95

Who's That Lady?
Andrea Jackson
ISBN-13: 978-1-58571-190-1
ISBN-10: 1-58571-190-X
$9.95

2007 Publication Schedule (continued)

July

Heart of the Phoenix
A.C. Arthur
ISBN-13: 978-1-58571-242-7
ISBN-10: 1-58571-242-6
$9.95

Do Over
Celya Bowers
ISBN-13: 978-1-58571-241-0
ISBN-10: 1-58571-241-8
$9.95

It's Not Over Yet
J.J. Michael
ISBN-13: 978-1-58571-245-8
ISBN-10: 1-58571-245-0
$9.95

August

The Fires Within
Beverly Clark
ISBN-13: 978-1-58571-244-1
ISBN-10: 1-58571-244-2
$9.95

Stolen Kisses
Dominiqua Douglas
ISBN-13: 978-1-58571-247-2
ISBN-10: 1-58571-247-7
$9.95

September

Small Whispers
Annetta P. Lee
ISBN-13: 978-158571-251-9
ISBN-10: 1-58571-251-5
$6.99

Always You
Crystal Hubbard
ISBN-13: 978-158571-252-6
ISBN-10: 1-58571-252-3
$6.99

October

Not His Type
Chamein Canton
ISBN-13: 978-158571-253-3
ISBN-10: 1-58571-253-1
$6.99

Many Shades of Gray
Dyanne Davis
ISBN-13: 978-158571-254-0
ISBN-10: 1-58571-254-X
$6.99

November

When I'm With You
LaConnie Taylor-Jones
ISBN-13: 978-158571-250-2
ISBN-10: 1-58571-250-7
$6.99

The Mission
Pamela Leigh Starr
ISBN-13: 978-158571-255-7
ISBN-10: 1-58571-255-8
$6.99

December

One in A Million
Barbara Keaton
ISBN-13: 978-158571-257-1
ISBN-10: 1-58571-257-4
$6.99

The Foursome
Jaci Kennedy
ISBN-13: 978-158571-256-4
ISBN-10: 1-58571-256-6
$6.99

Other Genesis Press, Inc. Titles

A Dangerous Deception	J.M. Jeffries	$8.95
A Dangerous Love	J.M. Jeffries	$8.95
A Dangerous Obsession	J.M. Jeffries	$8.95
A Dangerous Woman	J.M. Jeffries	$9.95
A Dead Man Speaks	Lisa Jones Johnson	$12.95
A Drummer's Beat to Mend	Kei Swanson	$9.95
A Happy Life	Charlotte Harris	$9.95
A Heart's Awakening	Veronica Parker	$9.95
A Lark on the Wing	Phyliss Hamilton	$9.95
A Love of Her Own	Cheris F. Hodges	$9.95
A Love to Cherish	Beverly Clark	$8.95
A Lover's Legacy	Veronica Parker	$9.95
A Pefect Place to Pray	I.L. Goodwin	$12.95
A Risk of Rain	Dar Tomlinson	$8.95
A Twist of Fate	Beverly Clark	$8.95
A Will to Love	Angie Daniels	$9.95
Acquisitions	Kimberley White	$8.95
Across	Carol Payne	$12.95
After the Vows	Leslie Esdaile	$10.95
(Summer Anthology)	T.T. Henderson	
	Jacqueline Thomas	
Again My Love	Kayla Perrin	$10.95
Against the Wind	Gwynne Forster	$8.95
All I Ask	Barbara Keaton	$8.95
Ambrosia	T.T. Henderson	$8.95
An Unfinished Love Affair	Barbara Keaton	$8.95
And Then Came You	Dorothy Elizabeth Love	$8.95
Angel's Paradise	Janice Angelique	$9.95
At Last	Lisa G. Riley	$8.95
Best of Friends	Natalie Dunbar	$8.95
Between Tears	Pamela Ridley	$12.95
Beyond the Rapture	Beverly Clark	$9.95
Blaze	Barbara Keaton	$9.95

Other Genesis Press, Inc. Titles (continued)

Blood Lust	J. M. Jeffries	$9.95
Bodyguard	Andrea Jackson	$9.95
Boss of Me	Diana Nyad	$8.95
Bound by Love	Beverly Clark	$8.95
Breeze	Robin Hampton Allen	$10.95
Broken	Dar Tomlinson	$24.95
The Business of Love	Cheris Hodges	$9.95
By Design	Barbara Keaton	$8.95
Cajun Heat	Charlene Berry	$8.95
Careless Whispers	Rochelle Alers	$8.95
Cats & Other Tales	Marilyn Wagner	$8.95
Caught in a Trap	Andre Michelle	$8.95
Caught Up In the Rapture	Lisa G. Riley	$9.95
Cautious Heart	Cheris F Hodges	$8.95
Caught Up	Deatri King Bey	$12.95
Chances	Pamela Leigh Starr	$8.95
Cherish the Flame	Beverly Clark	$8.95
Class Reunion	Irma Jenkins/John Brown	$12.95
Code Name: Diva	J.M. Jeffries	$9.95
Conquering Dr. Wexler's Heart	Kimberley White	$9.95
Cricket's Serenade	Carolita Blythe	$12.95
Crossing Paths, Tempting Memories	Dorothy Elizabeth Love	$9.95
Cupid	Barbara Keaton	$9.95
Cypress Whisperings	Phyllis Hamilton	$8.95
Dark Embrace	Crystal Wilson Harris	$8.95
Dark Storm Rising	Chinelu Moore	$10.95
Daughter of the Wind	Joan Xian	$8.95
Deadly Sacrifice	Jack Kean	$22.95
Designer Passion	Dar Tomlinson	$8.95
Dreamtective	Liz Swados	$5.95
Ebony Butterfly II	Delilah Dawson	$14.95
Ebony Eyes	Kei Swanson	$9.95

DO OVER

Other Genesis Press, Inc. Titles (continued)

Echoes of Yesterday	Beverly Clark	$9.95
Eden's Garden	Elizabeth Rose	$8.95
Enchanted Desire	Wanda Y. Thomas	$9.95
Everlastin' Love	Gay G. Gunn	$8.95
Everlasting Moments	Dorothy Elizabeth Love	$8.95
Everything and More	Sinclair Lebeau	$8.95
Everything but Love	Natalie Dunbar	$8.95
Eve's Prescription	Edwina Martin Arnold	$8.95
Falling	Natalie Dunbar	$9.95
Fate	Pamela Leigh Starr	$8.95
Finding Isabella	A.J. Garrotto	$8.95
Forbidden Quest	Dar Tomlinson	$10.95
Forever Love	Wanda Thomas	$8.95
From the Ashes	Kathleen Suzanne	$8.95
	Jeanne Sumerix	
Gentle Yearning	Rochelle Alers	$10.95
Glory of Love	Sinclair LeBeau	$10.95
Go Gentle into that Good Night	Malcom Boyd	$12.95
Goldengroove	Mary Beth Craft	$16.95
Groove, Bang, and Jive	Steve Cannon	$8.99
Hand in Glove	Andrea Jackson	$9.95
Hard to Love	Kimberley White	$9.95
Hart & Soul	Angie Daniels	$8.95
Havana Sunrise	Kymberly Hunt	$9.95
Heartbeat	Stephanie Bedwell-Grime	$8.95
Hearts Remember	M. Loui Quezada	$8.95
Hidden Memories	Robin Allen	$10.95
Higher Ground	Leah Latimer	$19.95
Hitler, the War, and the Pope	Ronald Rychiak	$26.95
How to Write a Romance	Kathryn Falk	$18.95
I Married a Reclining Chair	Lisa M. Fuhs	$8.95
I'm Gonna Make You Love Me	Gwyneth Bolton	$9.95
Indigo After Dark Vol. I	Nia Dixon/Angelique	$10.95

Other Genesis Press, Inc. Titles (continued)

Indigo After Dark Vol. II	Dolores Bundy/Cole Riley	$10.95
Indigo After Dark Vol. III	Montana Blue/Coco Morena	$10.95
Indigo After Dark Vol. IV	Cassandra Colt/	$14.95
	Diana Richeaux	
Indigo After Dark Vol. V	Delilah Dawson	$14.95
Icie	Pamela Leigh Starr	$8.95
I'll Be Your Shelter	Giselle Carmichael	$8.95
I'll Paint a Sun	A.J. Garrotto	$9.95
Illusions	Pamela Leigh Starr	$8.95
Indiscretions	Donna Hill	$8.95
Intentional Mistakes	Michele Sudler	$9.95
Interlude	Donna Hill	$8.95
Intimate Intentions	Angie Daniels	$8.95
Ironic	Pamela Leigh Starr	$9.95
Jolie's Surrender	Edwina Martin-Arnold	$8.95
Kiss or Keep	Debra Phillips	$8.95
Lace	Giselle Carmichael	$9.95
Last Train to Memphis	Elsa Cook	$12.95
Lasting Valor	Ken Olsen	$24.95
Let's Get It On	Dyanne Davis	$9.95
Let Us Prey	Hunter Lundy	$25.95
Life Is Never As It Seems	J.J. Michael	$12.95
Lighter Shade of Brown	Vicki Andrews	$8.95
Love Always	Mildred E. Riley	$10.95
Love Doesn't Come Easy	Charlyne Dickerson	$8.95
Love in High Gear	Charlotte Roy	$9.95
Love Lasts Forever	Dominiqua Douglas	$9.95
Love Me Carefully	A.C. Arthur	$9.95
Love Unveiled	Gloria Greene	$10.95
Love's Deception	Charlene Berry	$10.95
Love's Destiny	M. Loui Quezada	$8.95
Mae's Promise	Melody Walcott	$8.95
Magnolia Sunset	Giselle Carmichael	$8.95

Other Genesis Press, Inc. Titles (continued)

Matters of Life and Death	Lesego Malepe, Ph.D.	$15.95
Meant to Be	Jeanne Sumerix	$8.95
Midnight Clear	Leslie Esdaile	$10.95
(Anthology)	Gwynne Forster	
	Carmen Green	
	Monica Jackson	
Midnight Magic	Gwynne Forster	$8.95
Midnight Peril	Vicki Andrews	$10.95
Misconceptions	Pamela Leigh Starr	$9.95
Misty Blue	Dyanne Davis	$9.95
Montgomery's Children	Richard Perry	$14.95
My Buffalo Soldier	Barbara B. K. Reeves	$8.95
Naked Soul	Gwynne Forster	$8.95
Next to Last Chance	Louisa Dixon	$24.95
Nights Over Egypt	Barbara Keaton	$9.95
No Apologies	Seressia Glass	$8.95
No Commitment Required	Seressia Glass	$8.95
No Ordinary Love	Angela Weaver	$9.95
No Regrets	Mildred E. Riley	$8.95
Notes When Summer Ends	Beverly Lauderdale	$12.95
Nowhere to Run	Gay G. Gunn	$10.95
O Bed! O Breakfast!	Rob Kuehnle	$14.95
Object of His Desire	A. C. Arthur	$8.95
Office Policy	A. C. Arthur	$9.95
Once in a Blue Moon	Dorianne Cole	$9.95
One Day at a Time	Bella McFarland	$8.95
Only You	Crystal Hubbard	$9.95
Outside Chance	Louisa Dixon	$24.95
Passion	T.T. Henderson	$10.95
Passion's Blood	Cherif Fortin	$22.95
Passion's Journey	Wanda Thomas	$8.95
Past Promises	Jahmel West	$8.95
Path of Fire	T.T. Henderson	$8.95

Other Genesis Press, Inc. Titles (continued)

Path of Thorns	Annetta P. Lee	$9.95
Peace Be Still	Colette Haywood	$12.95
Picture Perfect	Reon Carter	$8.95
Playing for Keeps	Stephanie Salinas	$8.95
Pride & Joi	Gay G. Gunn	$8.95
Promises to Keep	Alicia Wiggins	$8.95
Quiet Storm	Donna Hill	$10.95
Reckless Surrender	Rochelle Alers	$6.95
Red Polka Dot in a World of Plaid	Varian Johnson	$12.95
Rehoboth Road	Anita Ballard-Jones	$12.95
Reluctant Captive	Joyce Jackson	$8.95
Rendezvous with Fate	Jeanne Sumerix	$8.95
Revelations	Cheris F. Hodges	$8.95
Rise of the Phoenix	Kenneth Whetstone	$12.95
Rivers of the Soul	Leslie Esdaile	$8.95
Rock Star	Rosyln Hardy Holcomb	$9.95
Rocky Mountain Romance	Kathleen Suzanne	$8.95
Rooms of the Heart	Donna Hill	$8.95
Rough on Rats and Tough on Cats	Chris Parker	$12.95
Scent of Rain	Annetta P. Lee	$9.95
Second Chances at Love	Cheris Hodges	$9.95
Secret Library Vol. 1	Nina Sheridan	$18.95
Secret Library Vol. 2	Cassandra Colt	$8.95
Shades of Brown	Denise Becker	$8.95
Shades of Desire	Monica White	$8.95
Shadows in the Moonlight	Jeanne Sumerix	$8.95
Sin	Crystal Rhodes	$8.95
Sin and Surrender	J.M. Jeffries	$9.95
Sinful Intentions	Crystal Rhodes	$12.95
So Amazing	Sinclair LeBeau	$8.95
Somebody's Someone	Sinclair LeBeau	$8.95

Other Genesis Press, Inc. Titles (continued)

Someone to Love	Alicia Wiggins	$8.95
Song in the Park	Martin Brant	$15.95
Soul Eyes	Wayne L. Wilson	$12.95
Soul to Soul	Donna Hill	$8.95
Southern Comfort	J.M. Jeffries	$8.95
Still the Storm	Sharon Robinson	$8.95
Still Waters Run Deep	Leslie Esdaile	$8.95
Stories to Excite You	Anna Forrest/Divine	$14.95
Subtle Secrets	Wanda Y. Thomas	$8.95
Suddenly You	Crystal Hubbard	$9.95
Sweet Repercussions	Kimberley White	$9.95
Sweet Tomorrows	Kimberly White	$8.95
Taken by You	Dorothy Elizabeth Love	$9.95
Tattooed Tears	T. T. Henderson	$8.95
The Color Line	Lizzette Grayson Carter	$9.95
The Color of Trouble	Dyanne Davis	$8.95
The Disappearance of Allison Jones	Kayla Perrin	$5.95
The Honey Dipper's Legacy	Pannell-Allen	$14.95
The Joker's Love Tune	Sidney Rickman	$15.95
The Little Pretender	Barbara Cartland	$10.95
The Love We Had	Natalie Dunbar	$8.95
The Man Who Could Fly	Bob & Milana Beamon	$18.95
The Missing Link	Charlyne Dickerson	$8.95
The Price of Love	Sinclair LeBeau	$8.95
The Smoking Life	Ilene Barth	$29.95
The Words of the Pitcher	Kei Swanson	$8.95
Three Wishes	Seressia Glass	$8.95
Through the Fire	Seressia Glass	$9.95
Ties That Bind	Kathleen Suzanne	$8.95
Tiger Woods	Libby Hughes	$5.95
Time is of the Essence	Angie Daniels	$9.95
Timeless Devotion	Bella McFarland	$9.95
Tomorrow's Promise	Leslie Esdaile	$8.95

Truly Inseparable	Wanda Y. Thomas	$8.95
Unbreak My Heart	Dar Tomlinson	$8.95
Uncommon Prayer	Kenneth Swanson	$9.95
Unconditional	A.C. Arthur	$9.95
Unconditional Love	Alicia Wiggins	$8.95
Under the Cherry Moon	Christal Jordan-Mims	$12.95
Unearthing Passions	Elaine Sims	$9.95
Until Death Do Us Part	Susan Paul	$8.95
Vows of Passion	Bella McFarland	$9.95
Wedding Gown	Dyanne Davis	$8.95
What's Under Benjamin's Bed	Sandra Schaffer	$8.95
When Dreams Float	Dorothy Elizabeth Love	$8.95
Whispers in the Night	Dorothy Elizabeth Love	$8.95
Whispers in the Sand	LaFlorya Gauthier	$10.95
Wild Ravens	Altonya Washington	$9.95
Yesterday Is Gone	Beverly Clark	$10.95
Yesterday's Dreams, Tomorrow's Promises	Reon Laudat	$8.95
Your Precious Love	Sinclair LeBeau	$8.95

Order Form

Mail to: Genesis Press, Inc.
P.O. Box 101
Columbus, MS 39703

Name _____
Address _____
City/State _____ Zip _____
Telephone _____

Ship to (if different from above)
Name _____
Address _____
City/State _____ Zip _____
Telephone _____

Credit Card Information
Credit Card # _____ ☐ Visa   ☐ Mastercard
Expiration Date (mm/yy) _____ ☐ AmEx   ☐ Discover

Qty.	Author	Title	Price	Total

Use this order
form, or call
1-888-INDIGO-1

Total for books _____
Shipping and handling:
  $5 first two books,
  $1 each additional book _____
Total S & H _____
Total amount enclosed _____
Mississippi residents add 7% sales tax